CLUB OMEGA

Billionaires' Game Trilogy
Book Three

Marata Eros

Contents

VIP List	v
Synopsis	vii
Music	ix
Chapter 1	1
Chapter 2	7
Chapter 3	15
Chapter 4	22
Chapter 5	28
Chapter 6	35
Chapter 7	44
Chapter 8	52
Chapter 9	62
Chapter 10	70
Chapter 11	77
Chapter 12	85
Chapter 13	94
Chapter 14	101
Chapter 15	110
Chapter 16	118
Chapter 17	127
Chapter 18	137
Chapter 19	146
Chapter 20	154
Chapter 21	163
Chapter 22	171
Chapter 23	180
Chapter 24	189
Chapter 25	198
Chapter 26	208
Chapter 27	215

Chapter 28	224
Chapter 29	233
Chapter 30	244
Epilogue	250
Bonus Material	261
Acknowledgments	287
About the Author	289
Also by Marata Eros	291

VIP List

To be the first to hear about new releases and bargains—from Tamara Rose Blodgett/Marata Eros—sign up below to be on my VIP List. (I promise not to spam or share your email with anyone!)

SIGN UP TO BE ON THE
♥TAMARA ROSE BLODGETT ♥
VIP LIST
👇
HERE

Synopsis

Zaire Sebastian is emotionally exhausted. After two Club Alpha events going horribly south, *his* clients narrowly evading torture, blackmail and worse—he's regretfully letting Club Alpha go.

Or so he thinks.

Zaire's friends know he's got a heart for peoples' troubles. What they don't know is his rich lifestyle will soon come to an end. Not by design, but because it took everything to fight the court battle that nearly robbed him of Club Alpha before he'd paid it forward with Gia Township and Merit Lang.

He's broke.

Alexandra Frost has it all. Beauty. Prestige. A luxury travel social media account with five million followers.

She's rich.

Then a chance encounter with devastatingly handsome Texan Zaire Sebastian has their lives intertwining in unexpected ways.

Their association leads them on a path of self-discovery, danger and love. When Zaire unveils a monstrous secret, he doesn't know what to believe. Or who.

Will Zaire listen to instinct—or extract himself before it's too late?

Music

Sleeping Satellite
by Tasmin Archer

<u>Woodstock</u>
by Joni Mitchell

Dr. Robert Malone
https://www.rwmalonemd.com/

For giving me hope, and validating my intuitive reservations that I'm still free to possess.

One

Alexandra Frost - Patras, Greece

I hold up the serrated knife, swinging the dangerous edge slowly in front of my face while making intense eye contact with the woman behind the lens. "If I see an ounce of cellulite, it won't be steak I'm sawing."

Genevieve's face pops out from behind the lens. Pursing her full lips she smirks, ignoring my innuendo entirely as per usual. "We are *women*. We have asses; we have jiggly bits. In case you didn't get the memo." She quirks an eyebrow.

Carefully, I set the knife's tip on the edge of the brilliant cobalt spun glass plate and hold up a hand to shade my eyes from the brilliant sun glaring the last of its dying light.

"No squinting. Wrinkles." Genevieve reprimands.

Gawd. I scrunch my nose. "I'll just get those fixed when I'm old."

"Nope, be preventative."

I slide on my rose-tinted Vuarnets and stretch out, rolling my hips so that I'm lying on my side. Putting up with the slightly abrasive and dry epoxied deck of the infinity pool diving off the cliff below, I support my head with a palm and pout at G.

"Oooh, I like that anger vibe," G says, winking.

Naturally, that irritates me even more. "I want to fork in some steak," I say in a growl, hangry.

"After I"—G's camera clicks, snaps—the shutter whirrs, taking a million photos so we can grab a few that are stunning enough for my TikTok social media site—"finish a few more shots."

Five million people are voracious for my content. And I'm addicted to giving it.

I'm not much into self-examination. What I do—works. My traveling lifestyle keeps real relationships at a distance, which is the object of my frenetic pace. I travel so much for fun I felt compelled to provide a duality angle. "Content" for people to consume while also doing something I love: luxury travel.

Now I employ a small team of people who make all of that lifestyle easier.

Cook, security, wardrobe, private jet, and—G, my second cousin and best friend.

When she's not being a royal dick and haranguing me about wrinkles at the ripe age of almost twenty-seven, I like her fine.

Right now, she's being a food-block and that's a no *me gusta mucho.*

Genevieve straightens, placing a palm at her lower back and rising on her toes, stretching. "Okay, *gordo*, have at it."

"It's *gorda* because I'm a woman," I correct absently.

Sitting up, I bend both legs and tuck my feet into the crook of my knees so I'm sitting cross-legged and prop the plate in the little table I've made with my lap.

Instantly, one of the staff from the luxury hotel trots up with a fruity drink and a cloth napkin.

Saying thank you, I lift the delicately constructed tube of glass, take a grateful sip, and gaze west at the Ionian Sea.

The azure gem of water glints a deep, shimmering turquoise from where I sit, the hotel nestled into a cliff with brilliant white houses dotting the rugged terrain that surrounds the expansive structure making a horseshoe shape around the pool. The small homes look as though they've sprouted like pearls inside their shell of rocky backdrop. Made of lime and painted a striking ivory, their tall narrow windows reflect like eyes, guarding the houses against excessive heat and light.

I'm not worried about the sun. A hater of cold weather, I travel to warm locales when they're not at their most scorching and travel to northern locations in summer.

Generally, my solitary travels bring a sense of peace. Other times, like now—and it's rare—I have a pang that's almost painful to endure in its insistence.

Loneliness.

There's not a man around who doesn't eventually come to understand I'm filthy rich.

For a chick who's as young as me—I'm as jaded as they come.

Men are something that comes with a penis, and I appreciate that particular body part. But, and that's with a capital "B," I want more. Or—better yet—I want someone who likes me for who I am, not *what* I have.

Mentally, I grind through the reflective pause in my day, the hump of regrets, and attempt to focus on the pluses.

Money.

Power.

Freedom.

I don't *need* to work. I'm reasonably good-looking; I'm not beholden to anyone.

Sometimes, I sorta want to be part of a whole, have that other half to consider.

Not total freedom yet. Trust fund babies have to wait until their expiration date, and I have just over three years.

Sure, I spend what I get each month, but the big bucks wait for the milestone of 3-0.

Taking another sip, I taste pineapple-flavored vodka with finely pulverized bits of strawberries. Setting the drink on the dry deck beside the pool, I cut a piece of cooling steak, and spearing the small morsel with the tines, I slide it into my mouth and begin chewing, so hungry a growl erupts noisily as though choreographed.

Sensing G's presence, I'm unsurprised when she plops down beside me, cradling her Leica Q2 Digital. It was a pricey camera. Not that I cared.

G sinks her bare feet into the heat of the pool, tipping her head back with a long sigh of pleasure. She leans back, propping herself with a palm on the deck.

"Hungry?"

I nod, stuffing another chunk directly after the other and chewing as she hikes the bulky chunk of plastic and lens with her free hand a couple of inches off her lap, giving me steady golden hazel eyes, the corners of her mouth quirking. "No cellulite *I* can see."

I finish chewing, opening my mouth to spout sarcasm when the same waiter that got my cocktail asks, "Miss?" from above G, his dark brows hike in question.

G looks at what I'm drinking and replies, "I'll have the same, thank you."

With a sage nod, he retreats.

Companionable silence stretches between us for a minute or two as I work through my tender steak and watch jagged pieces of sunset spear the cliffs, sea, and pool deck with gold, tangerine, and finally—pink.

The waiter returns and hands G a clone of my drink and a second for me.

The waiter and I exchange my empty glass with the full one, and I repeat my thanks.

I raise the glass to my lips, taking another sip. *The taste is delicious.* "This is yum," I say aloud.

G murmurs her assent.

We sip and I eat. I tore through the breakfast hour with coffee and cream. Then lunch came and went. By the time I realized I was hungry, we were deep into my photoshoot by the pool.

Light is the master of all photography, G claims.

G grins when her drink is half-gone. "I can't lounge around and get hammered. I got to work my editing magic."

"Good." I nod a bit drunkenly. "Get to work on giving me bigger tits."

We laugh, clinking glasses.

She cocks her head, the six earrings that climb her ear winking in the fading light. "If a bitch has significant tits and is as skinny as you, they're fake."

I dump my gaze to my small chest that's held inside a teeny deep green string bikini top. Laugh again. "Suppose so."

"Your boobs look natural—besides, you have a perfect set. They're just small, like the rest of you."

I don't self-consciously curl my arm around my undersized bosom, but it's a hard thought.

A woman always wants what she doesn't have.

"Hey."

I look up from my tiny titties and meet her direct gaze. The shorn sides of her hair appear colorless in the twilight that makes the sea disappear in a black wash.

"You promote luxury *and* authenticity." G tosses my own words back at me.

"Right," I say, taking another sip of a cocktail that's so mouth-watering the combined flavors taste like candy. *A-mazing.*

I'm not hungry for steak anymore. Surprise, surprise.

"I think I'm getting buzzed," I announce. Lifting the finely made crystal tube and closing one eye, I peer inside the empty cocktail glass.

"Excellent," G replies with a twist of lips.

The waiter returns with a pitcher and begins to pour more pinkish liquid inside my glass.

Then my guard appears at his elbow, and the poor dude startles, a small drop of sticky pink lands on my arm, and without missing a beat, I lick it off.

G guffaws at my lack of manners.

Merit Lang, premier bodyguard to the rich says in a low voice, "Ms. Frost has had enough." *Ms. Frost has had enough,* I mentally repeat in his gravely bass growl.

I haven't had enough.

It'll never be enough. But when I'm sober and in my right mind, I've made it clear to Mr. Lang I don't need to have too much to drink.

Bad things might happen.

Things I don't want to see repeated.

"Of course, Mr. Lang," the waiter stammers.

Merit gives him a nod, shoots me a shrewd glance, then pivots away, his tall muscular body disappearing around the corner of the all-white hotel.

I'm lucky to have retained Merit Lang. He'd taken a sabbatical after guarding some dude last year who does something with silk ... oh yeah, Denver Arnault. But now *I* have Merit.

Just in case.

"You going to be okay while I take off and edit inside the perfection of my suite?" G asks.

"Hell yes." I raise my glass again, wanting to cry.

And not knowing why.

Two

Zaire Sebastian - Texas, two weeks ago

"How bad is it?" I ask, knowing the answer, dreading the answer.

"Bad—won't lie, Zaire. You're plum out of funds."

Dammit. There's no licking my wounds in private, the ideal scenario. My financial advisor had told me all along that saving Club Alpha by way of the court system was more about principle and less about saving money.

"You were aware from the beginning that attempting to exonerate your billionaire's game club was going to cost you dearly." Wayne's voice tries for conciliatory.

"Yes." I can't be consoled at the moment.

I brutally tighten the grip on my cell. "I assumed with Gia handling things virtually pro-bono, it'd wash." Naturally, I couldn't handle my own defense.

"The law didn't like your last two clients' predicaments."

The last few Club Alpha highlights (and lowlights) flash through my mind. "The events did shave danger pretty close," I reluctantly admit.

"Not at all your fault... but, the shark-lawyers tried their damndest to go after you as though it was."

Not offended, though I'm a former lawyer myself. "Doesn't matter—the feds still viewed the incidents between my two clients as a twofer—where there's smoke, there's fire. Even though I'd vetted Gia's background, and Greta before her, dark web shit was surfaced."

I drag a hand over my face, feeling a two-day beard, and sigh.

Life isn't fair. And that's the nuts and bolts of what's happening here. I tried to play cupid to the billionaires, and there was no anticipating that the lives they lived before becoming players were not exempt from the same problems that face people without money. Unfortunately for Greta and Gia, because they had fortunes attached to them—evil people hurt them and had continued to try to ruin the women for potential monetary gain.

"You did a good thing with Club Alpha, Zaire—don't go beating yourself up now. It's filthy luck."

I give a dismissive snort. "Or no luck at all."

"Truth," Wayne chuckles, but his laughter fades. "Have you considered—"

"No fucking way," I grate, heading that overture off by a mile.

I can't see Wayne's smirk, but it's there. "How did you know what I was going to suggest?"

"I've thought about begging from satisfied clients. For about one point five seconds." I can't do it. Pride, fear—misery, I can't come to Gia (who'd fought almost two years to save Club Alpha) and now say: hey, sorry about those couple of years you toiled your ass off, and thanks for saving Club Alpha's name—but I didn't have the capital to keep it going anyway.

Gia would reply: thank you very fucking much.

No, she wouldn't. Gia Township is too compassionate for that.

I'm not about to rob her and Denver of their new life, and they have a kid now. I knew Paco and Greta would spot me whatever I needed.

Same deal. Now *they* have two kids. *Not just no but* hell *no.*

Past clients who date even further back than the Gs (as I now think of the girls) have moved on and probably forgotten all about Club Alpha bringing them together—the defunct entity now going down in financial flames.

"Zaire."

I come back to the moment with a thud. "Sorry, what?"

"Said your name three times."

"Yeah, sorry—totally in my head, feel like I'm going to my own funeral."

"It's not *that* dire. I have a tiny bright spot in all these dark financial revelations."

I wait.

"Give or take a hundred-thou, you have one million dollars left."

My mind chastises me even as the thought forms: *pennies.* I suck an inhale. "And my investments?"

"You took huge penalties for early withdrawal to fund saving Club Alpha—we might scrape another sub-one hundred K out of that."

"So... a million-two?"

"Thereabouts," Wayne confirms in a resigned tone.

"Okay, my law degree didn't prepare me for this." I run a free hand through my thick, dark blond hair and tilt my face to the ceiling of my penthouse rental, feeling the four walls beginning to close in. I slowly add, "Won't lie—feel like I'm suffocating."

"You have your health. You've sold all your assets, and you're free—young."

Thirty-three and counting.

"Had to dump everything to get money," I recount in a flat voice as I look around my at-the-moment, spartan digs.

Wayne's sigh is aggrieved. "Zaire, go to the gym with Merit before he leaves for his next assignment. In fact, take some of that money and do the Europe trip you keep threatening you'd take when there was a lull in clients."

Never thought there'd be a permanent lull. Ever.

"Yeah, thanks for the pep talk, Wayne. I guess some money is better than none."

"Don't be a dick. Some regular folk would think a million and change is not the end of the world."

I hear his words, just don't believe them. I'd become accustomed to a certain lifestyle, complacent in its longevity.

As long as I'm not on the self-delusion train, I can admit that my life has never been a true financial struggle.

My affluent parents had said they'd pay for university if I studied law.

I'd studied law, anticipating I'd hate it from day one. And it was no surprise when I did.

Came up with the idea for a billionaire dating game with Club Alpha. Got wealthy and paid my parents back for the college I'd hated.

Didn't want to be beholden. My dad had never quite forgiven me, believing Club Alpha was a young man's privileged folly.

What about the *real work* I ought to be accomplishing? he'd asked. Until the money rolled in and his tune had changed.

Of course, the money's not rolling in anymore, is it?

Nope.

Wayne's right. I'll attempt to kick Merit's ass, and at least, my aggression will be spent.

For today.

My body shakes from exhaustion, rivulets of sweat streaming down my bare chest. "Fuck, I needed that, you douche."

Merit Lang and I face each other, both our chests heaving from the exertion of hand-to-hand moves and a chaser jujitsu round.

"Wow," Merit says, whipping a towel around his neck and holding the ends, "you get that pretty, southern boy accent when you're pissed off."

I glare at him because I'm just pissed off on principle at the moment.

"You don't usually go so hard." Merit smirks, his dark eyes in utter contrast to his pale blond hair, cut in a classic flattop style.

I'm flattered by his bitch-slapped red cheeks, and I note I'm not the only one sucking oxygen and sweating like a swine. I worked him, and that's saying something because Merit is an expert in weaponry and using his body as one.

"Needed to get after it. Got the *worst* news today."

Merit's light brow pops. "Yeah? I'm father confessor," he announces, snapping the slightly damp towel between us, and the tail cracks loudly from the momentum.

Raising my hand, my middle finger springs from my fist.

Merit laughs.

He'd been on the books to be my bodyguard for a future Europe trip. Because I'd had the money to hire someone like Merit Lang. "I can't afford to hire you."

Merit shrugs. "I *am* for hire, you know." A wide grin spreads across his face. Pegging his hands on his hips, he begins a slow twirl and jerk.

"Can't afford any of y'all."

"Us all?" Merit halts his stripper act, stabbing a thumb

dead center in his chest, and I'm grateful Merit doesn't press for every detail.

I wave that away. "Guards. Bodyguards."

The grin splits his face again. "Bud"—he stabs a finger in my direction—"you don't need protection. I about got you where I want you."

Snorting, I rise from my perch on the hardwood bench and pluck an ice-cold water from the beat-up shorty fridge that corners the dojo mat. The orange extension cord leading from the fridge is set up like a dangerous snake for us guys to trip over as we exit the space.

Nobody sets this anomaly to rights. We begin to walk toward the door and unconsciously step over the duct tape that does a poor job covering the cord.

Merit Lang and I have been meeting at this gym for a decade. The crummy gym doesn't align with people who are wealthy, and some small part of me has always wanted this down-to-earth tether, a small rebellion if you will. We've been meeting here consistently, except when he was in France for a few months, years ago. Come to find out, a lot of horrible shit went down during that stint.

"Small world" deets; Lang had been a part of what took care of that little French problem the second time around. After a moment's internal debate, I figure Denver Arnault had his hand in it as well. Personally or impersonally—I don't know, but I suspect the hell out of the first rather than the latter, especially given Gia's involvement. If there were men who had harmed his wife, they would pay. That's just how Denver rolls.

"Thanks for the vote of confidence, but aside from general self-protection, I'm not rich enough for the wrong kind of notoriety, and there's no woman in my life…" I give a shrug, pissed and more sad than I want to admit.

Sad that I don't have anything for what I put out.

Pissed because I'm not liking the pity party trend I've sunk into.

Merit frowns. "It's none of my business, but you *told* me what your finance dude said."

I explained the part I *was* willing to admit in four sentences or less, and even that partial admission beats like wings begging escape from inside me.

He spreads heavy arms away from his muscular torso. "Clear your fucking head, man. Take the time away, blow some of the money."

"Feels wrong when I don't have that much compared to what I did."

"Come on, Zaire. You're still a millionaire, technically. And for the record, it blows the judge didn't have the feds cover your expenses when you weren't culpable."

"I wasn't guilty of anything. The win on that front had felt almost anti-climactic." I lift my shoulder then let it drop. "I'll return to the workforce. In what capacity, I don't know." Gone is the certain, confident, inspired guy I was before the dismantling of my company. I was proud of what I'd built with Club Alpha, the premise, the satisfied clients. Everything.

This new guy—I don't know him. I want *me* back.

"Hey," Merit says, sudden inspiration lighting his face.

Now it's my turn to give him a questioning expression.

"I'm heading to Greece for a month. Want to be a dick and tag along?"

"Shit, man, *I'm* a dick?" I thumb my chest, feeling an amused expression seat itself on my face.

"Yes," Merit instantly agrees.

I gift him a sour look as a thought occurs to me, and I groan, feeling like a classic asshole. "I didn't ask about Chloe or your new assignment, or Denver…"

"Yes, King Dickery." But Merit's smile softens the words before he adds, "Chloe's okay."

Much lies unspoken, but when a woman survives an attack of the kind she did, time would be the only healer and —the love of a good man.

Merit's that and more.

We share a weighted look.

"She'll be coming along, of course."

I nod.

Merit continues smoothly, as if the devastating memory of Chloe's attack hadn't just stained our minds, and hikes his square jaw. "Babysitting a rich social media tycoon this go."

I shrug. "They're all rich."

"She's old money, but that part's not as clear as the rest."

"What rest?" I ask, vaguely intrigued and happy for the distraction from my gloom and doom perspective.

"Ya know the old saying: You can never be too rich, too young, or too thin?"

"Yeah."

He points a finger at me and mimes pulling the "trigger."

"That's Alexandra Frost."

A few heartbeats of time slide between us. "Okay, I'll waste some money."

Merit and I reach the door, and I grasp the handle when he claps me on the back, "Who knows, maybe it won't be such a waste after all."

Maybe.

Three
Alexandra

I lean against the thick, deeply profiled hotel door and think jealous thoughts.

Uncharitable ones.

See, it's like this. Merit saw me to my room, first going inside and making sure no villains were lurking.

There weren't.

He'd come back from his routine inspection and given me the nod. That's his way. Merit Lang is economical with his words.

Translation: He doesn't talk.

It's his girlfriend, Chloe—she's the one who's got me seeing green. *She's* got big boobs.

Actually, tits notwithstanding, it's that she's got something I don't have: a man.

A *real* man.

Shoving off from the door I pad across the room, noticing my gait wobbles only a bit from imbibing in my pair of fruity cocktails.

It's not that men are actually fake, I muse—obviously,

they're breathing, living humans—it's just there are so many *players.*

I come to stand before the full-length mirror that one of my people brings and sets up before I even see the room at whatever luxury hotel we land at.

My eyes run over the reflective surface, noting the lights. I'm not sure what technology they used to manufacture this mirror, but the perimeter has integral LED strip lighting embedded within.

I peer at my reflection, sighing at my disheveled look. After two stiff drinks, a big steak, and all-day shooting, I'm deflated.

My bikini is a deep forest green color with high multi-strap sides on either hip.

I cock my head, giving the design a critical look. Weird tan lines for sure. Not that it matters because no one has seen me naked in... well—in a long time.

Stripping the barely-there bikini bottom off, I pull the string end for the bow that secures the top at my middle back, and the small bit of fabric pulls away, releasing my boobs from their prison.

I haul the tied portion of the halter over my hair and dump the top piece on the floor, critically perusing my nakedness.

G's right. My boobs are barely a "b" cup but stand at attention with perfect perky globes, creamy against the tan I've fought so hard to obtain, given my redhead status. Said deep auburn hair is on top of my head in the popular "messy bun" look. The ends of my hair are lighter and more coppery than the roots—a consequence of the sun.

If I'm being honest, my most arresting features are my brown eyes. They're so dark a brown that, though the pupils are in there somewhere, a person would have to hunt to find them.

Almost the same shade as Merit's eyes, I think. In fact,

when he first met me, he'd said: my sister from another mother, I guess since he's so blond and our eyes match. My parents both have naturally light blond hair, and they've commented before how much of a shock it'd been when I was born a ginger.

My height comes from some Scott way back in the annals of time, I guess, standing almost five foot nine. Freckles stand out against my dusky skin as they march across the bridge of my nose.

As my gaze lowers, I notice my narrow landing strip is the same shade as my eyebrows—a dark, true copper. Lots of girls go hardwood floors, but I find that a little prepubescent for my taste.

Women are meant to have hair in certain areas. I just don't want it everywhere and paid for full-body electrolysis years ago. My smooth skin does not have to be shaved, and I don't miss the chore.

Walking away from my reflection, I insert my closet slobbery and kick my bikini more or less in the general direction of my dirty clothes pile I've assembled before making my way to the shower.

My hair's filthy with pool, dust, and sunblock, and G had mentioned tomorrow as a "hair down" day along with sarong, sunglasses, and an "around town" shoot.

I'll wash my hair tonight. There's not a single wave or curl to my stick-straight hair. It's an asset because straight hair is so popular on social media. Middle part, all one-length.

Of course, trends change like the wind, and next year, curly might be in vogue; then I'll be screwed.

I'd like to say that I'm *so* different than what's currently trending. But I'm unique—just like everyone else. I give an ironic smile. It's not *enough* to be pretty or rich on socials. A person must also be interesting in a way that not *everyone* else is.

No pressure.

With the proliferation of filters, beauty, and body shaping apps, my omission of makeup has been seen as a novelty. I don't use filters, but I will instruct G to brighten a really dark pic.

Unwinding my topknot of hair, I groan when all the weight is loosened and the tendrils fall to just above my waist in a curtain like heavy silk. Shaking my hair out, I snag a brush from the ten-foot-long Carrara marble vanity and begin brushing through my locks until the snarls from the day are gone.

My eyes scan the bleached, rough, tumble travertine walk-in shower, and I decide it's an all-four-heads day.

Stepping inside the huge square space, I move clockwise and begin at my left, turning first one tap to hot, then move to the next one, and so on until all heads are spraying a fine rain that lands directly in the middle where the drain is located.

I step within that vortex of water and stand still under the steaming spray. The fine needles of water beat against my skin from all directions. Tilting my head back, I let the water run through my hair until it's suitably drenched and open my mouth, letting the spray run inside then run out. Tipping my head down again, I shut my eyes, allowing the water to hit my face, and for a shining crystalline moment, I don't have any thoughts.

Zero.

Of course, that can't last, and my mind takes me places I'd rather not be—with thoughts that find me when the distractions of my life fall away.

Familiar guilt assails me, and no matter how I try to run from the memories, I can't. Shattered bits and pieces of that long-ago event coalesce around my mind in brittle chunks of memory.

Bridget was my friend.

Until she died.

And I watched her final breath, her broken, bleeding body wheezing after what the murderer had done—like the others.

I shut the horror down, throwing a big metal door in place; a mental barricade of sorts. That thick metal partition clanks into place, saving me from my own recounting.

I quickly work the fragrant soap everywhere and step out of the shower, shivering because I don't deserve a hot shower.

Turning it to cold for the last five minutes is penance.

For what I did.

For what I didn't do.

———

My cell chime wakes me up, and groggily, I crank open my eyelids, disoriented for a moment.

Propping myself up on an elbow, I accidentally knock my cell to the floor and, with an irritated exhale, scoop it up. My iPhone verifies my face, apps springing to attention on my screen.

Tapping on the TikTok musical note icon, I start scrolling my comments.

There are the regular haters who take time out to let me know all the bad they see in me and what I do.

Your tiny tits, says one guy, should be blown up with a tit job. After all, he claims, *You're rich enough to afford one.*

Block.

The next hater comments that he'd love a chance to see if the curtain matches the drapes.

Briefly I peruse his bio and note he's an old fucking goat and thinks he'll class things up a little by asking (but not asking) if my pubic hair is the same color as that on my head.

Dick.

I hit the *block user* button again.

My last post was a simple video by the pool where I talk about where I'm going today—asking my followers if they want to see what I see.

Overwhelmingly, everyone does.

Also—people decided they like the purple bikini from two days ago most. *I'm not surprised; jewel tones set off my hair,* I think matter-of-factly.

Yesterday's deep emerald bikini will be today's upload. We always delay our videos by one day so "fans" don't know exactly where I am.

Merit's idea. He'd said he didn't want to kill an "enthusiast," read: a nutjob.

I don't want him to kill anyone either. But better to have a dude like Merit when I need one than to not have one when I do.

Speaking of. I sweep my feet to the floor and stumble into the bathroom, racing through my morning hygiene routine. Taking a last critical glance at my hair, I find I'm loving the new product I've been using that accentuates glossiness. My neck looks bare and boring so I toss on a platinum, diamond-by-the-yard choker by Tiffany's.

Stepping back from the vanity mirror, I give a nod, liking the simplicity of my outfit.

What there is of it. Today's brilliant, a pure white bikini is in high contrast to the deep violet and lavender swirled sarong I have knotted at my elevated hip. Six-carat diamonds studs are plugged into my earlobes and underscore the sizzling but icy look I'm going for.

G will dig this ensemble for photog.

Moving out into the cavernous main room, I search for my flip-flops with the Swarovski crystal accents on the thong portion and find one in front of the mirror and one by the bed.

Turning, I shift my foot and put on the one by the mirror backward.

Pfft, I snag the other one and face it forward, cramming my foot into that one, noticing my bright white French pedi will expire soon.

My stomach growls, and I think G will have my head on a lance if I eat before the shoot. *She likes my starved look*, I guess. Coffee and cream again. She can't bitch about liquid.

I snort. *Probably.*

Smiling, I move quickly to the door and toss it open.

A tall man stands before me with his hand raised as though poised to knock.

"Shit!" I yelp and slam the door in his face, throwing the lock, and slap my palms against the surface.

Who the fuck was *that*?

A few seconds drum by before a knock sounds.

I jump, heart hammering, and say through the door, "Who is it?"

"Zaire Sebastian."

Who? Inhaling deeply, I try to calm my shit and state the obvious, "I don't know you."

"I'm aware. Pretty tough to meet you with the door in the way, darlin'."

Ooh, a sexy southern boy.

Merit's warnings ring in my mind. "How do I know you're okay?" I roll my bottom lip between my teeth, gnawing lightly.

"You don't, but Merit Lang thinks I am."

Oh. Feeling a bit sheepish, I slide the bolt back and slowly open the door, giving him a one-eyeball view.

His smirk is a mile wide on his handsome face.

"So, who are you?" I ask again.

"Your new bodyguard."

Four
Zaire

Typical male assessment: Alexandra Frost is hot.

Untypical male assessment: she's not hot in the obvious ways. Most men—and I'm usually not an exception—are a piece and parcel man.

They like tits. Or they're ass men. Or legs.

We all like the obvious. If the male species didn't, there would be no perpetuation of mankind.

I've seen the best-looking females. It was my job to have a critical eye. Billionaires don't have to be with "ugly"—men or women.

It's a challenge for me *not* to assess this heiress as I would a client first instead of assessing her as a man would a woman.

When she speaks, I realize I was quiet for too long.

"Merit Lang is my bodyguard."

Right. The reason for my visit. I shake off my inner musings. "He apologizes." I pause, not sure how to explain things without surfacing personal details I don't own.

"I'm all ears," Alexandra says in a droll tone.

I'm taken aback by a voice on the lower contralto range that doesn't match the doll-like body and face. Skin that is sun-kissed fights with burnished copper hair in a most interesting way. Freckles are carelessly sprinkled across the bridge of her nose like brown sugar.

I spread my arms away from my body, trying not to stare at her like a lech and struggling.

Come on, Zaire, you know you don't fluster easy. My case of nerves is out-of-character.

Maybe it's because I have a different role. Merit had been crystal clear on what that role would be.

I run through his words in the split second before answering her.

"Listen," Merit had said, *running agitated fingers through his platinum crew cut, "Chloe's dad had a heart attack—she can't deal, man. I gotta split this detail."*

We both know why.

I feel responsible because Chloe got in the way of players I didn't even know were part of my elaborately orchestrated, final Club Alpha game involving Denver Arnault and Gia Township.

Though the reality is no one could have ever anticipated the events that unfolded.

Doesn't quit my guilt over it.

"I need you to babysit Alex for a couple days—maybe a half dozen at the most."

Six days or less of watching a social media, vapid, shallow rich girl pout and make duck faces.

I mentally sighed. "I'll do it." I felt my face screw up into a frown. "I've never guarded anyone before."

"I texted her, let Alex know you were coming—that it was an emergency."

We exchanged a look. "Not pro, Merit."

He lifted a shoulder. "Forfeited my salary." His black eyes returned to mine. "Asking a personal favor, Zaire."

"Fuck—you don't need to call chips in, partner—I'm in, I

just don't want..." I couldn't finish my thought.

Merit Lang did. "You didn't hurt Chloe, Zaire. It was just the most evil luck on the planet."

Nothing lucky about a woman being gang-raped and dumped in front of a man who would have died to defend her.

Nope.

"Well?" Alexandra breaks into my thoughts, crossing her arms.

"Chloe had a family emergency. He had—Merit needs to see her home, get her settled."

I glance at the white face of my Patek Phillip watch I haven't pawned yet and reply, "He said six days, at most."

"Okay," she says slowly, and her expression moves through the emotions of surprise, irritation, then acceptance. "I don't know Chloe very well, but—yeah—I get it." She gives a nervous laugh and adds in a low voice, "I mean, I don't really need a bodyguard."

I run my eyes down her slender body and think how easy it would be to subdue her. How easy it would be for any man who had a mind to.

Decide I don't like the direction of my thoughts.

"Merit could have texted me," she says like an afterthought.

I frown. "He did." I stroke the brim of my hat out of habit then add, "He *said* he would. Merit is a follow-through type of guy."

Just as the last word falls from my lips, a chime sounds at Alexandra's hip.

"Excuse me," she says politely.

I have to admit Alexandra's not the woman I expected her to be.

Scooping the phone from a hidden pocket on a sarong she's wearing, I note her perfect rack.

Never been a fan of globe-type tits. One doesn't need

money to have class. I like Alexandra better for not slicing and dicing her body for trumped-up shit.

"Damn," she says softly.

I wait, though asking is on my tongue.

"He *did* text." Her face rises, her dark chocolate-colored eyes meeting mine, and I'm struck by their similarity to Merit's.

I put my hands at my hips. "And?"

"He said a big dude with a cowboy hat, boots, and tight jeans would show up, claiming to be my bodyguard."

A laugh shoots out of me like a cannon.

Alex startles, hand to chest. "You scared the shit out of me; you laugh so loud."

I grin. "Only when I mean it."

Her eyes find mine. "Do you always mean it?"

Slowly, I nod. "Yes." I extend my palm and ask, "You mind?"

"You want to see his text?" she laughs.

"Yes, darlin'. I want to read Merit's interpretation of my looks."

"Your vibe-check."

I raise a brow.

A pretty blush colors her lightly tanned skin a subtle peach across high cheekbones. "You know, if you're legit."

Smirking, I keep my hand out.

I tap the screen, and his message says exactly what Alexandra recited.

Except for one comment at the end.

"Tell that asshole not to read your texts."

I glance up and bark another laugh. "That prick."

Our eyes meet. Probably shouldn't have indoctrinated Alexandra so quickly.

"My apologies, ma'am."

"Oh. My. God."

I can see from her scrunched-up nose I stepped in something.

"I'm not my mother."

"I'm southern," I say by rote.

Her smile is slow but savory as she peruses my outfit. "I can tell. You're going to sweat like a pig in the Grecian heat."

"Said by someone who's never been to Texas in August."

Alexandra smirks.

I hand her cell back.

"You have me there." Her eyes run over my body, and I've never been more glad of the work I put in with Merit and the boys back home than I am at that moment.

When her shrewd assessment returns to my face, I stare back.

"You look like you can handle yourself."

She has no idea.

A deep red eyebrow arches. "You're his substitute bodyguard?"

"In a manner of speaking."

"You guard a lot of people?'

My mind runs over all my clients and the intricate webs I wove to put them in just enough peril to test their metal—vet them for the billionaire who put fifty million in the pot for a chance at love.

"Yes."

"All right, Zaire—let's go."

"I'll be around, Alexandra," I say, making a little spin with my index finger in the air.

She gives me a brilliant smile. "Call me Alex."

I shake my head, and her smile slides to a frown. "A boys' name doesn't belong on you, darlin'."

"What does belong on me?" She blinks long ginger eyelashes, gorgeous without a hint of makeup.

Now we're talking. Then I remember myself. "Your full

name," I answer neutrally when every fiber of my being rejects the words for ones with far more heat.

She pivots and begins walking away.

I follow the sway of her hips and wonder a lot of things. Many of which have nothing to do with guarding her body—and everything to do with her body.

I didn't confess to Alexandra I've never been a bodyguard.

How hard can it be?

Five
Merit

"It's done," Merit tells his best friend and usual mark for guarding.

But not at the moment.

"Good," Denver Arnault replies.

Merit can feel the palpable weight of his pause before just making out Denver's softly uttered French curse word. "Gia needs this. And honestly—so do I."

"I know," Merit replies easily. "Life's fucking messy, Denver—I get that better than most. I just didn't dig the lie. I don't like using a contrived trauma to set Zaire up."

"Understood. If there were any other way—"

"—Zaire's a master of weaving scenarios. I can't believe we've been able to progress this without raising his suspicion."

Merit makes a low sound of disdain. "We're not chump change."

Denver gives a dark chuckle. "No, we are not," he agrees harshly. "We've been through some extreme circumstances, Mer."

Gruesome tasks surface in his mind, and Merit finds his consciousness is untroubled by the deeds of his past.

They were necessary.

When Chloe is tucked into the deepest crevice of his body every night—his heart, those dirty deeds of before become inconsequential.

"And this girl—Alexandra Frost"—Merit's laugh is short—"she's a lightweight social media star, not a target for anyone." Merit recognizes that's not a completely fair assessment of Alexandra Frost. In fact, his comment might be unfair.

He's caught an unguarded expression on Alex's face in the short time he worked for her that gave him pause.

A haunting behind the social media facade. Something stalks Alex—a memory from the past. An event, Merit would have sworn it.

His gut instincts are sharp, primal.

But Merit had *scoured* the past of Alexandra Frost. He wasn't having the ghosts of this heiress' rising from a surprise grave.

There's no deep traumas, no assaults from men, none of the things that plagued Zaire when he was working his magic for Club Alpha.

No drug use, though there was a shady window of alcohol overuse. However, Alex was disciplined enough to enlist Merit to cut her off from over-imbibing—which he had.

Merit had inserted himself with stealthy, "natural" deliberation so she would need his bodyguarding services when the time was ripe.

His name, services, and likeness had saturated the media for months after the debacle with Zaire's final Club Alpha couple, and suddenly, he'd found himself sought by all the mega-rich.

There was no one questioning Merit's skill set. It had been vetted in a public-as-fuck internet meltdown of epic proportions.

Once Alexandra Frost secured him in a bidding war, Merit had orchestrated this elaborate ploy to require Zaire to step in.

Could Zaire "pretend" to be a bodyguard?

Probably.

Could he fuck up someone's shit?

That's a resounding *yes*.

If there was any perceived chance that there would be real danger to either of the "players," Merit would know.

Merit senses Zaire will meet his animal side as Denver and Gia's deep pockets fund the ultimate Club Alpha—leveraging the very premise Zaire invented, against himself.

Zaire believes he's been circumspect with the slow financial slide of Club Alpha.

He was.

But those of them who give a shit about Zaire as a human being dug deeper than his pat answers of giving up Club Alpha because the time was right; because his good name and that of his matchmaking venture had been cleared.

Nope, he and Denver got the undertone loud and clear. Investigated his shit and turned up a million-ish is all Zaire was going to get after the feds dragged his ass through mud he had no business getting dirty in.

"You sure this Alexandra Frost is a good match?" Denver asks.

He gives a grunt. "She's not one of those vapid twats that shakes her ass on all the socials to gain followers because that's *all* she can do."

"Vapid twat?" Denver chokes on his laughter, and Merit gets a visual of Denver covering his mouth with a fist.

Merit gives a disgusted grunt. "Yeah, fuck. I get *so* tired of that garbage."

"Twats?"

Never that. Merit has one he's especially fond of, a memory of Chloe's wide, gray-blue eyes trusting him while he loves her with his body. He banishes the vision for the moment, and his next comment is said with more bite than he intended. "Fuck off, Denver."

"Excellent." The humor leaks away, and after a moment of silence, Denver says, "She needs to have a brain, have some looks, and not be a selfish bitch."

His new tone is serious, vagina discussions now closed.

"She's all that. Gave her the litmus test."

"Oh?" Denver asks in an amused lilt.

"Yeah, the Merit Lang special."

"Small or big?"

"Both."

"Do tell, Mer."

Before he can, Denver quickly adds, "Was it the door?"

Merit laughs before he can help it. "Yup."

"She said thank you?"

Alex had. "Yes, and the four women who went through before her did not. I was a non-man." Merit laughs without humor.

"If a woman will be thankful in small areas, it shows attentiveness." Denver's voice is thoughtful.

"Yeah."

And the big one? Denver asks with his weighted silence.

He fills that quiet with his answer, "She didn't come on to me. Even when she didn't know about Chloe."

"And when she did?"

"That too," Merit answers. "She wasn't the typical rich, jet-set heiress bent on getting fucked because she whistles the loudest."

Denver grunts at the crude metaphor. "What's her best thing?"

Merit mentally reviews what he knows about Alexandra Frost and decides almost instantly. "She works hard."

"And doesn't need to," Denver finishes, stating the obvious.

"No."

"Perfect," Denver says.

Merit shrugs. "I thought so."

"Great. Now we just keep away for six days."

"I'll keep tabs on them. If it looks like it's going pear-shaped, I'll step in, but within a day I'll be inserting some fun."

"Some problems?"

Merit chuckles. "Oh yeah. Ones that'll get Zaire's full attention."

"Good."

They're quiet for a beat of silence; then Denver breaks it, "Gia wants me to tell you *thank you*."

"Thank me when Zaire's okay. When he's him again."

Merit swipes his cell to hibernate just as Chloe comes up behind him and winds her arms around his waist.

He sets the phone down to concentrate on other things.

The most important thing.

Alexandra

As I walk away from Zaire Sebastian, I try to act like my insides aren't on fire.

Impossible.

At first, I was pissed off because Merit just dumped me on some dude I don't even know.

Then he put me at ease almost instantly.

A man.

Sure, I've slept with guys—but I don't get too close. Sometimes I just need, need—fuck if I know.

Physical closeness? I'm aware a shrink would say I had intimacy issues. *Why?* he or she would ask—*Why do you fight intimacy?*

I can't say.

It's like an extreme case of potty training. A one-day train. Where the worst thing you can imagine—the unimaginable—will happen if you pee your pants.

If you open your mouth.

If you *tell*.

My hand goes to my mouth automatically, as if that small gesture can hold back the grief that begs for physical escape.

"Alex," G calls from down the hotel corridor.

My face jerks up, and I can't squelch the treacherous vapors of my memories fast enough, G must see a shadow of the horror on my face, and her expression washes to worry.

"What's wrong?" G's hand drops to her side with the camera clutched in her grip.

I make a spontaneous decision. I lie.

"That fucker Merit dumped me on some other guy."

Confusion trumps worry.

Good.

Deflection at its best.

"What—why?"

"Some fam emergency."

After a moment, G says carefully, "You didn't really need a bodyguard, I guess."

Not really, though my recent direct messages have been creepy as hell. All the big people get those weirdos who threaten them.

But when I had a few DMs that really shook me and I'd seen all the news stories about *the* Merit Lang, I decided a little backup would be good.

So far, in the couple of weeks he's been guarding me, there hasn't been a spot of trouble.

Looks like I was worried for nothing. "Well," I evade, "he did send another guy."

"Oh," G brightens. "So, he didn't totally abandon you."

My mind conjures up the six-foot-three of Zaire Sebastian: dark blond hair curling just above his ears, a hat that appears molded to his head—and jeans doing some molding of their own to his slim hips and tight butt—and a nice package, I couldn't help but notice.

Yeah.

What color were his eyes?

I laugh softly. The color of *be careful,* Alex.

Six
Zaire

It's clear by now that I'm not cut out for bodyguard work. My skin's been crawling off my body while I watch Alexandra.

And she's not doing anything wrong.

Except her *not* doing anything means everyone is watching her not do anything.

Damn.

My eyes shift to the second cousin, Genevieve "G", who's got rainbow hair—the latest craze—and a stack of a dozen earrings lining the edge of each ear. Wild looks aside, her character is sound.

I know because Merit gave me the ten-second rundown before he tossed me at Alexandra.

G, by all accounts, appears to look out for Alexandra.

My eyes take in the women as they confer after each photo op before my attention shifts to where they stand. I hate the unprotected breaks to discuss each photo session out in the open. *How does Merit do this job?*

I couldn't. Yet, I said yes to this if only for a few days.

I must have been insane.

Their two heads press together, one multicolored, the other a deep copper penny ginger as they check out the latest batch of pictures. Alexandra nods and points to the wide digital lens, clearly liking one shot and not another.

I dab my forehead with a sodden handkerchief, melting back into the shadows cast between two bright white homes where intersecting hot pink bougainvillea is tucked and draped between the pair, forming a casual "arch" as the homes are so close that calling the space between the two an "alley" is a generous identifier.

As I watch Alexandra from my dim hiding place, the relentless sun beats down on her lightly tanned shoulders.

I couldn't help overhearing her and G discussing the sparkly sunscreen, and a smile tugs at the corners of my mouth from the fresh memory.

Alexandra only allows sunblock if it contains sparkles. *Sun-kissed shimmer,* I remember her calling it.

My eyes move over the acres of uncovered skin revealed by only a brilliant white bikini top.

People stream past the pair, giving curious glances but defaulting to the indifference so typical of Europeans who politely don't intrude.

I catch sight of one man who walks by.

Slows.

My body automatically tenses, assessing. His attire is not untypical of the region but makes my nuts sweat just looking at it.

Alexandra hadn't been wrong when she said it was hot here, but not quite as hot as Texas in late summer.

White suit jacket paired with a pale pink button-down and expensive loafers in a buff color, surfaces him as money. My gaze crosses broad shoulders and biceps that strain against the linen fabric. Built. Over six-foot and under thirty-five.

He's dressed too expensively for me to worry about

robbery. He's probably thinking he has a shot at an obviously pretty woman.

I'm not a fan of his perusal.

My eyes move over Alexandra again. *Not just pretty*, I think —*unique*.

Mentally, I run down the list of the small staff Alexandra employs. They number five. Chef, G (photog and relative), wardrobe girl, personal assistant, and myself (pseudo bodyguard).

This guy doesn't fit any of those roles, and as far as I know, Alexandra doesn't have a bunch of groupie friends she brings along for built-in entertainment.

And no steady man.

Still, I hesitate. Interrupting won't come off well if I interfere, proving I'm an amateur because a passerby has a few words with Alexandra.

I've intellectualized it, but my disquiet deepens. Shifting my weight, I watch.

*

Alex

Frustrated, I let my hand fall from shielding my eyes from the sun, which just seems to be a different strength here in the Mediterranean than where I live in New York City.

My eyes sweep the general vicinity. Nothing. Zaire is supposedly watching me.

I give a little snort. *Ditched.*

Then I feel myself frown. To be fair, I never searched out Merit when he was on bodyguard duty. He always had the "brother" vibe for me. Not that Merit Lang wasn't a great-looking guy, he is. There just wasn't any undertone with Merit, and—he's all-business anyway.

I get the feeling that he doesn't mix business and pleasure

and have to admire the devotion he has to his girlfriend, Chloe. He would never stay a nanosecond past his shift and verifying I was secure inside my hotel room.

He'd immediately raced off to be with her. The media had protected Chloe's identity, but I'd eventually discovered she'd been the poor woman who'd been attacked then left for dead.

At Merit Lang's feet.

I totally understand that he might have a hero complex or something. Not that *I* should be throwing any stones.

Not since Bridget.

My stomach executes a small flip.

It'd never occurred to me to put the moves on Merit. First, he had the relative vibe. Second, even if he hadn't had the relative vibe, I wasn't some tacky rich bitch bent on making a guy feel obligated to sex me just because he was worried about retaining his position.

Cheap and not real flattering.

It's not that I don't have needs. I totally do. I want to be held by a man, loved by a man—filled by one. But unlike "regular" women, I have to be careful, protect myself. A semi-famous, rich young woman can't just have sex with anyone. Contrary to everyone's assumptions about wealth, yes—it's definitely ideal to have more money, but money doesn't buy things like happiness or freedom from others' opinions about who you are, what you do, etc.

In fact, having a bucket of cash seems to have the opposite effect, causing everyone to suspect you of the worst things by default due to your wealth.

Gretchen spends three hours a day just on DMs and comments. Blocking, answering, and deleting. I don't know how I'd do what I'm doing without a personal assistant.

Oh yeah, I wouldn't. If I had to do all that work, there would be no content for anyone to view.

"Are you listening?"

No. My head whips back to G from searching dim nooks and crannies between brilliant white houses, and I feel a subtle heat surface on my cheeks. *Caught.* "Yes."

G's nose twitches as she taps the view lens with a bright blue nail tip to emphasize my rudeness.

She gives me a look of pure disbelief.

I duck my head. "Okay, no."

"What's got your panties in a distracted twist?"

I flip my palms over, noticing the heat is making my head swim. "Let's move to the shade."

G adjusts her wide-brimmed hat. Her tattoo sleeve with a brightly-hued parrot is barely discernible under the pure zinc she applies to keep the tat completely protected from the sun's hot rays.

"Pfft. Okay, wussy."

I give a slight smile but gratefully move to the shade cast by a tiny terracotta overhang that juts out just enough on both sides of a door so we can flank the sides and not block the entrance.

G follows me, ticking off our ops as she walks, "We have an ocean view backdrop and that gorgeous shot of you with the orange trailing flowers…"

"Bougainvillea," I supply, slumping against the wall and planting a sandaled foot against the surface.

"Yeah, those. Whatever. They're like weeds around here, but I don't even have to use a filter for color saturation; they're naturally gorgeous." She bites her lip then adds fretfully, "But maybe they won't compliment your hair color."

My eyes close, and I state, "I'm not dying my hair."

"Is that a dis?"

Snapping my eyes open, I catch G's grin. And her middle finger.

"Classy, G." I laugh. "You know I *adore* your unicorn hair."

She winks. "Right." *Sarcasm.* "Somebody's got to keep you in line."

Right.

"Are you peckish?" Her critical gaze scans my body. Then she slowly nods. "You're peckish. Let's do the restaurant set next."

"Pushy."

"Tell me I'm wrong?" She widens her arms, lens strap swinging.

I smile. *She's not wrong.* I drove myself through the day with no food and just the cream in my coffee as per the usual. Normal routine, but with the sun and all the walking... I'm starved.

I push off from the wall and begin walking the three blocks to the restaurant Gretchen had scouted for me. It has some of the foods I like.

I'll need to order a classic Grecian dish to taste as well. My followers demand it.

I give a lopsided smile. Who am I fooling? *I* demand it. I want them to feel as though they're vicariously living through my travels. The following I've amassed has the feel of extended family. Usually, they love what I'm doing and what I share.

Except a few who hate, of course.

But all influencers and media queens have those. After all, as the old adage goes—you can't please everyone.

Just then, a guy walks by with the traditional tall, dark, and handsome looks. My eyes float down his body and note he doesn't appear Greek but has that subtle European vibe I've come to recognize.

Normally, I'd breeze by, but he gives me such close scrutiny I slow my walk to a stroll and stare back, untroubled by the visual contact.

Zaire's somewhere, I tell myself. It's broad daylight; he's handsome—let him look.

"Excuse me," he says in perfect English.

I stop.

Won't kill me to be polite. Besides, he's so obviously gorgeous it's not going to burn my retinas to dally.

"Are you Alexandra Frost?"

Oh *shit*. A little thrill of adrenaline zings through me. My truthful nature nails me to the spot. "Yes, I am."

His smile chases a somewhat solemn expression from his face in a slash of perfect white teeth above a chiseled jawline. "Excellent."

Poise asserts itself as I admit, "I'm afraid I'm at a disadvantage." G moves up beside me as I spread my palms away from my sides.

He walks closer, and I relax. Nobody this gorgeous and refined could be anything other than all about the good.

My hormones—I mean eyes, drink him in.

I love a guy I can wear heels with and still be shorter. Just a pet peeve, and though I have bejeweled, flip-flop two-inchers on, I'm shorter.

Check.

"I'm Bryce Davenport."

Huh. Not a very Euro name. Accentless on the English.

"Oh—I don't think I know you." I feel myself frown.

He waves that away. "We move in the same circles, but I don't believe we've met."

Davenport, Davenport—my mind roars through all the "names" of the wealthy people I've been around my entire life and comes up blank. I think I'd remember Bryce Davenport.

"Our parents went to the same boarding school."

Click. A memory assails me: my father showing me a yearbook from his senior class.

Got it... maybe.

I smile. "Yes—I do know the name."

Turning to G, I say to Bryce, "this is my cousin—"

"Genevieve."

I laugh, and G's eyes round. "How do you know Genevieve?"

He gives a casual shrug of his broad shoulders. "I'm a big fan, and you talk about those who assist you with your socials."

Instantly, I'm nervous, reviewing all my content through his eyes and coming up short.

But Bryce disarms me immediately, "I love 'traveling' with you," he says, dropping air-quotes around the word *traveling*. "My work keeps me busy, but at a thumb swipe, I can be wherever you are, enjoying the sights, sounds, and tastes of places I can't easily be."

Bryce's indigo-blue eyes hold no guile as he captures my gaze.

My shoulders unknot, but at that exact moment, an epic fail happens: my belly lets out a huge bellow.

Oh my God. I slap my palm over my bare stomach. "That's great," I say in a quiet voice.

G starts guffawing.

I give her a side-eye death glare meant to maim.

Bryce's midnight blue gaze never leaves mine. "Sounds like you could do with a lunch," he quips, eyes traveling my stomach.

Not at all embarrassed. *Nope.* "Actually, that was where we were headed," I explain, trying to smooth over the lame belly roar.

Another smile flashes on his handsome face. "I have just the place."

I mention where we'd planned to go.

Bryce shakes his head. "This is a literal hole in the wall, but the food is sublime—amazing."

My mind latches onto the direction shift for my social—

after all, it's so much better for a gorgeous guy to eat with me than without one.

Too bad I can't separate the two. I'm always angling for content. I can't extract that desire from just living.

I should, but not right now. This chance meeting is a win-win. "Okay," I give a grateful smile, Bryce seems to know the area, and his parents were friends with mine.

I feel safe. Admired.

Not a bad mental place to be.

The three of us walk to the Greek dive, and I almost forget about where Zaire Sebastian is.

Almost.

Seven
Zaire

Fuck, darlin', don't go with him.
Then she does.
Dammit.

I can just imagine what kind of pick-up he gave Alexandra to have her wander off with him—must've been good. Because Merit had made no bones about what *he* required from Alexandra to be the best bodyguard for her—he'd given Alexandra the protocol on her daily routines.

And Alexandra is not fucking sticking with it. Taking off with a fella from out of nowhere is *not* safe. That maneuver does not follow the daily protocols.

I visually tag them, keeping to the shadows wherever they fall.

Alexandra doesn't head in the direction of the restaurant that's on the itinerary.

Nope.

Taking a sharp turn into a narrow uphill alleyway, she exits the main road entirely.

G actually turns around and spots me. She tips her finger from her forehead in a mock salute.

Dipping my chin in acknowledgment, I can just make out her eye roll before she turns and follows the pair.

Lengthening my stride, I traverse the worn cobblestone-lined road for the shadowed narrow strip of uneven stones that climb the hill.

Slowing at the corner where the road stops and the alley begins, I spot Alexandra, G and the mystery yahoo at the top of what turns out to be steep stairs.

It's not lost on me that there are two points of easy entry and exit and no more.

Don't like that.

My attention swivels behind me to the open road, my gaze returning to the top of the flight of misshapen and worn steps where I can't see beyond G, Alexandra, and the stranger.

The other access point is a mystery, and my earlier unease plucks away at my usual clear-headedness. The stress is real, considering I don't want anything to happen to Alexandra, nor do I want to let Merit down in his absence.

Independent and separate from each other—they're both counting on me.

I hike.

Staying far enough back from the small group I can make their figures ahead without drawing too much attention to myself, though I believe blending in would be more obtainable if I'd give up my ten-gallon hat.

No fucking way, never going to *not* be Texan enough for that kind of traitorous wardrobe fail.

I love Europe.

But I love Texas more.

I hit the top step, not out of breath but the war with sweat wholly lost. I concede victory to the weather, leaning against the corner of the building that anchors the spot where steps halt and an even more narrow alley appears.

Only a sliver of my body is visible. I remove my hat and pat my forehead down with my handkerchief.

A wooden sign swings from a small, pastel pink house. The color sticks out in sharp contrast with all the surrounding houses done in bone-bleached white.

Trofi.

Food, I loosely interpret, though the letter that looks like an "F," isn't one.

The man pauses, pointing to the small pink cottage, and Alexandra nods, she and G walking inside before him.

As soon as they enter, I extract my cell from the back pocket of my linen-blend pants and run through the geography of the immediate area.

Local dive, I discover.

I walk to the front of the building, eyes scanning what's across the street.

A bank of shade beckons from beneath an overhang heralding an entrance to a residence, the shockingly blue door shouting its color against the bleached-out exterior paint of the tiny house.

With another glance at the open door to the restaurant, I note Alexandra is sitting with G and the unknown male.

I stride across the street and wait, getting more pissed off by the moment.

Not that I have a right to.

Alexandra has to eat. G likely needs sustenance as well.

Hell—even I do.

I'm just insulted as fuck that Alexandra can't be a tiny bit more about her own self-preservation.

And if I'm honest with myself, some of my negative passion comes from her being with another man.

But I'm not.

Honest with myself.

Alex

My chatting falters for a moment, eyes drinking in Zaire sauntering across the narrow street and taking up post directly opposite the little hole in the wall I find myself in.

G follows my gaze, but Bryce is turned away for the moment, giving our order to an older lady in Greek.

Zaire's words come back to me from earlier today.

The part of the conversation where I wasn't paying close attention felt like a rehearsal from what Merit had explained already.

Don't linger in the open.

Pay attention to your surroundings—stick to the itinerary.

Well—I blew *that* all-to-hell.

Wrenching my eyes away from where Zaire stands, hands hooked in belt loops of his tight, ivory linen-type pants, I can just make out his hard jaw, obscured by the biggest cowboy hat I've ever seen in person.

Smoothing my hands over my sarong, I smile at Bryce as he turns back to me.

He's *so* handsome, my mind convinces me.

I don't look at Zaire again.

Instead, I take in the five beat-up wooden tables, each painted a different pastel color and topped with the same, electric blue checkered plastic tablecloth.

In the center of each table is a small dove-gray jar labeled "salt" and a half-burnt candle in a crackled glass holder.

Quaint. Different. *Not* rich girl surroundings.

I love it.

The older lady shuffles in and sets a huge woven basket of steaming Koulouri in front of us.

"These are so yummy," G announces, grabbing a huge one at the top of the pile and tearing off a chunk.

Somewhere between a pretzel and breakfast bread, Koulouri is a Greek staple, especially with coffee.

"Come on, Alex—live a little. You won't grow a buddha belly from just one of these beauts."

Bryce's eyes run down my body, lingering between my breasts and halting at the subject of G's comment.

Love a guy looking at my stomach. *Always great.*

I restrain a snort.

"No buddha belly there," he says with a smile.

I return his smile.

"So what are you doing here, Bryce?"

He leans back in the chair, crossing his legs at the ankle, and replies, "Business."

"Oh," I say, thinking he really cleared things up with that vague-ass comment.

"Wonderful, that told us a lot," G huffs, verbalizing my thought.

I cover a grin with my hand.

Fishing out a Koulouri from the stack, I take a bite, loving the fragrant, melt-in-your-mouth freshness and crunch of the sesame seeds.

"Wait!" G says.

I give a little jump.

She hops up and starts taking photos.

"Hey!" I say, covering my lips as I chew. "My mouth is full!"

"Not doing your zero carb nonsense today. I *must* offer proof," G says as she squats, getting nostrils shots and all kinds of unflattering poses.

"G!" I cry, figuring my stomach is roll-ish and I have crumbs where I shouldn't and... *shit.*

She pivots as though she'll snap a pic of Bryce and he turns his head at the precise moment G attempts to capture him.

"Ah! Come on—I want to have the 'I-met-a-stranger-that-isn't' documentation."

His smile is tight. "I said I'm a big fan of Alexandra's socials, not that I want to *be* in them."

G pouts. "Okay, but *damn*." She huffs over to her chair and mutters something about joy-sucks.

I pat the seat of her chair next to me. "Sit down, G—we can take an hour to eat without you having to get candid, ugly shots of me." I raise my eyebrows.

"You couldn't look ugly if you tried."

"Truth," Bryce agrees, snagging his own Koulouri.

"I want butter," G mutters, dusting the loose sesame seeds from the exterior of her Koulouri.

"Not very European of you," I comment, thinking about Europeans' lack of interest in dairy, water—and ice, especially.

I'd kill for water to be served without asking. Instead of the usual answer when I ask if I can have water, it's always, "Live or still?" From a bottle.

Never ice.

How about tap? Sometimes frills get old. They take more time than they're worth. I'm not so un-self-aware I don't realize I'm bitching about stupid shit.

"Wait a sec," I say.

Bryce looks at me expectantly.

"What did you order for us?"

He grins, perfect teeth inside a very white smile.

I decide he's too perfect then instantly feel bad. *God.*

My eyes start to flick to Zaire outside, and I have a sudden thought—is he hungry?

"It's a surprise," Bryce comments, clearly pleased with himself.

My eyes shift to him.

"I heard what he ordered because *I* was listening," G says smugly.

I resist flipping her off.

Then the wonderful aroma of lunch hits me before it even arrives, and I instantly recognize my fave dish. "How did you know?" I ask Bryce, turning my pleased face to his.

"I know what you like to eat because you go into great detail about it."

Oh.

The elderly lady sets down a huge plate of Souvlaki, and my mouth waters.

Usually served with Pita bread, we had the Koulouri instead so the gorgeous skewered pork steams enticingly as my nose defines the different ingredients.

The *tzatziki* sauce is inside a large glass container with three small ceramic bowls for each of us.

I drag the wooden ladle inside the large bowl and transfer a generous portion into my small bowl. Made with yogurt, cucumber, and mint, it is the best compliment to the savory notes held within the Souvlaki.

Next, our waitress sets a wedge of mozzarella with ruby red tomatoes, drizzled balsamic, topped with fresh herbs on our table.

I look up at her, happiness crow's feet surround her kind brown eyes, suggesting a good life. "Thank you," I say in English, hoping she understands my meaning.

She smiles, nodding.

Bryce repeats my thanks in Greek.

I give him a grateful glance.

"Heaven," G announces, giving a small moan as she takes the first greedy bite.

Agreed. "Thank you for this—I meant to try a new dish and always end up going back to Souvlaki." I shrug.

"It's *my* favorite." Bryce winks.

I sweep my eyes over his figure and say casually, "Doesn't look like you're sampling much of the cuisine here."

He shakes his head. "I adhere to a strict gym schedule no matter where I travel and try to eat light."

So does Zaire, I think.

Sliding a chunk of meat from the skewer, I dip the succulent pork into the sauce and take a delicate bite.

Takes some discipline, considering I want to cram the entire morsel inside my mouth and choke to death as I shovel food.

I laugh.

"What?" Bryce asks, slowly chewing his piece.

"I'm starved and trying to pretend I'm not," I admit easily.

Chuckling, he says, "Don't on my account. I'm not for women who deny their appetite."

"That's sexy, not gonna lie," G pipes in, her rainbow-colored hair shivering as she laughs.

We consume in happy silence for a few minutes, and I'm just thinking food coma is a possibility when Bryce drops a small bomb.

Or a big one.

"Why don't we invite your bodyguard in to dine with us?"

My heart speeds.

He noticed Zaire?

My head turns as I look outside, hunting for where he stood before Bryce ordered our food.

Zaire's not there.

Eight
Alex

I won't lie, I'm a bit panicked. Zaire said he'd make himself easy to spot. Like Merit, Zaire concurred that him being identified as my bodyguard is more of a benefit to my safety. In fact, he mentioned, very briefly, it's okay that potential problem-types get the idea they can't just approach me or do whatever because Zaire's presence would give them pause.

Bryce's chuckle breaks my chain of thought.

I narrow my eyes at him. "Are you serious?"

"Of course." His wide navy eyes are innocent. "I bet he's hungry too."

"He's a guy—of course he is," G adds, smirking.

"I don't see him." I bite my bottom lip, giving a visual eye-sweep at the street again.

"I'm right here." Zaire's deep voice is low, controlled—coming from somewhere behind where I sit.

Whirling in my seat, I find Zaire standing there, appearing reserved and calm, huge cowboy hat tipped low on his forehead, shadowing his expressive eyes.

Our older waitress stands behind him, beaming like she just won the lottery.

I laugh softly. Zaire must have poured on the charm because he'd been allowed to enter from the back.

My eyes move behind him. I don't spy a door.

Considering I'd made a last-minute decision to come, and this restaurant was *definitely* not on the itinerary, Zaire flew under the radar really well. Not that I'm surprised he has the skill set to stay hidden, I'm just wondering why Zaire made a point of saying he'd be in plain sight then skulks around.

Hmmm.

The two men regard each other for a bloated moment. Then Bryce invites, "Come—join us."

Zaire gives a polite smile and replies, "On duty, sorry." He lifts a broad shoulder then lets it drop. "Ignore me."

Why does that make me feel bad? "Oh!" I give a little gasp at my own rudeness, "Zaire Sebastian, this is Bryce Davenport."

Zaire moves his eyes everywhere but at Bryce, and I note his gaze bounces from the open door to somewhere behind our waitress then finally lands on Bryce before he commits to stepping forward.

Bryce stands, and they shake hands in a single, hard pump —Zaire has Bryce by a couple of inches, but they're both tall guys.

Zaire moves to a table that is almost against the wall and, with great deliberation, removes his hat and sets it on the table. His hair is adorably mashed where the rim of the huge brim rested. Short dark blond curls where his hair is slightly longer cup around the top of his ears. But there's nothing little boy about Zaire.

He's all-man.

Bryce sits back down, and Zaire leans back against the chair. He doesn't look at me, though. He watches the exit and entry. A lot like what I'd seen Merit do. But Merit never got this close.

He always kept some distance between us.

My mind dances around unrealistic possibilities. What does that difference mean that Merit installed distance between us but Zaire doesn't?

Probably nothing, Alex.

I smooth suddenly damp hands over my sarong as Bryce returns his attention to me.

"Let's get together tonight, talk about your socials."

My brows meet. "What about them?"

"I've got some interesting propositions."

Okay. "I'd like to—let me check with Gretchen; she manages my world." I laugh.

His smile is shameless, wide. "Oh, well—I already spoke with her, and she said you were free if you *wanted* to be." He lifts a dismissive shoulder as if to say, *no big deal if it doesn't work.*

My head snaps up and I fight to look unperturbed. I'm not a fan of what feels like Bryce going behind my back—that Gretchen would clear my schedule without so much as a text.

A small trickle of unease slides down my spine.

I don't look at Zaire or G. But I badly want to know what Zaire thinks and recognize I never thought about Merit in the same context. *Zaire* doesn't *care, Alex.* He's a hired guy. Like wardrobe, Gretchen—hell, *your cook.*

"You do cross your 'Ts' and dot your 'Is,'" G comments with a contemplative glance at Bryce.

Bryce nods. "I assumed once Alexandra made the familial connection, we'd be able to visit about work things without too much concern."

Except that I'm not really into someone showing up and offering insights into my business. I'm a young woman and wealthy.

So? Some might ask. What should be impressive for them

to know is that I don't *have* to work. However, I pursue a living that's aside from my inherent wealth.

Not to be arrogant, but I might not *need* to listen to Bryce. Why? Because he's a *man* and certainly he has more business savvy because of his gender? *Pfft.*

I try not to let my feelings show, but I can't deny Bryce Davenport just put a damper on the impromptu lunch and doesn't even seem to understand it. Which somehow makes his assumptions worse that he might not get how all his showmanship comes across.

What makes him special enough to warrant me listening? Because my parents knew his? And *why* did Gretchen say I was free tonight?

Maybe I didn't *want* to be.

I slide a look to Zaire, and his eyes are on me with an unreadable expression.

Does *he* think Bryce is being pushy?

I do.

But maybe I'm being an ungracious bitch. That's possible. Or probable.

Why do I give a shit what Zaire thinks? That's the most important question.

"Listen, if that doesn't work?" Bryce cocks a dark brow, obviously interpreting my silence as less-than-positive, and spreads his neatly manicured hands away from his body in a study of nonchalance.

Our eyes meet and heat climbs to my cheeks. Suddenly, I feel like an ass. He took me to lunch—our parents knew each other, and I'm hog-tied by convention and playing mental volleyball about what Zaire thinks.

I usually do better than this. "Sure, no, it's fine." I force a smile, feeling slightly ashamed at my own behavior.

G snorts. "Yeah, Alex—get a life."

I have a life. It's not exactly the one I want, but it's living.

I don't look at Zaire.

Won't.

Zaire

What a prick.

My eyes run over his expensive, fitted suit—his feigned charm.

It's clear to me that Alexandra's not vested in this aggressive dick. Yet he pushes.

Why?

I can't guard and do intel at the same time. If I still had the resources I created from Club Alpha, I'd know what brand of underwear this chump favors.

But I don't have that clout anymore.

In fact, I have to keep that fact in the forefront of my mind. I have a million-*ish* cold hard cash, and not a penny more.

I had billionaire clients. *Had* is the operative word.

Tuning into their conversation, I listen to every word. Who does Bryce Davenport think he is?

Alexandra Frost is a self-made girl. Not her money, no. But what she's doing with her social media empire, yes.

Last night, when I'd technically been off-duty, looking into Alexandra Frost had been easy.

Too easy.

She's way too simple to locate—track. Look at Davenport and what he'd accomplished. He'd weaseled his way into a lunch with her and made the run-in appear spontaneous. But when push came to shove, Davenport had already contacted her assistant, and whatever he'd said had made Gretchen clear Alexandra's schedule.

From her expression, Alexandra wasn't a huge fan of all the behind-the-scenes workarounds in her social life. If I were her, I'd be feeling "managed" about now.

Either way, I respect her cool response to his insertion into her business mechanics.

G watches Davenport the same way I do—cautiously, adding credence to my innate sense of distrust.

Of course, I'm attracted to my "VIP" as Merit refers to the bodies he guards, and that emotional signature is a big no-no.

Alexandra Frost doesn't feel like a VIP. She feels like a woman I'm interested in, and suddenly I want Merit to return, badly.

I would then be free to pursue Alexandra.

Sudden regret fills me when I'm reminded that I'm not going to be interesting to Ms. Frost.

She's worth billions.

And I'm not—not anymore.

My attention touches on Davenport again, leaning forward in animated conversation with Alexandra.

He has a hidden agenda, and I don't know what it is.

I aim to find out.

Alex

I'm careful with my appearance. I even applied makeup. Wearing my hair down, I take a critical look at myself in the corner mirror in my hotel suite.

My linen pants are wide-leg in a true beigey/sand color. A spaghetti strap, cropped blouse and tied at the waist in deep navy collects my cleavage in nothing short of a miraculous way, setting off the deep copper of my waist-length hair. The hem of the top exactly ends at the waistband where my pants begin, a sliver of tanned belly revealed with movement.

Nude, stiletto, open-toe, skyscraper heels put me at almost six-foot-two—Bryce Davenport will be my rival in height.

Zaire's even taller, my mind interjects.

My reflection shows my pursed lips.

Turning, I take in the scope of my penthouse suite. It's such a large space; we won't have to go beyond its confines for our little chat. Visually sweeping the room, I'm happy with the plush yet simple furniture in neutral tones and a full wet bar. Though there's no way I'll imbibe.

Especially tonight.

Sighing, I step away from my reflection. My mood is trash because Gretchen and I had it out, and I can't reclaim my former lightness from earlier today. Remembering our convo makes me feel bad.

And vindicated.

"Why would you clear my schedule?" I'd asked her, face-to-face.

Gretchen spreads her hands away from her body, "Have you met him? Bryce Davenport is so charming. He knew your parents and wanted to pick your brain for business ideas—Bryce wanted to surprise you for lunch."

Bryce.

"He surprised me, all right," I'd replied dryly.

One of the reasons I've dug Gretchen from the beginning is she's got a good head on her shoulders, keeps my shit straight.

This entire episode had given me pause.

"Alex," Gretchen started, bringing my full attention to the way her eyes seemed more pinched with her dark brown hair pulled back in a severe French braid. "All of us who work with you adore you." Her eyes trained away from me only to come right back, caging me with her truth. "And you never do anything with any *man. I wasn't going to roadblock the possibil-*

ity." Gretchen was playing cupid now. There's a reason for my lack of a boyfriend, but I remained silent as she went on. "This guy's okay; you didn't have anything else going on, and G always races out to party without you."

Gretchen was right. But having my plans made for me nagged. Actually, it pissed me off. "Not again," I said, lifting a palm. "Bryce Davenport is hot and handsome, and we have that history, but I don't like anyone orchestrating my time, except me."

Gretchen stepped forward, towering much taller than my five-foot-nine frame, and folded me against her. "You know I love you," she whispered fiercely.

"That's why I don't fire you." I sounded sullen, even to me.

Gretchen leaned back, searching my face. "I'm really sorry. Don't break up with me."

I'd smiled. "Nope."

A knock sounds at my door, and I move over the plush carpet and weave through the understated lounge furniture to stand before the door.

My heart's not into meeting Bryce, though every bit of me understands how flattered I should be.

He's wealthy.

Bryce is handsome.

By all appearances, he is absolutely interested in my work and has insights to offer because of that alleged interest.

I fully acknowledge those are all positives.

So why are my thoughts consumed by Zaire's final off-duty goodbye glance being speculative before leaving me at my hotel room door? Zaire hadn't said one word about my "lack of self-preservation" as Merit had called my tendency to be oblivious of my surroundings.

The absence of commentary had made me think more about it, not less.

There'd been lots of thoughts swirling behind those expressive greenish-hazel eyes.

None that were voiced, though.

Zaire's pause had been lengthy. And I knew, *knew*, he hadn't wanted to leave me here alone when Bryce showed.

G had taken off to party, and we hadn't really discussed the whole "Bryce" thing. She's probably so thrilled there's a guy in the wings she thought lack of discussion was better than her peanut gallery commentary.

I line up one eyeball at the peephole, and Bryce's arresting smile comes into view.

Retreating a step, I open the door with a return smile.

"Hello," he says, dark blue gaze gleaming as he runs his eyes down my careful outfit, "May I come in?"

I get a little flutter in my stomach at his perusal. "Absolutely," I wave a palm behind me and take a step backward, swinging the door wide and already thinking about what refreshments to offer, having ditched the idea of alcohol for myself.

Bryce steps through.

I shut the door, automatically sliding the bolt home.

Turn.

He steps into my space in a finely executed dance-like move.

With intimate, ferocious eye contact, Bryce wraps his fingers around my throat and pins me to the door I just closed.

When I open my mouth to scream, he tightens his grip, suppressing my airway.

I choke, rising to my tiptoes.

"Quiet, Ms. Frost."

My eyes lock with his, adrenaline making my toes and fingers tingle. The lunch we shared earlier begins to rise in my once-calm stomach.

"Shut your shallow mouth and listen well. Your life depends on it."

I can feel the strength in his hand. The weight of truth in his words. I'm stunned, scared and, in the worst way possible, want Zaire.

After Bryce's next words, I couldn't want Zaire less.

"This is about Bridget, and you *will* listen without interrupting me."

I do listen without interrupting, my terror overshadowing every other thought.

The joy of my life is fleeting, snuffed out with the mention of her name.

NINE
ZAIRE

Hated leaving her there. I know that dickhead will want a nightcap. He had the feel; he intimated as such, rearranging Alexandra's schedule without her knowledge.

And if Bryce Davenport actually gives a ripe shit about Alexandra's business, I'm a priest.

Better phone Merit.

I stride across the hotel room, jerking my suitcase from the folding stand of support straps, and slap the heft onto the foot of the bed.

Disengaging the locks with a loud snap, I rifle inside. Digging through the integral zipper pocket within its depths, I grab a burner and flip it open.

No charge, of course.

Moving to the wall, I impatiently unwrap the packaging and fling it as I plug one end to the phone, attaching the other end to the voltage adapter, and finally stabbing the other into an electrical outlet.

I travel with burners—always. But Merit had given me some of his before he took off. I'd told him it wasn't necessary;

he'd tasked me with Alexandra's safety for less than a week. What could happen?

Today, that's what.

Removing my hat, I set it on the bed beside the suitcase and wait through three rings.

"Lang," Merit answers.

"It's me."

"Okay."

Fucker. "I'm the Alpha of the Club," I say in a bored voice.

"Hey, Zaire."

"You could forgo the super-spy routine."

"Nope, if you were under duress, I couldn't be sure. You might really dig that line if you ever were."

"This isn't something I plan to take up for a lifetime," I say in a dry tone. God knows I'm already stressed out and I've been on the job less than forty-eight hours.

"But you're calling."

"Yes. There's a dickhead circling."

"What—like a vulture?"

"Something like that. I don't have any of my resources, but the fella's name is Bryce Davenport. He claims to be the kid of a former schoolmate of Alexandra's parents."

"Sounds reasonable." Merit pauses, and I knew it wouldn't take much time for him to dream up my possible reasons for phoning. "You got a feeling?"

"I understand that's not real. Instincts don't count."

A moment hammers between us then, "They *do* count."

"All right," I say slowly, "Davenport pops up while Alexandra's on her way to the 'itinerary' restaurant, and his appearance seems a little too easy to me."

I can almost hear Merit's mental wheels turning. "Don't love it, not gonna lie."

"I'm phoning because I didn't like him almost on sight.

Not after he spotted me and told Alexandra her bodyguard should come in for food."

Merit's derisive snort blasts through the phone lines. "Did ya?"

"Yes. On my own terms. I had already been headed in from the back—and I hadn't made my presence known up to that point, secretive."

"No need," Merit instantly dismisses. "Her entire followership knows she has security and even knew who I was. I ghost when I have to. Otherwise, like I mentioned before, my face being seen when Alex is running around being social media queen is just fine. Let them see there's a consequence if they've got something in mind other than some distance worship."

"Right."

"Okay, fucking talk."

"Working the Club Alpha circuit, I had to use my gut instinct a lot. Sometimes, a woman or a man would be swell on paper and then, on meeting, turned out to *not* work for the client at all. It's hard to quantify."

"Meeting them was about *your* instincts, like a crosscheck," Merit accurately guesses.

This isn't something I like to admit; my gut feeling is a gray factor. But I had the satisfied clients to vouch for its validity. But I called Merit because of a hunch, so some confessing's in order. "Yes."

"So your instincts say what?"

"That he's dangerous."

"Good enough for me. Is she with him right now?"

"Yes."

"And you can't stand it?"

Not a bit. "That's the short of it. Just have this feeling I can't ditch."

"Describe it."

I analyze the hunch, the way Davenport interacted with Alexandra. I hit on something. "He was acting."

"Everyone does." I hear the shrug in his voice.

"No, sir. Not like this fella. Davenport wants everyone to think he's gone on Alexandra, that they had this casual run-in. Davenport talked about following Alexandra on her social, that he lived vicariously through her travel, but he just happened to be here on business."

"Plausible."

"I know this seems impossible."

Merit snorts. "Kinda paranoid for you, but lay it on me."

"I don't think he's actually *into* her. It's almost like he was gauging her reaction and filing whatever that was away for later reflection."

Merit's silence is lengthy.

Just when I'm about to fill the conversational void, he says, "Do you know where the escape-pack is stowed like we discussed."

I think of the touristy "visit Greece" lightweight pack with its sparse survivalist contents.

"Yes." That Merit asks about the pack deepens my unease.

"Go over there, knock, and if Alex's okay, she'll answer."

I stand, burner clutched in my hand. "If she doesn't?"

"Alex isn't a saint, y'know—she could be *involved* with this dude."

I grind my teeth. Not pleased with Alexandra boning the guy and having no right to feel that way. "Is that normal behavior?"

"No. Alex is a nun compared to my other clients."

Hmm. "Why? She's a hot woman."

"Interested?"

Yes. "No."

"You've got Chloe. That's why Alexandra isn't on your woman-dar."

"Yeah, but she's more like a little sister to me. Alex is good-looking, there's no doubt. She's just too like me in some ways."

In no way. I bark a laugh. "Don't see that."

Merit ignores that last. "Apologize if she's asleep."

Turning my wrist, I note the time as nearly ten o'clock. "Too early."

"No. G likes her up before dawn for the early morning light. She's usually in bed."

Great. "I feel like a dick."

"You are."

I grunt. "I can't sleep worrying about them together." I sigh. "I did my normal workout—past my norm so I could wear myself out." My arms and legs still feel fatigued.

"How'd that go?"

Still alert and bright as hell. "Fuck off, Merit."

"Just as soon as you do."

I grin, the expression fading as I contemplate interrupting Alexandra for what will probably be *nada*. "I'll let you go; I need to figure this out."

Alex

His dark eyes, a blue I thought was riveting a minute ago, pierce me to my marrow.

"How do you know Bridget?"

His smile is cruel.

When the knock sounds, I jump and give a soft sound of distress as his fingers tighten around the column of my neck.

Bryce's eyes lift from my face, moving to the door.

"Whoever it is, make them go away."

He releases me, and I open my mouth to scream, he slaps a hand over my lips, and tears spring to my eyes.

I was going to get help.

Clearly, Bryce saw my intent.

"I will megaphone your involvement in her death from the rooftops if you don't give an academy award-worthy performance." His eyes find mine like a heat-seeking missile. "Right. Now."

He steps away.

The knock comes again.

Heart pounding, I take a painful swallow, resist touching my tender throat, and turn.

Rising on my tiptoes, I peek through the peephole for the second time in minutes, the small hair's at my nape rising as I give my back to Bryce.

Zaire's perfect hazel eye meets mine.

Oh shit.

"Just a sec!" I call out.

He's not a stupid man. He will instantly know I'm shaken up.

I turn, giving a wide-eyed stare at Bryce. "Zaire will know I'm"—I try to search around for a word and finally finish with —"flustered."

But "devastated" is more appropriate.

Bryce's scathing midnight stare sweeps my face, and a small devil's smile creases his face. "I don't care. Convince him, Ms. Frost."

I drop my hand from my throat and unlock the door, sweeping the solid wood-paneled plank wide.

Zaire fills the doorway, and not for the first time, I notice he's a big guy. But his presence doesn't overwhelm me.

Tears fill my eyes, but when Bryce's arm winds around my waist and he subtly pinches my side, I don't allow the wet fear to climb from my eyes and rush down my face.

Zaire's bright hazel eyes move to the intimate gesture Bryce makes. Like we're *together*.

Our eyes lock for a moment, and I swear to God I witness an emotion flash in Zaire's eyes. Did I see right? Am I just hopeful? Was the fleeting emotion jealousy?

Before I can know for certain, Zaire says, his eyes moving to my face again, "Just checking on you before I turn in."

He already checked on me when he'd left me here for the night.

Help me, I silently scream from the depths of my soul.

"I'm good."

His eyes halt at my words, climbing over my changing expressions more slowly.

A thrill shoots through me at the chance to be rescued. Then I remember the horrible secret I keep and how Zaire knowing would not be any kind of rescue at all.

I would safeguard that knowledge in the face of anything else.

You don't want him to know what you did, Alex.

My silence has made the decision for me. Instead of telling Zaire like I yearn to do—that Bryce Davenport is clearly a part of something awful, that he choked me—I smile instead and tell Zaire I'm just fine, playing the part of a woman on a date that might end spicy.

A fabrication so big I feel myself strangling on the noose of it.

To his credit, Zaire doesn't offer any judgment about how I'm behaving. As though he's untroubled by my superficial acting, Zaire retreats from his position inside the doorway and sets his hat back on his head, tipping the wide brim at me.

I hold his eyes, so scared I can barely breathe.

At the last possible moment, that astute gaze tracks to my neck, lingering.

Zaire's eyes flash to my face and see something I'm incapable of hiding—maybe subconsciously, I didn't want to hide my surfaced emotions.

Without warning, Zaire rushes the door, slamming it wide, the doorknob hits the wall with enough momentum to impale.

Bryce tosses me so violently to his left I stumble, falling against a highbacked lounge chair and hitting the armrest with bruising force.

I scream as pain sinks into my side.

The men charge each other.

Ten
Zaire

I'll never blow off my instincts again. From the instant Alexandra says "hold on a sec!" I know something's up.

Not sure how. Not sure *why*.

Maybe the tell is the thinly veiled tension loaded like a cocked gun in the sound of her voice. Not that any of that matters once I see Alexandra's tight expression.

And her neck.

A necklace of angry red marks mars the lightly tanned skin. Fingerprints.

But it's her eyes that tell me the story.

Fear and secrets are crammed together, taking up a huge amount of the real estate of her expression.

"Checking on you before I turn in," I announce in a strictly perfunctory way. 'Cause I know what I'm gonna do before I do it. Bright adrenaline thrills through my limbs, readying them for action.

Davenport slides an arm around Alexandra, and she can't hide the wince.

"I'm good," she assures in an unconvincing tone as her eyes shift away from my hard scrutiny.

The next part isn't bodyguard shit; it's Zaire Sebastian acting on a gut feeling.

Hasn't let me down yet.

I close the distance between Alexandra and me in two strides, flat-palming the door so hard I vaguely notice the sharp crack as the knob spears the wall.

That fucker throws Alexandra to the side, and she screams in clear pain.

I wanted to catch her—arrest her fall, I did.

Can't.

Davenport engages me instantly.

He executes a leg sweep to the knee and I pivot at the last moment, the glancing blow delivering a jolt of pain.

I drive my knuckles into his throat. Not enough to kill, just enough to get his strict attention.

Coughing, Davenport grabs my forearm with both hands.

Twists.

I slam my forehead into his.

He releases me, and we stagger apart.

"Wait!" he lifts a palm in supplication, hand to throat, gagging.

I don't, shoving him in the center of his chest, preferring Bryce Davenport down, not up.

Stumbling backward, he falls on his ass, instantly scissor kicks his legs, and springs back to standing.

My hand shoots out, delivering a punishing strike to the jaw.

Head snapping back, he grabs for my hat and jerks the brim down, causing momentary blindness.

Shaking my head, the huge hat flies off, and Davenport gets a sucker-punch to my gut.

Breath gone.

I hit him again. Hard.

Davenport goes down.

He holds his palm up again. "Wait," he says from his knees.

Then he does the one thing that does halt my momentum—because make no mistake—I was on my way to beating the fucking shit out of this asshat.

A badge gets tossed out in front of him like a white flag of truce.

Eyes trained on his face, I scoop the thing off the ground, taking a painful first breath as I do, the contents of my stomach begging to come up.

Straightening, my eyes gloss over the badge.

Federal Bureau of Investigation.

Fuck. Me. Running.

I'd dicked with enough feds during the Club Alpha siege to know a real badge when I see one.

"International," chock, cough, spit, "division." His gaze meets mine.

Ignoring Davenport, I move to Alexandra, her wide eyes leaking tears, hand at her side.

Dammit. "Where are you hurt?"

She attempts to shove off from the side of the chair she's propped herself against and whimpers.

Gathering her slim body against my own, I notice she's only wearing one shoe.

Her head rests against my chest, and I sweep her up in my arms. Striding to the nearest couch, I lay her down.

Turning on my heel, I stare holes through Bryce Davenport.

"Talk. Now."

His eyes narrow on me. "I don't owe you anything, Zaire Sebastian."

"Yes—you do." I nod. "You've abused my client."

Davenport's eyes flick to where Alexandra is lying then

return to me. "Hurting her wasn't intentional. You barged in. Violent intent. I responded accordingly."

I cock my head. "Why are the feds here? In Greece."

"Close the door, Sebastian."

Walking backward to the door, I slam it closed with a heel as Davenport gets to his feet.

Naturally, I walk over and insert myself between him and Alexandra.

"We are on a decade-long sting, and Alexandra Frost is believed to be a key witness."

I hear Alexandra's sharp inhale but don't turn away from Davenport. Not for a second, badge or not.

"Then it's typical for you to choke women?" I cross my arms.

His face reveals nothing. "Don't judge my methods, Sebastian."

"I'm afraid that you don't get to justify FBI protocol when it has to do with my VIP." I pronounce the acronym like "snip."

His lips curl. "VIP?"

My return smile is just as tight. "You understand my role and how it relates to Alexandra."

"Of course. I *know* who you are, Sebastian."

Here it comes.

"I know about your little club," he articulates.

"Bryce," Alexandra says in a low voice.

He begins to walk to the couch she's lying on.

"Nope." I shift in front of him.

Chests almost touching, I say, "Chat from here."

His dark blue eyes flash to mine. "She's a material witness. Alexandra Frost is key to solving a criminal ring of the first order. It's big, Sebastian—way bigger than your angst about my treatment of Ms. Frost."

Nothing is bigger than Alexandra. And I won't lie to myself—the realization of that fact is some scary shit.

"Wait a second," Alexandra says.

I turn.

And it happens that fast.

The press of a gun's business end is cold against my temple.

"Get the fuck out of here, Sebastian—let it happen."

My eyes drive to his, the shadow of the barrel never wavering in my periphery. "What am I supposed to let happen, Davenport?"

"Her death. We make Alexandra Frost go away, and there's no trace."

My death as well.

That's when my suspicions are confirmed. The real Bryce Davenport is six feet under. Somewhere.

And if I live through this, I'll never question my instincts again.

If we live through this.

And I want Alexandra to live, badly.

Alex

I can't breathe very well.

Partly because I'm terrified but partly because I'm pretty sure my ribs are bruised.

Or broken.

"Bryce," claims to be FBI. I'm pretty sure the FBI doesn't choke "material witnesses."

"Wait a second," I say. Because I want to tell "Bryce Davenport" to go to hell.

I don't want to revisit my abandonment of Bridget.

Ever.

Then Bryce puts a gun to Zaire's head.

Oh my God.

Sucking in a painful breath, I hold it, sliding off the couch, and stand behind where Zaire's as still as a statue. "Kill me, but you won't get away. The sound will carry."

Davenport's dark chuckle fills the space. "I'm not on my own here, Sebastian."

Zaire's body tenses, and he slaps the gun up, driving the tip toward the ceiling.

The report is so loud I yell as the gun sights down on Zaire again.

Scrambling from the couch, I run for the door.

A second shot hits the doorframe, sending splinters of wood flying beside my head.

I yelp, ducking as I grab the frame and hurtle myself into the hall.

Grabbing my side, I race down the long corridor, turning left toward the short hall that contains dual elevators.

A third shot rings out.

Mewling, I sprint around a corner, gasping through the pain of my side, and get to the elevator where I kick off my remaining high heel.

Zaire.

Painfully, I turn and look behind me.

Hard footsteps approach, and I know I'll die in the middle of a hotel corridor in Greece.

Zaire appears around the corner at the end of the hall, covered in a fine mist of blood, a bruise forming on his jaw like a dark, ugly flower.

Intense eyes that are more green than brown find me.

With a gulping sob, I stumble toward him, and he meets me halfway, wrapping strong arms around my waist.

"Ouch," I say softly.

"We need to go."

I lean back and look up into his face. "What?"

"I don't know what the fuck is going on, but Davenport or whatever his name is will be after you."

I shake my head. "Is he FBI or—" My frantic eyes search his face. "*What* is he?"

Zaire doesn't release our locked gazes. "I need to know why there would be a man trying to impersonate the FBI to get to you."

No.

His eyes linger on my expression for a moment more, lips forming a grim smile. "But not right now. Right now, you're not safe until I get you somewhere that is."

Zaire transfers his hold to my elbow, swiftly leading me to the staircase beside the elevator.

"W—"

"No elevators. It'll be the first place they look."

My face swivels to his. "*They?*"

Zaire spins me, and I gasp at the sudden pain.

His astute eyes imprison and condemn me at the same time. "Whoever the fuck wants you dead because of something you know—something you've seen." A flutter appears in his jaw. "Now, we're going, and then you're going to tell me what the fuck is going on."

"Is he dead?" I whisper.

Zaire grunts. "Close enough."

The blood spatter on his face isn't his.

It's Bryce Davenport's.

Eleven
Zaire

I am as honest as I want to be – translation: not very fucking honest. I don't tell Alexandra that I beat "Davenport's" head in with the butt of the gun, taking off without so much as a check-the-pulse hesitation.

Nope, that explanation is a bit too bald for where our relationship stands at the moment.

Somewhere between client, want, and turmoil.

I can't tell Alexandra there was no pause—that I couldn't think of anything else except she was outside my purview, secure in the knowledge of what Davenport had admitted—there were others at his beck and call.

And Alexandra could be running straight into the second net of would-be attackers.

"G—I have to tell G that she's in danger." Alexandra's liquid black eyes look into my hazel ones.

"Negative," I say, hauling her as carefully and quickly as I dare.

She grips my shirt, giving a small shake of her head. "Please, she doesn't know about any of this."

That's fine.

I look up and down the stairwell, determining to exit the floor above where we need to be.

The other players won't expect that. They're not interested in Alexandra's small entourage—they want *her*. I give a terse explanation of that as I half-carry her, guiding us through the fire exit on the level above the ground floor.

The instant I get us somewhere secure, I'll be digging into this shitshow.

Merit Lang will hear from me as well.

For now, we get the fuck out of Dodge. "Hang on," I say, moving to open the door when a furtive noise reaches me.

Instantly, I reverse direction, simultaneously shoving Alexandra behind me.

A man with a black skull cap telegraphs his intent, stepping forward with his right foot and pulling his left arm as he shoots the limb forward.

I jog my face to the right, missing the blow.

Grabbing his wrist, I twist then shove him backward in one fluid movement.

He rises to his toes at the top stair of the tight landing, throwing his muscled arms wide to regain balance.

Stepping forward, I blast a strike dead center on his chest.

Large body bucking, he begins a slow pinwheel backward, attempting to arrest his fall with a lurching grab at the handrail.

Turning, I rip open the door, grab Alexandra, and pull her through.

She groans.

It's now a part of our terrible reality that to help Alexandra escape from this place, I must hurt her in the process.

Hurt is better than dead.

The instant we're through the door, I turn and swing the bolt to latch it. Nobody will use that as an escape route.

Swinging my gaze, I search for what I need.

Find it.

The fire alarm says *pull* in Greek. I don't need foreign language skills to make that work.

Lifting the solid pane of glass, I yank the lever down.

Instantly, a shrieking alarm blares from all directions in what sounds like decibel one million.

Alexandra slaps her hands over her ears.

Grabbing her elbow again, we begin to descend the steps leading to ground level. To witnesses. To relative safety.

"Zaire," Alexandra whisper-shouts.

"We'll talk when we get out of here," I say, my eyes moving everywhere at once then returning to her pinched face.

"Can you make it downstairs?"

I'll carry her if it comes to that.

Alexandra rolls her bottom lip between her teeth, worrying at it. "Yes, I think."

We begin walking down the twenty-foot-wide steps that curve gracefully to the main floor in a tapered flare, widening at the foot.

I have my arm around Alexandra's waist and the other on the rail. Most of her weight is being hauled by me.

"Why was that guy going after us?" Alexandra shouts above the wailing siren when we've almost reached the bottom.

Lifting my hand from the solid brass rail, I put my finger to my lips.

Her dark gaze moves to mine.

I shake my head. Trying to convey without words that we can't talk.

Shouldn't.

The alarm is a siren's wail as people stream out from the hotel in all directions.

I pull Alexandra into the center of the throng, attempting

to blend our escape with the pouring mass of people exiting the hotel doors.

The fresh air hits us. Sweet floral notes travel the heated air, perfuming the outside as though we're safe and should linger, enjoying the night.

We're not safe.

I keep us moving. Taxis and übers pile up alongside the curb.

I maneuver away from the first five cars and open the passenger back door of the sixth.

"Get in," I tell Alexandra.

"I don't know that I can." Her breathing is shallow, and her left hand is high against her side.

I feel my scowl, torn between duty, concern, and protection. "Did you break your rib?"

Alexandra shakes her head. "I think it would feel worse if I had." She bites her lip.

I watch the gesture. In the middle of this fucking nightmare, I'm riveted by her mouth.

"Okay," I say, snapping out of it, I hold her elbows, wrapping my fingers around her forearms, and gently deposit her on the seat while she breathes through the motion.

"Swing your feet over."

As she does, I notice she isn't wearing shoes. Gone are the really impractical high heels, though the alternative is bad.

I meet the driver's eyes.

He looks Greek, and I don't speak the language. "Do you speak English?" I ask.

He nods.

Thank God.

I close the door and jog around to the other side, open the door, and pile in, slamming the door and instantly engaging the locks.

The driver turns smoothly to face us, pointing a gun at Alexandra.

She screams.

I punch his chest in an instantaneous strike.

His shoulders cup, and I take the gun, reversing the target to his face, flicking the safety off.

"Get the fuck out."

He pauses.

I hike the barrel an inch, keeping his torso as the biggest target.

He gets out.

"Make sure the door's locked," I tell Alexandra.

She hits the lock, and all four doors click a second time.

Shit. An obvious problem presents itself as I watch the driver through the glass.

"Hold the gun on him."

"Oh my God." Her voice shakes.

"Don't have time for fear right now." The driver is outside the car, shouting—trying to gain help.

Can't look at Alexandra. "I need to get in the front seat and get us the fuck out of here."

"O-okay," she stammers.

Butt first, I pass her the weapon. "Safety's off."

"Oh my God," she repeats. "He's yelling for someone to come help him."

"No hypocrisy there," I announce in a droll voice as I hop over the seat and land in the driver's side.

They've left no room in front or back of the vehicle.

Shifting into drive, I bump into the car in front of me, slowly nudging it into the next.

I shift to reverse. Rinse and repeat.

Cranking the wheel hard and to the left, I blast out from the small outlet I made for myself just as a guy who's not our "driver" jumps on the hood.

Alexandra shouts a warning.

Wild eyes meet mine through the dirty glass.

Perfect.

Fuck. "Put on the safety!" I roar, praying she does, or I might get my head blown off because my next move is fishtailing the car back and forth to lose the asshole on the hood.

Asshole lifts a gun as one hand hangs onto the seam where hood meets windshield.

"Hang on!" I slam on the brakes.

Alexandra gives a gasping yell from the back as Asshole flies off with a rough tumble, disappearing from view.

Setting the car in drive, I move forward. The car lifts like it just went over a soft speed bump.

Oops, I think with grim humor.

"I'm going to be sick," Alexandra announces from the back.

"Not yet," I say.

Her harsh laugh holds a note of hysteria as I haul ass out of the semi-circle porte cochère.

Tramping on the gas, I fly down a road that leads to bigger ones. *One way*, my mind says. The narrow road winds in a loose corkscrew.

Alexandra must be hanging on by a thread.

"You okay?"

Silence.

"Alexandra!" I yell.

A heartbeat's time then, "Yeah, I'm all right."

"Talk to me," I say.

"About what? About the fact that there are certifiable killers after me? Or that I left my cousin back there to die—my staff." She gives a sad laugh.

My eyes are trained on the last bit of road that will open to the main thoroughfare.

"Or the best thing ever—that my bodyguard, who isn't, has to risk his life?"

The last part of her small speech is muffled.

My eyes flick to the rearview mirror.

Alexandra holds her face inside her hands.

"I'm going to stop at the first autohof I can get to..."

"Those are in Germany," Alexandra comments listlessly.

"Darlin', whatever rest stop thing they have is going to see these plates switched out first thing."

She drops her hands, black gaze seeking mine. "Okay," she says meekly.

"We can't use any of your credit cards."

Her palms give a small, helpless lift then drop to her thighs. "I didn't grab my handbag—I don't even have my cell," she groans, clearly defeated.

I remember I tossed on the escape-pack after pulling it out from where it was stowed as "Davenport's" brains were making a solid mess on her hotel room floor. "Good." Our eyes meet again. "You probably have location tracker enabled."

"I don't know."

"Yes, then." I shake my head, *disaster averted.*

Her arms cross and she winces as I get up to speed, the inky scenery of true night blurring past the car like black water. "And you don't?"

My eyes flick to hers then back to the road. "I use a burner."

"Oh." Alexandra lightly gnaws at her lip, distracting me again.

"Secret spy stuff?" She leans back, and I note she doesn't have her seatbelt on.

"Buckle up—and, no—it's not 'secret spy stuff', it's just rudimentary untraceable protocol. Basically, if it's electronic, I won't use it. Not right now, anyway." Club Alpha taught me that and a ton of other shit I don't have time to think about or employ. I try to reassure her with, "We've got time before I stop—car's full of fuel."

Her demeanor shuts down into a sort of stony silence.

But I *have* to know why this mess is unfolding. Doesn't matter that I want Alexandra—that there might be something between us because, God knows, I felt the chemistry.

If we're dead there's no road to explore.

The why *is* important. Why the *fuck* are people coming at an heiress who is a social media princess? The *not*-FBI agent, Davenport—planned to shoot to kill.

Those are facts.

She pierces the silence, "It's because I saw something I wasn't supposed to. And I left my very best friend. I"—she looks at her hands instead of my eyes—"*abandoned* Bridget."

"Who's Bridget?" I ask slowly.

Tears well then fall, one lonely wet drop after another.

"My sister," she whispers.

I frown at the admission. "You're an only child. Merit looks into his clients. He gave me the rundown."

"She was my surrogate."

My stomach bottoms out as words piece themselves together inside my head. "Surrogate for what?"

I don't want to know.

I must know.

"Everything," she says so softly I strain to hear.

Twelve
Alex

Now I've done it. I'll have to confess my part in the murder of my sister.

That makes it real.

Too real.

We drive for miles in silence as I gaze out the window into the abyss of night, trying to figure out a way to explain things —when no explanation is good enough.

In the distance, solar vapor lights begin to appear, dotting the perfect scenery. Their unforgiving glare appears like the many-seeing eyes of a fly. I shiver at the macabre mental image.

"We'll stop up ahead," Zaire says.

I feel like I'm on a pirate's plank, always walking that narrow stretch of wood but never falling into the water.

"Okay."

His eyes meet mine in the rearview, and the knowledge is there. The unspoken future of secrets unrevealed.

Zaire pulls into the brightly lit rest station. Like most in Europe, they're half-restaurant, half-fuel station, with bathrooms, and totally all-purpose.

He turns off the engine then turns.

We face each other, and I bite my bottom lip again to keep it from trembling, a nervous gesture I hate.

"Alexandra, look at me."

Slowly, I lift my chin and meet his eyes.

That hazel gaze doesn't condemn me. It holds compassion. I glance down briefly then back up.

God. My lips part to speak.

"It's okay. We don't have to hash things out right now. I'm going to change plates, and then we drive." His lips twitch at the corners. "Sit in the front seat—I'll grab food; you can't be seen." Even as he says that last, his eyes are sweeping the large lot full of cars and trucks.

My insides sink. My escape will be noted when Bryce (or whoever that jerk was) is found dead.

I carry the knowledge that it's likely Zaire killed him, though he didn't elaborate.

That makes Zaire a murderer and me his accomplice. But who am I fooling? Did I think hiring a bodyguard meant they'd slap someone who tried to hurt me?

I just hadn't thought the potential all the way through. Nor had I entertained this scenario. Had I imagined a rabid "fan" theme playing out? Sure, in theory, it sounded plausible that a social media "follower" would get too close.

Not the trail of bodies beginning to pile up from Zaire defending me. "Bryce Davenport." The driver. The guy at the stairwell in the fire escape passageway. And I have the feeling those won't be the last.

Zaire Sebastian was supposed to be a fill-in for Merit Lang. Now we're on the run, and I have to bare my soul to a guy I don't know.

Who I want to *get* to know if circumstances had been different. Like, *biblically*... get to know.

"Hey."

My face jerks in his direction. "Yeah." I feel my blush to the roots of my hair.

"Jump in the front seat. I'm not trying to scare you more than you already are, but we need to get out of here, pronto."

I nod, and we exit the car at the same time. I shut the back door and hop into the front passenger seat.

He moves into the shadows where a ton of cars are parked in a single-file line.

Zaire removes a long slim rod I can't quite make out from the pocket of his lightweight jacket.

Screwdriver, I guess.

After a tense minute, Zaire returns, moving to the back of the car.

Another couple of anxious minutes wash by, and Zaire reappears, opening the driver's side and throwing the screwdriver on the floorboards in the back seat. "All set."

His eyes meet mine, his tall body leaning against the door frame. "Getting food then we split."

I squeeze my legs together. "I need to use the restroom."

Zaire sighs, blasting his fingers through his curly dark gold hair. "I know this goes against everything you're used to, but can you go in the bushes?"

I glance outside in the dark. No TP, no—*gawd*. "Yes. I can."

His eyes search my face then move to my hair. "Dammit." His face tightens before he seems to come to an internal decision. "Wrap something around your hair and take this." He hands me a Euro. "It costs to pee." Zaire smiles.

I smile back. The circumstances are so weird. "Because my hair's red?"

He nods. "You're *so* far from a nondescript female."

I duck my head, hoping that's a compliment and feeling ashamed to wonder at a time like this.

"I'll get food. Meet me back here in five."

"Okay," I say, slipping out of the vehicle, I quietly shut the door and begin to unbutton my blouse, leaving me wearing only a cami.

Shivering, I wrap my blouse turban-style around my head, using the long sleeves to knot it and tuck it into itself at the base of my skull while I walk toward the glare of the lights.

As I approach, I hear the faint hiss from the bulbs and search for a sign that says anything like bathroom.

I can speak and read Spanish, but that doesn't really help a person in Europe where English and the native language of whatever country you're in is typically all that's spoken.

Thankfully, my foreign language skills aren't necessary because there's a sign picturing a man in pants and a woman in a skirt that seems to be the universal cue for bathrooms.

Thank God.

I'm sure I needed to go for a while, but between the adrenaline of escaping and the low throb of my ribs, peeing took a backseat.

Looking to my left, I just make out Zaire's broad shoulders disappearing inside the building where I recognize the Greek word for food above the door in a neon script.

I squint, believing *hot* to be the word that comes right after.

Moving into one of the turnstile thingies so common in subways, my legs come into contact with another and I stop, feeding a Euro into the coin slot. The metal limb of the mechanism clicks then releases, allowing me to push the bar with my hips as I move through.

Men are on the right, women on the left—all one bathroom. Frowning at the community setup, I walk to the left where a sign holding a stick figure with a dress is hung.

I stride to the furthest stall within the line-up and step inside, shutting and locking the door behind me.

Emptying my bladder is a wonderful simplicity, and I

breathe a grateful sigh of relief. The instant I'm done, the commode automatically flushes, I'm wiping and standing.

I've just buttoned my pants when I glance down, and underneath the stall door are two feet presenting themselves.

Men's feet.

Adrenaline makes my fingertips tingle; my prior calm instantly vanishing.

He tries the door, and the latch rattles within the bracket.

"I want... date you," the man announces in broken English.

Oh my God.

His fingers curve around the top of the stall. He starts rocking the stall door back and forward with his body weight.

The latch holds.

Flicking my eyes at the next-door stall, I gauge the space.

Dropping to my knees, I skirt along the filthy bathroom floor and GI crawl beneath the partition that separates one stall from the next.

Just as I pass through and get to my hands and knees, the door to my stall bashes in with a well-placed kick.

I stifle a scream as I jump to a stand, ripping the adjunct stall door open, and dash out as the dude is searching the stall.

Sprinting to the row of turnstiles, my eyes latch onto a flapping half-door meant for an exit. I shoot out of that just as the guy grabs me from behind, cinching strong arms around my waist and lifting me off the ground.

Directly in front of me, Zaire fills my vision, his face a mask of thunder.

"Zaire!" I try to yell; a hand claps over my mouth.

I kick backward and strike something.

The hold loosens. I make a fist and cover it with my other hand, blasting my elbow backward into his gut.

Zaire grips the bar that holds the door and heaves himself

over the top in an elegant push of strength, punching the guy in the face as he lands.

I give an abbreviated shout, sinking low.

With me out of the way, Zaire lands another kick at the guy.

He goes down in a heap of twisted limbs.

Zaire turns, gathering me close, and presses my face against his chest.

I suck in a sob as all the emotion that's been bottled up inside me since this horrible night began threatens to boil over.

"I got ya, darlin'."

Taking me by the hand, Zaire pushes me in front of him, and we move through the door, leaving the moaning jackass back on the bathroom floor.

His grip is tight as we stride to the car.

I get inside the passenger seat and he the driver's side.

Taking the blouse off my head, I slip my arms through the sleeves, re-buttoning it partway.

Zaire turns on the engine and slowly pulls away as my heartbeat tries to slow from its jackhammering rhythm.

"We are so goddamned lucky it was after midnight and the bathroom wasn't manned."

I gulp. "I didn't do anything. He tried to get inside my stall—"

Zaire's face whips to mine then back to the road. "What?!"

"Yeah." My voice shakes. "I had just finished going, and this guy just shows up in front of my stall saying he wants to 'date me.'"

Zaire snorts. "That's the lamest come-on I've ever heard. I hate the community gender-neutral bathrooms in Europe," Zaire adds. And the ones that are beginning to sprout up in the states.

"You don't think it was them, do you?" I ask softly.

"No way," Zaire immediately says.

With a relieved exhale, I lean my head back against the seat. "Good."

"He was just some opportunistic rapist."

I lift my head again, turning it to look at him. "How do you know he wanted to rape me?"

"Because, darlin'..." Zaire glances at me then back at the road. "No actual decent man interrupts a woman while she's relieving herself then finds it necessary to mention they want a date."

"It was scary-weird. And women are vulnerable when we're going to the bathroom. We have to get half-undressed to go. It's dumb." I give him a narrow look.

"Don't get mad at me because I'm a gander."

"So, I'm a goose?"

Zaire laughs from his belly.

My eyes wander to his strong hands gripping the wheel and his abraded knuckles.

"Oh my God," I say softly, gently touching the barely scabbed-over wounds. "Your skin's gone."

"Yup."

"I'm sorry," I whisper.

His eyes move to mine. "Don't be. I signed up for it."

Why? "Why?"

Zaire concentrates on the road. "At first, I thought I was helping out Merit. Y'know—helping out a friend."

"And now?"

"I'm in way over my head. I should have never said yes to any of it."

"You hate me." Guilt swamps me. Zaire protected me, hurt himself. We're on the run from murderers—and I still haven't told him the ultimate sin—how I wronged Bridget.

"No, darlin', on the contrary." His eyes seek mine in the dimness of the car's interior before returning to the road.

"What do you mean?" But I think I know. I've known all

along and was just trying to deny it. Because I don't want intimacy with anyone, no matter how right they might be for me.

Intimacy translates to baring one's soul—confessing things better left buried.

"What I mean," Zaire says with care, "is I have feelings for you—a client." Silence presses against us before he continues, and I hold my breath. "And there's something else."

My heartbeats begin to race. "What?"

"You might have that secret you'll be telling me, but before this thing between us—*if* there is something?" His eyebrows rise.

I mutely nod.

"Goes any further, I have a confession that might make you back out before we begin."

I can't imagine anything making me walk away from Zaire in this moment. There'll be stuff he'll hear that might make *him* walk, but not me.

"I'm broke."

What? "Do you think any part of what is between us might be about money?"

"As a man who's interested in a rich woman, it's a blow to the old ego—I won't lie."

I blink. "I have enough money for both of us."

"That's the thing, darlin'." Zaire smirks. "I don't want to be a money-grubbing loser."

Unlatching my seatbelt, I knee walk, depositing myself beside him.

"Unsafe, Alexandra."

Carefully, I slide my arms around his neck. "I don't care."

The car slows.

Zaire carefully pulls over to the shoulder, putting the car in park, and against all that is prudent, he drags me onto his lap.

Our lips brush. Then Zaire takes my mouth like I hope he'll someday take my body.

Thirteen
Zaire

I can't fight my feelings any longer. Alexandra Frost is not a temp job done as a favor for a friend any longer.

When I got a load of that fucker jerking her from the ground with the intent to do bodily harm, something inside me snapped.

I understand a relationship blossoming right now might screw everything six ways to Sunday, but that's never stopped me before.

Zaire Sebastian is a risk-taker, and she's worth the risk.

The steering column is hell on Alexandra's back, so I draw her against my chest, splaying and pressing my fingertips between her shoulder blades, smashing her tits against me.

We groan at the intimate contact, and leaning back, she somehow manages to squeeze her leg from between us to the right of my hip and straddles my lap, bringing her closer to my huge erection.

Capturing her eyes, I ask silent permission, and Alexandra's soft expression gives the yes I'm waiting for.

Hand diving between us, I cup the warmth of her sex.

With a sultry gasp, Alexandra throws her head back with a hiss.

"This isn't smart," I whisper against her neck, rasping kisses along her throat as my fingers find her joy button and begin to work the tight bundle of nerves right over the top of her thin linen pants.

"Don't care, too freaked out."

Works for me.

My cock's in the way of my goal: getting Alexandra off.

Right now.

With every evil thing after our asses, I'm on the side of a thoroughfare, fingers busy with a girl that's clearly out of my league, and feel compelled to pleasure her in the middle of a firestorm.

Alexandra begins to rock her hips in time with the rhythm of my finger on her clit, and I cup her nape with my free hand, pinning her in place up high, steering wheel supporting her back and my fingers driving against her high and hard.

Lips pressing against her neck, I lick, peck, and suck, finally giving a small nip right at where her collarbone meets the slender length of her throat.

With a hoarse shout, Alexandra stills, beginning to come.

Tramping down with my finger, I slowly knead and flatten my finger, and she whimpers, pussy clenching so hard I feel the sensation through her pants. I catch the erotic noise with my lips, eating the sounds of her pleasure while I slow the rhythm with my fingers as she groans.

Working my fingers from her nape into her hair, I fist the silky strands, turning her head to capture another kiss on her soft lips.

"What. The. Hell was that?" she asks in a dreamy voice.

Taking a stab at facts I reply, "An orgasm."

She gives a throaty laugh as my cock throbs with unfinished business, but for once, blue balls are just fine.

The anxiety has been eased from her face. Witnessing Alexandra's complete trust in me as a male is—Worth. The. Pain.

Our silence begins as a comfortable tranquility before sanity returns to us in raw chunks of consciousness.

Her expression goes from dreamy, post-orgasmic ecstasy to a slow broil of embarrassment. "I can't believe I just dry-humped your hand."

She moves to scramble off my lap.

I grip her hips. "Don't."

Her face whips to mine.

I cradle her slender jaw with my hand, moving the pad of my thumb in a tender caress up and down the length. "I'm stoked."

Body relaxing against mine, her lips lift at the corners. "Stoked?"

I nod. "Thrilled, happy, joyous—*turned on.*" I raise a brow and her cheeks heat, showing color I still manage to make out within the car's dim interior.

Leaning forward, Alexandra turns her head, resting her profile on my shoulder.

I cup the back of her skull, wrapping my other arm around her upper body.

"I don't know what's wrong with us. We kinda lost it."

A short laugh escapes me. "Stress reliever."

Alexandra sits up, backlit by a streetlight in the distance.

Cupping her shoulders, I give a gentle squeeze. "There's been something between us from the minute we met."

She nods. "I didn't—this sounds so lame." Alexandra bites her bottom lip, and I find myself distracted by the nervous gesture yet again. "I didn't feel like this with Merit."

I snort. "Thank Christ."

Her teeth flash brilliantly at me for a moment; then she

grows serious. "Merit's like this really great older brother who also happens to be my friend."

I cock an eyebrow.

"Okay." She tucks a tendril of hair behind her ear that makes me wish I'd done it instead. "He's reserved, but I thought he could be my friend if he hadn't been guarding my body."

"And what a body it is," I say softly, pressing a gentle kiss between her breasts.

She crosses her arms over where my lips just were and gives an embarrassed laugh.

"Stop that."

Carefully, I remove Alexandra's arms, setting them on her thighs that still straddle me.

Winding my fingers around her wrists, I hold her immobile and duck my head between her breasts again, nosing the material of her tank top aside. I kiss every bit of skin that I can reach.

"Do I seem"—I pause, pressing another hot kiss on her silken skin—"like I'm *bothered* by your breasts?"

"They're so small," she whispers.

I jerk my head up.

Grin.

"Let's see." Gripping the fragile edges of the blouse, I tear it open, popping buttons.

Alexandra gasps.

They fly, pinging off the hard surfaces of the car's interior and dropping noisily to the floor like scattered, plastic rain.

Using my thumbs, I gently push her breasts from the bottom of the cups of her tank top and fold the material underneath.

I give her bare, perfect tits critical attention.

She moves to cover herself again.

I hold her arms again. "Don't darlin', just let me worship your assets as they were meant to be."

"Worship?" her voice quavers.

I don't break from the suspended lust seeming to hang like an unfinished impulse between us.

Sliding my large hands along her bare ribcage, I pull her forward, and Alexandra helps, arching her back slightly to my seeking mouth.

It is true. Alexandra does have a small rack with perfectly formed, high and tight, edible nipples.

Everything a man could want.

My right hand leaves her ribs in favor of cupping the underside of her perfect tit, and squeezing slightly, I take the nipple into my mouth, sucking gently at first until her breath changes from even to erratic, giving me the *go* I was waiting for.

Still sucking the nipple, I take even more of her breast into my mouth.

Her slender fingers move through my hair, tightening in the short strands, drawing my head down harder.

Fighting her hold, I switch to the other luscious orb and repeat my hot, wet attention.

Alexandra groans.

I lift my head.

"Okay," she says, voice shaky, "maybe you like my boobs well enough."

"I do." *Like I said.*

Women are insecure for the wrong things, I think.

She gives me a fierce hug. "What are we going to do?"

I can think of a few things that aren't fully practical at the moment. Instead, I say, "We get going until we find a place to hang our hat. Regroup, get ahold of Merit—go from there."

With a lot of shifting, Alexandra manages to slip from my lap and attempts to straighten her clothes. After a few seconds, she looks at the state they're in and laughs, giving up. She shoots me a regretful look. "Buttonless blouse and damp panties. Nice."

"*Very* nice," I emphasize.

Taking her hand, I lift it to my lips and press such a light kiss it's hardly more than heated air.

Slowly, her eyes rise to meet mine. "Wow, are you for real?"

The moment swells, and then I answer, "Yes."

She nuzzles her cheek against my hand then reluctantly releases me.

I turn on the engine and pull away.

Allowing a few minutes, I steal myself to prompt her, but Alexandra begins talking on her own. I've wanted to know the history that haunts her. When I do, I almost wished I hadn't.

The stakes grow higher with every word that drops from her mouth.

Alex

How can I follow up that amazing thing that just happened between us with the sordid tale—my part in killing my own sister?

Because Zaire is a wonderful man. A beautiful male. He needs to know what I did. Why I push myself so hard.

Why I don't feel I deserve happiness.

When I'm busy, I won't have time to think about what I've done—what I didn't do. It's how I stave off the overwhelming guilt threatening to consume me.

I stare at my fingers as they twist in my lap. "Bridget was always my friend. She'd show up at least twice a week from the time I can remember."

Stealing a glance at Zaire, I watch his steadfast eyes remain on the road.

"I was older when I found out she wasn't just some kid of my dad's friends. She was my sister. Well, half," I correct in a whisper.

"How old were you?"

"Around ten." I pick a thread off my linen pants then give him uncommitted side-eye before continuing, "That's when the abuse began," I say, dropping the verbal bomb in a low voice.

The silence is deafening.

I take a deep, painful breath. "I held her when it was over."

Tears run from my eyes as I add in a whisper, "I washed the blood from her thighs."

How many times was that?

"Fuck," Zaire says.

Just one word uttered. So bleak, so disgusted, so defiled.

Just. Like. Me.

I nod, because it's not possible to speak.

When I can go on, I've never wanted to do something less. "Of course, even though I was young, I knew whatever was happening to Bridget was wrong, that someone was hurting her in a sick way."

I sniff the sob back then plow forward. "So... I went to our father." I turn to face Zaire, eyes so full of tears he's only a dark shape across the seat from me.

His swollen glance is full of compassion before he's forced to return his attention back to the road. "What did he say?"

My pause suffocates the inside of the car like a bloated, dying bug.

The next confession will be the worst of all. It *is* the worst. The most criminal—the most cowardly.

"He said—" I gulp back over a decade of guilt and remorse. "He said it would be me if it wasn't Bridget."

Fourteen
Zaire

"This is related," I say, my eyes touching on Alexandra then away. "There's no way these circumstances aren't."

"That was years ago," she confesses.

"I feel like I'm running on part-information, Alexandra." My gaze returns to her then lands on the dark ribbon of road ahead. At these speeds, I can't afford to look away for too long. "I'm not trying to dismiss the tragedy of this," I continue in a low voice, "that a man could do that to a young girl." Makes me sick. In fact, no torture is too small in my imagination to perpetrate against a man who would commit that atrocity.

"You were young too, Alexandra—you couldn't defend her, and I have to ask." This time I do swing my head in Alexandra's direction, giving intense eye contact. "Why the *fuck* did your dad let men abuse Bridget?"

Alexandra shakes her head, hands twisting on her lap. "You know that old perv who had the island?"

Jeffrey Epstine. Notorious. "Hell yes," I drag a hand through my hair. "Epstine. Sick fuck."

"Dead fuck," Alexandra restates with a shudder. "My dad was somehow in their debt; they were blackmailing him."

A disgusted grunt shoots out. "He sacrificed Bridget for their sick agenda?"

"Yeah," she answers in a miserable whisper.

"And when you advocated for Bridget with your dad, he threatened *you*."

With another anguished nod, Alexandra buries her face in her hands.

"Hey." I reach out with my free hand, lightly gripping her nape. "When did these rapes happen?" I ask in a quiet voice.

Alexandra's shoulders lift in a helpless shrug. "The shit show had been going on for a while, but I don't think the rapes happened right away." Alexandra leans the side of her face against my extended forearm. "Bridget would return after—quiet. Wouldn't look at me, just wanted to go lie down in the twin bed across from mine." Her next inhalation is shaky. "Then one day, Bridget came back, and instead of her silence, she sobbed." Alexandra shakes her head as if warding off a witch's spell. "I've never seen anyone cry like that." She lifts her head from my arm, leaving the flesh cold where her profile had just warmed it.

Gazing through the window, looking at nothing but pitch-black scenery blurring past, she goes on, "It was like pieces of her were breaking up and shattering before my eyes." Alexandra looks down at her lap again. "And the blood. There was so *much* blood."

Her eyes flick to me then away.

"Girls are not meant to have sex; *women* are," I affirm, the disgusting memory of one young girl comforting another without the benefit of adult knowledge. "Bridget was forced; those acts leveled against her were beyond criminal, and that's *why* there's a law to protect minors."

"It doesn't stop men from raping and molesting—or the women who help them."

I squeeze her nape gently, feeling a stab of intense shame for my gender. "*Evil* men. Men who don't protect but take advantage."

"And there's my part. I kept silent and comforted her after they hurt her because I was too scared to act."

My grip tightens and her wide, ebony eyes move to mine. "And what the fuck should you have done at *what* age?"

I release her, and a frustrated exhale shoots out.

"Twelve," she answers softly.

Giving a disgusted hiss, I toss my head back against the headrest, unable to wrap my head around all the young girls who are harmed by those who should be protecting them.

The realization that this thing's coming full circle isn't lost on me. "I'm not a believer in coincidence."

Swiping at her cheeks, Alexandra gives me watery eyes. "I don't understand why I'd be a target *now*."

"Did the threats stop after Bridget... died?"

"You mean my dad?"

I nod.

"Bridget never came back. One time, she never walked back into our room." Trembling fingers wipe the river of tears as they fall. "Oh God—you know, she *never* blamed me. Bridget told me once, 'At least, it wasn't both of us.'"

"Why would these fuckers take a tycoon's daughter? Talk about playing with fire."

"That was part of it, Zaire—don't you see?"

We exchange a loaded glance as I take a turnoff from Adriatic-Ionian motorway, advertising lodging. Actually, the symbol for hostel is a vague outline against the red backdrop of the octagon sign.

Good. Cheap and anonymous.

"It's because she wasn't legitimate. My dad never explained the 'half' part of our relationship."

"Your mom's still alive though?"

"Yes." Her laugh is sad. "How do you know so much?"

I smirk. "Google."

She gives a minute shake of her head as though to silently say, *of course.* "They've been separated for years."

I can see why. "Does your mom know about Bridget?"

Alexandra nods. "She'd have to know. Before my parents split, my mom was around when Bridget came over."

"Why would your father want you to even know about Bridget?"

"I suspect his empire was threatened after our introduction."

Ah. "He's Mr. Benevolent, revealing a secret sister." I use my turn signal, carefully navigating the foreign roads and heading down a steep hill where the hostel sign softly glows. "Then, when things get saucy, he throws Bridget under the bus; but not before letting you stand witness so you live in fear of the same outcome. A passive threat."

"I've been afraid ever since," she admits.

"Like waiting for the other shoe to fall. Diabolical and abusive."

"My dad must hate me."

"No," I answer in a clipped word, turning into the narrow parking lot and slotting the stolen car in a murky spot at the back of the structure. "I think he hates himself more. He has the public daughter and the one he sacrificed to the perverts from the island. How can a person live with those actions?"

"I got away the instant I could. But this Epstine thing is so much deeper than just Bridget."

"It's been a few years since that went down."

We look at each other.

"The timing's right to start taking out witnesses without

the connections being surfaced," I say, cupping my chin, rough with more than a five o'clock shadow.

"Like me," Alexandra whispers, pulling her wrecked blouse over her perfect chest.

Yes, I think but don't say. Alexandra doesn't need me adding to the already staggering weight with the death squad chasing her down.

We exit the vehicle at the same time.

Alexandra's laugh is defeated. "I don't have any money. For the first time, I don't." She lifts her hands, and her blouse falls open, revealing a hot thin tank top thing, opaque and so thin a material it allows her nipples to show through the fragile fabric.

My eyes linger where my mouth sucked, and I think of Davenport and how he behaved like he wanted to dive into her panties when, all along, diving wasn't his main agenda.

Fisting the silk folds of the blouse together, she asks, "Now what?"

"I have money."

Reaching down, I lift a pantleg to reveal a money belt designed for calf application.

"Wow," Alexandra breathes. "James Bond shit."

The corners of my lips lift. "Not really, but practical."

Jerking the thing open, I fan out the rainbow-hued euros. "Take two hundred euros."

"Okay." She gives me a curious look from red-rimmed eyes. "That's all?"

"It's a hostel, not a hotel."

She huffs, cheeks heating. "Fine."

Alexandra plucks the euros from the fan I made, and I neatly tuck the rest inside the money belt, redoing the buckle.

"How much do we have?" she asks.

"Five thousand."

Her look is eloquent.

"Before I made money with my company, I didn't have much. You'd be surprised how far a person can go on five K."

She puts the money into her pocket, clear curiosity etched on her features.

"No," I cup my fingers, "Give it to me and wait outside. You're more distinctive looking." My eyes run over her burnished ginger hair. Nope, she stays out here.

Alexandra walks outside the door that leads into the small entrance lobby and wearily leans against the wall. "Okay."

With a last glance at her, I walk inside, sighting the hostel clerk right away, and approach the elevated counter.

Not suspicious at all, right up midnight's ass.

Sure, Zaire.

"Γεια," he says in a bored tone.

Good to know Greek is still spoken even though Croatia is a hard thought away. I'll have to change out currency when I'm there, or I won't have money.

We won't. Me and Alexandra.

"Do you speak English?" I ask in the shittiest Greek known to man.

"Yes." A smile ghosts his lips at my expense.

"Thank God."

He gives me a toothy grin.

"I'd like a room if you have one?"

He nods. "Off-season."

Right, blistering summertime.

He staggers me with a cost of ninety euros.

I slide two, golden-colored fifty euro notes across the scarred countertop.

He asks if I need the change.

With a hard plow of my Adam's apple, I answer, "Yes, I definitely want the change."

Might need to eat, though I'd been able to buy a few

staples at the last rest stop before having to do the turnstile leap to clean that prick's clock.

I scrub a hand over my exhausted face, taking visual surveillance around the small space. Tourist trinkets, t-shirts, and a limited food station meet my eyes.

I grab the change and shove it into my front pocket. He gives me a key card, and I walk out of there.

Alexandra is where I left her, and without a word, I take her hand and lead her to the door of our room.

I paid extra for a room that wasn't shared.

I don't tell her that. Or that bedbugs are a high probability. Or any of the other depressing shit I know about hostels.

Sliding the credit-card-shaped, stiff, plastic rectangle through the designated slot, I wait until small dots blink a bright green.

The door latch sounds, and Alexandra pushes inside.

I press the rocker light switch shaped like a fat wedge, and low LED lights flood the space as our hands break apart.

I'm pleasantly surprised.

Everything appears orderly, and the place holds the fragrance of astringent laundry detergent.

Unlike a snooty aristocrat, Alexandra moves straight for the bathroom, flicks on a light switch, and softly shuts the door.

I follow, giving a soft rap of knuckles against the closed door. "I'm going to hide the car."

The temporary spot was good for the now, but not for the later.

"Okay," I hear her faint reply through the cheap hollow-core door.

Leaving like I came, I lock the door and pocket the card key. Jerking the fob out, I press the unlock symbol and jump into the stolen vehicle. Turning on the engine, I allow it to slowly crawl around to the back of the hostel and find a narrow spot running parallel to the building and angle beside the structure, exiting through the passenger side.

Jogging around the building, I sigh, as tired as I've ever been, and passing the door to the room, I return to the lobby.

When the bell sounds as I open the door, the same clerk is there. He sees me, and his eyebrows shoot up. "Everything to your satisfaction?" he asks in formal English.

"Yes, everything's good."

His shoulders ease.

"Just need to get a few things."

Walking to the clothes rack, I move to the section for shirts marked "small" and rifle through until I find a color I like and grab it.

Taking it to the counter the clerk robs me of another twenty-five euros, and I trot back to the room.

I repeat the key card entry and open the door, quietly entering.

Hearing the shower, I close and lock the door behind me. Sloughing off the jacket, I toss it on a lone chair angled in a corner.

Walking over to the bed, I sit on it, hands dangling between my legs, and hope there's hot water left, not begrudging Alexandra one second of her wet, cleansing comfort.

The water seems to patter on forever. Finally, the shower shuts off, and a few minutes later, Alexandra exits in a billow of steam, beautifully pink and treacherously clothed.

A cheap undersized white towel clings to every curve, skimming her high thighs and barely covering the sweet treasure between them.

I decide I'm not that tired as a hard-on springs to attention.

And she's aware enough to notice, eyes sliding to the

healthy erection that unsuccessfully attempts to tent my snug pants.

Walking toward me like a prowling cat, Alexandra comes to stand about three feet from where I sit at the edge of the bed as I catalog her every breath.

The towel drops.

And along with it—all my ideals.

Fifteen

Alex

Time stands still as, with a racing heart, I allow the towel to drop from my tight grip.

I've never had a man look at my body the way Zaire does.

Ravenously.

Not in the way lust makes me feel wanted but like a man who wants to try a dish he's never eaten and has always desperately wanted.

Zaire's slow perusal I can withstand, his silence, I cannot.

My lips part to speak just as his eyes close.

I approach him and stop when I come to stand between his legs, my most intimate part at chest level.

His eyes open, and he raises his hand, cupping my hipbones.

Zaire pulls me nearer and does the unexpected, laying his profile over my pubic mound.

My breath escapes in a surprised hiss, fingers finding his curly hair and slipping within the strands.

"You are beautiful, darlin'." The heat from his words warms my secret flesh.

Is it possible for words to make me feel beautiful when I confessed horrors a mere hour before?

Yes.

Because they're spoken by someone who means them. Within days, Zaire Sebastian has peered into my soul, divining things about myself I didn't know.

Zaire committed a terrible act to save me. Not because he was my bodyguard but because we were meant to be.

This is my hope.

Turning his head, he grasps my butt cheeks, pressing his lips against the top of my slit, finding the swollen bundle of nerves. With exquisite slowness, he flicks his tongue over me, and I groan, unconsciously pressing him deeper into my slickness—damp from the shower, damp with my arousal.

Splitting my legs, Zaire lifts his mouth and stands, hiking me as he does.

I wrap myself around his waist.

"Clothes," I say breathlessly.

Turning smoothly, he sets me down on the turned-down bed and removes his shirt, lifting from the collar, dragging the material over his head, and tossing it in the general direction of a tiny dining table.

He kicks off his shoes and releases his cock from the prison of his pants. "That feels better," he murmurs.

I give an enthusiastic nod. It's been over a year since I was with anyone, and that was only because I had enough liquid courage to see it through. Sex is all mixed with the violence of what happened to Bridget, and I can't easily separate the two.

Zaire banishes this thought trend as he walks to where I lie, my eyes tracking his movement like a sly feline.

Raising my hand, he takes hold, lifting it as his eyes take in my fingers, travel to my face then finally begin to travel the length of my naked body.

"Where were we?" he quietly asks.

"You were gorging on my pussy," I say without a hint of embarrassment. We're beyond that, Zaire and I.

He chuckles. "And I want more." His pupils dilate as Zaire lowers himself to the bed.

I place my hand on his chest.

He slows, looking deeply into my eyes. "You're not ready? Because every signal says green light."

"I am—but can they find us?"

"Yes, but I think we have time for this and some shut-eye." He closes his eyes for a moment then opens them. "I'll do whatever you need."

A fat tear brims, rolling down my face.

"Don't cry, darlin'—your tears wreck me."

"I'm not crying because you're hurting me or I don't want to do this. I just can't believe anyone would want me after what I confessed."

Zaire lifts my hand again, kissing the top of each finger then pressing his lips to the inside of my wrist, hesitating before he releases the erotic pressure.

Our eyes meet, his darkened by desire and resolution.

"You were not responsible for what happened to an unprotected girl when you were one yourself."

I nod, tears scattering like warm rain.

Zaire draws me against his body, hugging me to his bare muscled chest, his heart beats against me, and I close my eyes from a comfort the simple rhythm brings to me.

After a few moments, I draw away, and his eyebrow rises.

"Okay," I say through the frog in my throat. If we come together, it'll change my life.

This isn't casual; I can see it in *his* face—I can feel it in *my* heart.

When he continues to stare, I clear my throat and repeat, "Yes."

"That's what I needed to hear."

Zaire's hand cradles my jaw, allowing his fingers to trail down to my collarbone, running between my breasts, he flattens his palm between them. Lowering his head to my nipple, he gently sucks the erect peak into his mouth.

Arching my back, I lose myself in the sensation as Zaire attentively laves my nipple.

While my breaths come short and hard, he releases the pressure of his hand and cups my left breast, squeezing gently until the flesh mounds into a small mountain.

He repeats his rapt attention on that peak as well.

My fingers dive into his hair, and his arms sink behind my back, drawing me so tightly he can barely perform what I so badly need.

"Hang on, darlin'."

His hands run down my back and grip my butt, lifting my hips. As he does, his mouth finds my heat, and I cry out when his tongue lands on my clit.

Hips bucking, he drapes his arm over my belly and sinks two fingers inside me.

"Zaire!" I gasp.

He doesn't halt, pumping inside as he relentlessly attacks my clit until, a moment later, I still, the air in my lungs frozen before the second orgasm of the night crashes into me—through me.

Releasing my hips, Zaire places his palms on my thighs and spreads me vulnerably open. His tongue pressing inside of the same place he'd just had his fingers, catching each deep pulse as I have them until they begin to grow softer.

I lie there, learning how to rebreathe.

Gazing down the line of my body, he lifts his face, chin glistening from me blowing apart all over him.

I whisper his name, holding out my arms in invitation.

Zaire comes to me, seating himself between my legs, and

the top of his cock easily splits my wetness, the first inch diving inside.

Wrapping my body against his, Zaire secures my spread wetness with a subtle forward rock of his hips, spearing me more deeply as I lift to meet his entry, silently begging for more.

We kiss, and I taste myself and him as our tongues twine.

Zaire pushes forward until he comes to the end of me, and we throb together, our bodies married as close as a man and a woman can be.

When he begins to move again, I shiver within his tight hold from the sensation alone.

Pressing back my hair from my temples, he forces intimate eye contact.

I nod. His hands tighten as he moves within me until he suddenly halts. "I can't last, darlin'," he whispers.

"So don't," I say.

"I want you to come. I *need* you to." Releasing my face, he stabs his elbows on either side of my body, and without breaking eye contact he begins to swivel his hips in a glorious uptick of motion, his cock rubbing that spot up high. Over and over.

"Yes," I breathe, helpless not to close my eyes to the purity of sensation.

"Come for me, darlin'," Zaire whispers against my temple.

The erotic command summons a surprise orgasm that sweeps through my body, rendering me with liquid passion as I widen my legs, folding them over Zaire's back as he pumps deeply within me.

After a few hard strokes, his body planks, and I feel the throb of his release.

Zaire doesn't immediately collapse on top of me, but softening, he slowly withdraws then smoothly rolls me on top of him.

My hair falls forward, offering a curtain to the outside world and sequestering us together.

For a handful of seconds, we lie like that, together but not.

His hand parts the waterfall of my hair, and he runs the tip of his finger along the bottom lip I constantly gnaw at when I'm nervous.

Applying pressure, he sinks the tip inside.

I kiss his fingertip and he smiles.

"Wow," Zaire says softly.

"Profound," I laugh.

With a little shake of his head, he turns me on my side, brushing my hair from my face.

We stare at each other for a heartbeat when Zaire finally says, "I don't have great words to quantify how you make me feel."

I lightly touch his spent erection. "Here?" My smile is light, casual.

His face is not casual or light.

Zaire shakes his head to the negative, forming a fist, he places it directly over his heart. "Here."

―――

Zaire

"I took you dirty," I lament.

Alexandra grins, and clear pink color breaks through her light tan to cover her cheekbones. "I didn't mind."

Thank God. "At least I managed to wash my hands and face."

"Zaire," Alexandra's smile fades, "the circumstances are extraordinary. We can't expect to be this perfect dating couple." Her eyes sink to her feet. "Or whatever we are," she mutters.

I turn from stuffing some of the outrageously-priced clothes I bought at the tiny hostel souvenir shop inside the pack and meet her eyes. "Nope." I stride across the small room and grip her shoulders. "Listen to me, and listen well."

Alexandra's dark eyes widen as I give her a small shake.

"I am *not* playing you. I have no room here"—I tap my temple and go back to holding her with my hands—"to do that. I wouldn't do it anyway," I finish in a low voice. "I'm not hardwired that way. Life is too short and all that jazz."

She gives an abrupt shaky laugh. "I don't know what to do here. Being chased by psychos with a man I hardly know that I let..." Alexandra starts biting on her lip and abruptly stops, clearly second-guessing our interlude.

"I wanted it," I say emphatically.

"Duh, all guys do," Alexandra says.

"Look at me."

Her black irises latch onto my expression.

"I. Am. Not. Leaving."

Alexandra swallows before replying, eyes dipping from mine, "How can you..." she lifts a shoulder, and I release the curve of flesh and bone, dropping the bend of my finger beneath her chin.

I lift her face until her eyes lock with mine. "How can I know it's more than this one time? That it's not a one-time-stand in the middle of a battle?" My brows drop. "I know I want to be with you."

My hands fall from her shoulders. "Do you want to be with me—because that might be the better question, darlin'?"

"Of course I do."

"There's no 'of course' about it. I'd be a clown to assume I could have something serious with you. Look at you," I say, sweeping a palm down her body that only now wears clothes.

She gives a self-conscious laugh. "I amassed my following

on being 'naturally pretty'." Alexandra's fingers drop from air quotes.

"When all the while, you felt ugly," I state like the fact I believe it is to her.

Her face jerks up in surprise. "Yes," she agrees quietly.

"You *are* gorgeous, Alexandra." I give a rueful shake of my head. "And that certainly helps me want you." Her silence is painful before I continue, "But looks fade, as my pop used to say." I splay my palm above her heart. "A good person is worth more than all the external beauty in the world."

She grabs my hand with both of hers and lays her face against it.

I pull her into an embrace meant to be tight, not crushing.

But crush her, I do.

I never had anything to lose but the millions I gave up to the courts and the feds during the war to save Club Alpha.

The importance of money fades as Alexandra stands within the circle of my arms, my protection.

Happiness doesn't have a price.

And if I can feel this with assassins on our tail, imagine what Alexandra and I could be without their threat?

Sixteen
Alex

"I know we had to go," I say, leveling a yawn after the brutal cell chime wakeup with only two hours of sleep behind me.

"I noticed you're not a morning girl," Zaire comments with a barely-there lip lift.

Understatement of the year. "Huh." I shift in the front seat while dawn seeps across the landscape, marking the shadows to burnished cream as we roar past.

"No way. But G has changed my circadian rhythm," I announce, and as soon as I do, panic seizes me.

G. I had forgotten her in the race to get out of the hotel.

I slap a hand over my mouth.

I was screwing Zaire, and maybe G is hurt or worse.

"What?" Zaire says, and his hand reaches out, gripping my shoulder.

"G," I choke out.

"It *will* be okay."

Nothing feels like it will ever be okay again. I drop my hand, devastated. "You can't know that, Zaire."

His hand falls away, returning to the wheel. "When you were in the shower, I got ahold of Merit."

"Oh my God—why didn't you tell me?"

Zaire looks straight ahead, and the flavor of what he will say assails me. "It's not good, and I didn't know how much you could take. After Davenport then the dicklick at the rest stop..."

My heartbeats stack like out-of-control pancakes. "Just tell me."

"Well, since this is obviously a huge cover-up, they've painted us as the ones who committed the crime against Davenport."

"What?" I nearly scream. "How—*no!*" I shake my head, lashing my hair back and forth as I do. "He's not even a real dude—he tried to *kill* you for God's sake."

"I know this, Alexandra," Zaire says in a calm voice, accent eerily absent.

"Let me out, I have to get back there, see G—figure out, tell my tiktokers I'm not some murderess, I—"

The car slows then carefully exits to the shoulder as traffic whizzes by so quickly the car moves as they speed past.

Zaire puts the car in park and turns to face me.

As I search his expression, tears hunt their way to my collarbone, wetting the cheap bright green t-shirt Zaire bought for me.

He takes my hands.

"No."

"I'm sorry."

"No—Zaire, please, please, *please*."

His bright hazel eyes shut for a long second, and when he opens them, I sense what he'll tell me.

I throw my arms around his neck in a stranglehold. "Don't say it," I command in a fierce whisper.

"I have to. I can't withhold the truth. Not if I want to be with you like I hope to be."

Slowly, I unwind my arms from his neck and sit back on my heels.

Eyes locked, Zaire says, "G is gone, Alexandra."

I cover the sob that threatens, and all I can do is shake my head.

Deny.

He takes my hands again. "Your staff... are all gone."

"I thought—I thought you *said* they wouldn't"—I gulp back my emotions like a bitter pill—"care about hurting them."

"I was wrong," Zaire unflinchingly concedes.

My heart sinks. Guilt rides my mind like a drug I can't escape.

"Merit told me they framed us. We took off—"

"We were trying to survive!" I cry.

"Yes." Zaire scrubs a hand over his face. "My only concern was getting you the hell out of there, alive."

"I—I," panic hits me square in the chest, and suddenly I can't breathe.

His strong hands grip my shoulders. "Alexandra!"

"Can't," *breathe*, I think. My breaths pile up in an airway that narrows with every passing second.

Releasing my shoulders, Zaire slaps me, making my head rock back, and I begin to slide.

He catches me as I fall, and with a crashing slide of emotion, a sucking whoop of precious oxygen comes, then another.

"Zaire!" I wail.

He pulls me tight into his body. "Don't ever make me do that again."

I sob, hanging onto his ruined shirt, wanting to die.

Wanting to live in spite of my shame.

Zaire

"I've got to ditch this car for another one before Merit's people intercept us."

Alexandra leans against the glass, hand tucked beneath her chin, legs curled to echo the same posture.

Since I slapped her, Alexandra's been quiet, streaks of tears drying on her face like painted grief.

It's a first for me; striking a woman.

I wouldn't have thought it possible just a day before. But watching Alexandra's wide eyes while she clutched her throat, I knew the move would shock her into breathing.

The outline of my palm faded; the act has not.

I release a pent exhalation and try again, "How are your ribs?"

Alexandra's chest rises with a deep breath, and she lets it out slowly. "Sore. I'm okay."

Not broken, thank God.

"They felt broken when that jerk shoved me into the chair."

"Bruised ribs feel like broken ribs if a person doesn't know the difference."

Alexandra turns and gives me steady, red-rimmed eyes. "You know the difference?"

"Yeah."

Her lower lip trembles. "You hit me."

Fuck. "Yes."

"I don't know how I feel about that. Actually," Alexandra slowly admits, "I don't know how I feel about anything at the moment."

"I would kill anyone who touched you," I say with a hard edge to my voice.

She nods. "I know, you've proven that. I was hysterical."

"You weren't breathing. I can't get you medical attention. I... fuck—" After a heartbeat of weighted silence, I finish with, "—blew it, didn't know how to handle it."

I train my gaze on the road again. Flicking my eyes to the next rest stop, I notice the fuel in our stolen ride is on fumes.

"All right—for the record, I've never struck a woman before. I was keen on you *breathing*." I steal a glance her way. "I needed you to breathe, Alexandra." *Actually, I just plain need you.* "It doesn't absolve me."

She puts her hand out, and I take my right hand off the steering wheel so we can lace fingers. "You saved me, Zaire. Probably, there will be other mistakes that you make"—she turns to me, liquid eyes finding me within the dimness of the car—"that I make."

"I guess we just survive and see what's left," I say, flicking on the turn signal.

Alex

Zaire makes short work of spotting another vehicle.

"How do we just," I pitch my voice low, "steal another car?" My eyes dance around the packed parking lot where the door to enter the adjunct restaurant and bathrooms is a constant stream of people.

Zaire pushes his hair from his forehead in an unconscious gesture, looking so different minus his huge cowboy hat.

I mention it.

"Left it behind," he replies in a flat voice. "Davenport got a few good licks in when I was wearing it, and"—he turns, giving me a significant glance—"it's bad enough with your looks. I can't add my Texan spice to the recipe." He winks.

"Texan spice?" I snort.

Zaire frowns. "Don't make fun of Texas."

I laugh, and when his frown turns to a scowl, I laugh harder. "I'm sorry." I choke on my words. "It's just—I don't know—who *cares*?"

"I care," Zaire says, obviously miffed.

Naturally, that makes me double over.

"Alexandra," he begins in a chiding tone.

I wipe my eyes, straightening. "Comic relief."

"Clearly." Zaire's voice is bone dry. "I need you to steal the plates, and hopefully, the car I've got my heart set on is old enough for me to break into and hotwire."

"Old? Don't we want a newer car?"

"Nope, darlin', can't get those hotwired. Hell—can't even break into them anymore."

"Okay." I slowly look around. "And I'm supposed to be circumspect?"

Zaire's critical gaze moves to my hair. "Wear that scarf I bought for you."

Bleh, my mind supplies, and the irony isn't lost that it's the first normal thought I've had since this ordeal began.

Reaching inside the stolen car, I whip the deep emerald, polyester scarf from the floorboards, and with a sigh, I twirl my hair around itself and stick the tail deep within the knot, wrapping the scarf around my head and tying the ends.

I look down at my t-shirt then lift the tail of the scarf. They're the same shade of green.

When I look up, Zaire's ears are pink.

"You bought me green."

"I love you in green, darlin'." Then he runs his hand over his nape as the color spreads there. "Maybe I—"

"Hey," a voice sounds from behind me, and I whirl, my heart in my throat.

A guy around thirty or so stands there, appearing a little

out-of-place in blue jeans and wearing a hoody and Converse sneakers. *American*, his outfit screams at me.

Because in Europe they're casual dressers for nothing.

"I thought it was you." The smile is broad on his nondescript face.

At first, I draw an absolute blank. Then a moment later, anxiety swamps my guts. *Oh my God, he's a social media follower.*

I try not to be too obvious and show my feelings, but I sense Zaire tense beside me.

We can't have anyone noticing us right now, even though —normally I'd dig the coincidence.

"We need to be going," Zaire says smoothly from my elbow.

"No way, man—figure the odds of me running into *The Alexandra Frost*."

"I'm sorry, I don't want to put you off, but he's right," I say, almost saying Zaire's name aloud like a dumbshit, adding a hasty correction at the last second.

I sweep a palm at Zaire standing beside me.

"I gotta have an autograph and a pic. This is too fucking big to believe." His eyes travel my form hungrily, and I inch a bit closer to Zaire. There something vaguely rabid about this dude.

I'm not getting a great feeling. Of course, I'm so keyed up I can't tell if the feeling comes from the last twenty-four hours or has organically reared its head in the now.

Zaire takes my elbow and begins to drag me away. A small cheap backpack he's had from the beginning is flung over one shoulder, which reads, *Visit Greece*.

Not to be put off, the guy trots after us. "Come on, don't be a fucking lit Kami."

Great. The young version of a stuck-up "Karen." Not that anything matters but getting away from here.

I can do damage control if I live long enough to do it.

We're almost to the building, and since running into a social media fanboy wasn't on our agenda, I don't know what Zaire's contingency is for this.

We don't have time to think of that as three other guys approach us from the front.

Zaire and I slow our footfalls as he subtly draws me nearer to his side.

"Go ahead and stop there," one of the three instructs us.

Oh no. My eyes bounce between the trio.

Zaire does, moving in a loose circle, he stations me in front of him, keeping the dude that caught us off guard front and center.

"Listen." Nondescript strolls around to join the posse and holds up his palms. "The law in these parts has a five million dollar reward for you guys." His eyes twinkle at us maliciously. "Ya never know about people. Here you are, going all 'Charles Manson' on your staff." He gives a contemplative pause then says, "Nice, by the way."

His eyes travel me again, and I try to be brave, I do, but a little sound of distress slips out.

G was more than staff, you dick, I think.

Then his eyes shift to Zaire. "Me and my friends are going to kick *your* ass," he says as though that's been all neatly decided.

His attention turns back to me. "Then we're gonna take turns on Alexandra." He licks his bottom lip in obvious anticipation. "After all, the reward doesn't say nothing about handing you guys over in perfect shape." He grunts in self-affirmation.

"Zaire," I say in a voice gone low with my terror.

"Get behind me, Alexandra."

My gaze sinks into the headcount, four men in all.

Zaire can't do this—he can't protect me from all of them.

I keep contact with his body and slowly circle around until my hands are gripping the back of his shirt.

"Move back, darlin'," he says as though he's checking the temperature outside instead of facing down the dismal ratio before us.

"Yeah, *darlin'*, move back," the front man mocks, false grin gone.

Reluctantly, I give Zaire space, never feeling more alone than I do in that desolate foreign rest stop.

Zaire plants his legs wide, slightly relaxing his knees, and motions for them to draw nearer by cupping his palm in a *come on* gesture.

I retreat a couple more steps.

All four rush him at once.

I sway where I stand.

Lost.

Crushed.

Resigned.

Seventeen
Zaire

I've never felt more inadequate than I do at this moment—adrift, my tenuous hold on confidence slipping through my fingers like sand.

Alexandra's fear is palpable when she calls out my name.

"Get behind me, darlin'," I say in a careful voice—careful to contain my rage now that I've found someone worth protecting.

Anger won't save us; grit will.

Hell, even though I'm not worth much, Alexandra makes me want to be a better man.

My attention turns front and center.

The Mouth rushes me and reaches my position, forecasting his next move and handily gifting me with his arm as he swings.

Taking the limb, I pivot my opposite hand, bringing it down like a hammerhead on the forearm.

He shrieks like a schoolgirl, but I'm not done. Sliding my hand to his thumb, I leverage the digit backward, breaking it.

Shrieking anew, he nearly collapses as I continue to apply pressure to the hand. He drops to his knees, mewling loudly, as another prick strikes me between where the deltoid and bicep intersect, instantly numbing my arm to the wrist.

The third guy moves in tight, grabbing my other arm as number four will be the pounder.

Out of options, I drop. The surprise deadweight causes them to release me.

The fourth moves around where I land... to Alexandra.

Lying on my ass, I rock backward, my back a boat shape, and sweep one leg hard at the dick at my left, taking out his kneecap with a neat, side-strike.

The one at my right halts, losing his advantage of being the one on his feet, and pivoting hard, I repeat the same move to the one at my right.

He howls, dropping like a demented bowling pin.

I bound up just as Alexandra screams.

The last man standing cinches his muscled arms around her waist and lifts her from the ground.

I sprint to them.

Alex

Run, my mind screams.

In the next breath, my answer is just as quick, just as organic.

I can't.

Zaire's here, fighting for me.

For us.

I watch them come, and my fingers go numb with the adrenaline that descends on me.

Fight.

Flight.

I stay, though it's the hardest thing I've ever done when every instinct thunders at me to escape.

The loudmouth is forward of the other three and steps into Zaire, pulling his arm back to punch Zaire.

The limb shoots out.

Zaire grabs the offering, rotating his palm to the side in a hard chop to the dude's forearm, and rapidly slides his hand to the man's wrist, bending the thumb back to meet the arm.

The audible crack brings him to his knees in a shout of agony.

I cover my mouth. *Oh God.* "Zaire!" I scream as Number Two punches the side of his arm.

Zaire's grunt of pain is a muffled bellow.

Number Three takes his other arm.

No!

A guy at the back shifts his attention to me like a target through dual sights.

Zaire drops, his weight pulling him from their grasps.

He rocks backward, his left leg striking the knee of Number Two at the left. The joint buckles, and he goes down as Number Three bends over, clearly trying to wrench Zaire from the ground as Number four begins to move around them.

Zaire repeats the knee cap destruction with Number Three, and he falls backward, howling for all he's worth.

Pedestrian traffic has slowed to a crawl as people begin to belatedly realize something violent is happening.

My eyes move from the fallen assailants, and Zaire, who's still on the ground.

Too late, I see Number Four has committed to grabbing the prize.

Me.

All my life regrets spin through me like a mental cyclone and land on one that lingers in the eye of the storm that was a rational thought process moments before—*why didn't I take self-defense?*

Number Four hops over the jerks, and he's on me that fast.

I punch his chest in a completely reactive move as he tackles me around the waist, lifting me from the ground.

I scream, hanging over his shoulder like a sack of potatoes.

Men who were standing, watching Zaire defending against impossible odds, begin to move forward when a woman is being stolen in front of their eyes.

Zaire lurches from the ground in an unsteady stagger, our eyes meeting. "Fight!" he bellows as he runs toward us.

Tears spring to my eyes, arms locked beneath my attacker's hold.

I think of Bridget.

My cowardice.

I use the only weapon that remains. Turning my head, I gracefully take the shell of his ear between my teeth and bite down.

"Hey!" he squeals like the pig he is.

I bear down at the same time I jerk my head backward, tearing the flesh from the side of his head as I do.

The copper pennies of his blood fill my mouth, and I choke on the flesh, spitting the chunk of him away as he throws me.

I fly, arms reaching for nothing, and by some miraculous coincidence, I bash into someone and find the arms that hold me are Zaire's.

"Zaire," I whisper, throwing my arms backward and gripping the shoulders of his sweat-soaked t-shirt.

"No time for reunions, darlin'."

He sets me down, and I turn, still trying to hang onto him. But his hazel eyes aren't on me but the greater crowd of witnesses.

I suddenly want to be sick, the flavor of Number Four overpowering my taste buds.

The crowd of people begins to encircle us.

"Come on." Zaire takes my hand and steps over earless, who is caterwauling from his writhing position on the ground, clutching what's left of his ear.

I did that, like some kind of animal.

I swallow, and the taste of his blood is so gross my gag reflex kicks in, and I manage a coughing, pre-barf gag as Zaire tows me behind him.

Zaire doesn't risk a glance at me. "No puking." His grip on my hand tightens as he drags me.

I nod, swallowing my gorge, and shake my head like I've bitten into a lemon as we draw nearer to the other fallen jerks.

Dropping my hand, Zaire steps forward like a graceful dancer, kicking loudmouth in the face. His head snaps backward, blood flying from his mouth in a spray of red.

I clap my hands over my mouth, tears beginning to roll down my face at the raw violence necessary to survive us past this moment.

The other two attempt to stand, but their knees aren't cooperating.

Zaire's brutal attention turns to them, eyes glittering with his intent.

"No, no—*no.*" Someone mutters. I realize after a second, it's *me* who's saying the same word over and over.

Zaire lifts my chin. "I have to immobilize them, darlin'."

Oh my God.

His eyes lock with mine.

"Okay," I say in a bare whisper, giving a sort of evil permission.

Undaunted, Zaire repeats the move with each one.

Number Two makes a gurgling sound as he topples, jaw canted unnaturally to the right.

Zaire swings his leg at the last moment, turning the sole of his shoe so the toe points at the ground, and stabs Number Three with a hard tap of his foot to our assailant's head.

His head snaps back, neck clearly broken as the back of his head touches his upper back. Body falling backward, his uncooperative knees won't bow to his weight, and the tearing of his torn tendons give up their hold like crazed velcro.

Heat strikes me like a two by four of fire. Beginning at my feet, the sensation zings upward, enveloping my head in an inferno that pulses to the beat of my heart.

Dizzy, I give a small moan before I bend at the waist, vomit shooting out like a noxious volcano, splattering on the ground to mix with the blood at my feet.

The crowd muttering darkly penetrates the fog of my shock, and I realize the tide is turning, and it's not in our favor.

When we were being attacked, no one interfered, but when Zaire finishes the men who meant us harm—somehow —*that's* offensive.

I shakily straighten.

Returning to where I stand, Zaire's eyes run down me then land on my face. A heartbeat pounds between us then he says, "It's time to get the hell out of here."

Tears crawl pathways of grime over my face. I have enough presence of mind to wipe my mouth with the back of my hand. "They'll tell th-the men that are chasing us," I whisper.

"Yes."

Gripping my hand, he begins walking, sweeping the bloodied backpack off the ground as he passes where a stripe of gore runs through the word Greece.

I cough through the taste of blood and meat in my mouth and slap my free hand over my mouth.

Oh my God. I bit a man's ear off.

The crowd parts like we have the plague, the red sea of

bodies tilting as we move past, their image blurred through the wash of my tears.

Zaire passes the cars.

One is running, and the only person not enjoying the gruesome theater performance of my life is purchasing something at the counter.

"Quick!" Zaire says.

Jerking the handle on the passenger side door, I hop in, shaken to the core. My fingers grip the dashboard to keep from passing out, the edges of my vision dimming to gray.

Zaire pops into the driver's side and slams the door.

I hit the door locks in a purely reactive clutch of survival mode.

The man whose car we're stealing whips his face in our direction, notices strangers inside his ride, and slaps his things on the counter, rushing the door.

"Time to go," Zaire murmurs.

My eyes shift to the rearview, and the reflection fills with people moving our way.

Zaire sees them, reversing into the crowd.

They scatter at the oncoming car.

"Oh my god, oh my *god*—Zaire—look out!"

He overcorrects and the car slides sideways, then he jerks the wheel hard to the right to stabilize.

The car rocks to a halt, the nose now facing the road.

"Hang on."

Zaire tramps the pedal, and the car leaps forward like a jailbreak toad.

We sail out of the parking lot like a shooting star on steroids, backend fishtailing as we reenter the highway.

Zaire

Holy *fuckburgers*. That was close.

And now you're in a stolen car that everyone saw leave the parking lot, Zaire—good going.

Not that there was a choice.

Let the authorities come at them. It's part of the fun of escaping the murderers.

My eyes leave the road for a moment to glance at Alexandra.

Small abrasions cover every bit of her skin. Her hold is so tight on the dash her fingers bleed to white.

"You can let go now."

The pieces of adrenaline fall away like resistance flakes of panic as I watch.

Alexandra releases her hold, finger by finger, and when her hands are free of the dashboard, she gives a shaky exhale and softly falls back against the seat.

My eyes return to the road. A beat of silence presses between us then I ask, "How are you?"

In my periphery, her hands fist, and Alexandra presses them against her eyes. "How. Am. I. Doing?"

I wince at her slightly freaked tone but remain unapologetic.

Alexandra's hands drop to her lap, and she looks at me, aghast. "I don't know, Zaire?" She shakes her head, slapping her thighs. "You killed those men." She gives a shaky laugh edged with lacy hysteria.

"Yes."

"That guy was a fan," she says in a forlorn note.

Sobbing sounds close, and I won't have her feeling sorry for those hired fucks.

"If he was a real fan, I'm a woman."

A genuine laugh shoots out of her, and I love hearing it.

We've dealt with so much hardship in the last forty-eight

hours our lives have been a series of pieces of sleep mixed with harried meals.

And death.

"The main mouthpiece was hoping to separate you from me," I state.

Her brows come together. "I'm sorry—why? The people who are after me, Davenport—or whatever his name is, they're not ahead of us, we left them behind." She jerks her thumb backward.

I shake my head. "They *are* ahead. They're surrounding us. It's bigger than I've had time to wrap my head around."

Silence stretches between us for a few seconds.

"Zaire."

I turn.

"I can taste him in my mouth."

Jesus. "Does that mean you're going to puke again?"

We look at each other for a split second before my gaze shifts to the road again.

Alexandra's laughter lasts until it devolves into the tears I knew would follow.

"I want to comfort you, I do," I admit as the endless scenery rushes past us on both sides.

"I know," she replies, hiccupping back a sob, "but if you stop—we die."

Truth. "Yes."

"God, you don't even *try* to make things sound like anything else is possible."

"Does that piss you off, Ms. Frost?" The first stirrings of anger warm my words.

"Yes," she answers loudly, but her next admission is soft as she adds, "I wanted a life."

"You said you were existing before." Alexandra's post-coital confession has been tucked away as a secret inside one of the chambers of my heart.

"I was hoping—I could begin living."

It was me. *I* was the one that gave Alexandra that hope.

I creep my fingers across the seat of our stolen car, waiting.

After a few seconds, chilled fingers fill my hand as they thread together with mine.

"We can *live* together," I say as part-promise, part-optimistic prediction.

If we survive, I don't add.

Eighteen
Alex

We hold hands for a long time. Zaire releases my fingers only after skipping three rest areas.

He stops at the third.

"They'd figure I'd skip the first or possibly the second rest area."

"They won't think you'd go all the way to another?" I guess.

Zaire nods. "The poor sap we stole the car from had just filled up the tank."

"Thank God," I say without a hint of remorse.

"Yes." Zaire uses the turn signal, nosing into a decrepit, small gas station. Not the huge thoroughfare like where we were attacked.

The surrounding area is dim, lacking any true decent lighting as we navigate into the isolated parking lot with a dual pump and nothing else.

"Sketchy."

"Safer," Zaire responds, guiding the front of the car until it sits parallel at the fuel pump's raised concrete island.

Zaire turns off the engine, and it's only then I notice what kind of car we're in.

A fiat.

A giggle slips out then a gale of laughter.

Zaire quirks an eyebrow. "Darlin'," he begins slowly, "I cannot, for the life of me, find one piece of humor right now."

"I," the gales continue, and after a half-minute of solemn silence from Zaire, I finally manage, "We stole a *fiat*."

"Okay," Zaire says as though he's dealing with someone teetering on the brink of sanity (he's not wrong). Taking my hand, he lays his lips on the top. "Stay put, Ms. Frost."

The words are formal; the eyes he uses to study my face are not. They brim with intimacy, urgency, and resolution.

"Please Zaire, I need to use the bathroom." If I don't remove the taste from my mouth, I'll die.

Zaire's hazel eyes lift as he searches the small building that houses a cashier seeming to stand guard over assorted goods at the witching hour we find ourselves in.

"I'll be filling up, watching every move."

"Okay," I say gratefully.

We get out of the Fiat at the same moment.

"Alexandra," he calls out softly.

I turn, our eyes meeting above the car's roof.

"Try not to get raped, beaten, or lost in the next five minutes."

God. I give a long blink. "Just *five* minutes?" Keeping things light. But I'm starting to realize that Zaire isn't light, though he attempts to put out that persona.

I've come to realize it's merely a costume covering who he really is.

Zaire's eyes darken as I watch. "Forever is too much to ask."

He turns away to fuel up, and I walk toward the building I hope houses a bathroom.

I walk through the gas station's entrance and am greeted by a buzzing florescent burping out the last of its life with a low, irritating drone.

My eyes meet those of the cashier, maybe my age, descent unknown but dark-complexioned and halfway clean cut.

Shoulders easing, I give him a greeting, and he says, "Hi," back in English.

I take a chance, asking where the restrooms are.

His finger lifts, pointing vaguely at the very back of the structure where I can just make out a dimly lit hallway.

"Okay, thank you."

When I get inside the restroom, the mirror doesn't reflect anything I didn't anticipate, but when I see the state of myself—the rat's nest of hair, the dirty face—it's such stark proof of the last day's events I want to cry anew.

Sucking in a breath, I turn away.

Prioritize, Alex. Blasting on the hot water tap, I root around in the soiled backpack as the water grows warm, feeling around for anything that might resemble a toothbrush and touch a bit of cellophane wrapper that crinkles as I strike gold.

I extract the slim package and stare at it for a moment—how is it that Zaire has a brand new toothbrush?

Hostel.

On the heels of that revelation, an image of us making love rises in my tired brain. The memory feels like we came together years ago.

It feels like minutes ago.

With shaking fingers, I use the non-brush end of the toothbrush to stab through the plastic sheathing. Throwing the wrapper away, I dive back to scrounge some more, locating a tiny tube of toothpaste.

I can't stop the tear that leaks out but manage not to

dissolve into another sobbing fit for how grateful I am to be able to cleanse my mouth.

Mechanically, I work through brushing my teeth, and when I'm done, I deliberate.

Finally, I decide that, no matter what, me keeping a toothbrush for later use that cleaned a mouth fouled by skin and blood is a no-go.

I toss it in the trash can, gripping the rim of the sink.

Slowly, I raise my chin and stare at my reflection.

Face.

Leaving the hot water on, I run my hands beneath the torrent then stab the base of a metal stem coming out of a box affixed to the wall.

Dry soap falls from the box like fragrant sand, piling into a small pink mound inside my open palm.

Using the soap, I lather up, washing my face with the slightly gritty texture then rinse. I pat a paper towel over my face and use the crumpled paper to turn the doorknob and exit.

Zaire stands before me, and I startle, hand to chest.

"Oh my God," I say in the stark light of the interior hallway and finally see him revealed for the first time. "They hit you." Bruises bloom like ugly eggplant orchids all over his arms with a grape-sized bruise standing as a naked mar just to the right of his deep cleft chin.

His sudden grin sits weirdly within the sea of his injuries. "They got some licks in. There *were* three, you know."

Four, I think but don't say.

His eyes tenderly roam my face. "Don't cry, darlin',"

"Am I crying?" I touch my face, and my hand comes away wet. "I guess I just can't seem to stop."

With slow deliberation, Zaire wraps his arms around me. "It'll be okay."

"Are you saying that to make me feel better?" I ask against his neck.

"Yes."

I turn my face so my nose is stuffed against his throat; the beginnings of stubble tickle. "It's working," I mutter.

"That's all I want." Zaire pulls away.

We stare at each other.

He smirks. "Looks like you found the toiletries."

"I'd kill for a comb," I admit.

Zaire winces as he digs into his front pocket, extracting a couple of Euros.

For the first time in my existence, I ask a question I never thought to utter, "Do we have enough money?"

With complete seriousness, Zaire answers, "Barely."

He pushes money into my limp hand and folds my fingers over the note.

I clench my eyes shut. When I open them, he's in the bathroom, and I turn away to buy the cheapest comb they sell.

Zaire

"Now what?" I ask Zaire as we walk back to the gassed Fiat.

"We need to get to Croatia."

"Zaire"—I slow, stomach bottoming out—"that's, like, twenty hours away."

"I know."

Our eyes unerringly return to the Fiat.

"We have to ditch this car too?"

"Yup," Zaire says with his normal economy of words.

"I guess we don't have plates?"

Zaire gives a small, exhausted smile.

Hope trembles. "What did you do?"

"I borrowed some that were lying around," he confesses then shrugs. "It won't get us very far, probably only out of Greece."

I wrack my brain to think of the countries between here and Croatia.

My mind ticks them off: Albania and Montenegro.

An idea forms. "Let's take a boat to Italy."

Zaire shakes his head. "Nope—trapped on a boat? No way."

Shit, shit, *shit*.

"Let's get in the car and go."

I move to the back of the Fiat and look at the plates.

"Cashier won't notice right away," Zaire supplies.

I shut my eyes for a moment. I'm too exhausted to voice anything. I want out of here and somewhere safe.

"Alexandra."

My eyes spring open.

Zaire stands by the driver's side door as my gaze takes his beaten, tired body in. A memory of Zaire moving above me as he pinned my body with his own comes into sharp focus in my mind's eye.

I begin to walk to the passenger side, and opening the car door, I slide inside, bone-weary.

We drive off, and I stubbornly stay awake. How can I sleep after all the near misses and evil that's been pressing in at all sides?

Somehow, in a matter of minutes, I do. Sleep claims me without seeking permission.

Alex

"Alexandra." A gentle hand shakes me.

Blurry and disoriented, I swim to consciousness, pissed I fell asleep.

Or just pissed. I sit up, and Zaire has the car doors wide open. "I found another car."

"Okay," I say as fresh air hits my face. "Where are we?"

"Northern Albania," Zaire says, snagging the abused backpack from the floorboards.

"Wait," I say, and he turns.

"Have you slept?" *God, Alexandra, what do you think, bright one.* I swallow and try again, "Can I drive?"

His eyes are just two black holes in his face. The sun hasn't risen yet, and there's no light pollution on this deserted stretch sufficient to see his face.

"No, and we can't delay."

The port-o-potties cubicles have four occupants.

There are four cars, excluding the Fiat.

Zaire doesn't bother to shut the car doors, beginning to jog toward the lineup of cars.

I run after him, discarding my lethargy with each tread of my shoeless feet.

He tries the first car.

Locked.

Second.

Same.

His head whips in my direction for a moment. Then he returns to the task. Zaire tries the third, and I hold my breath, a lump of helpless anxiety lodged inside my throat.

The door handle sweeps up and Zaire slides inside.

I try the passenger side.

The handle won't engage, and my panicked eyes meet Zaire's through the glass.

"*μουνί.*"

Cunt, my mind translates because everyone learns the dirty words first in a foreign language.

Dear God.

A guy is running at me; déjà vu clobbering me with bone-jarring fear.

Zaire slams his hand on the locking mechanism and opens my door from the inside, smacking the interior door panel with his open palm and shoving.

I grab the side of the door and throw myself inside.

The owner of the car lands on the door, pinning my legs before I can sweep them inside.

"Zaire!" I scream in agony as the man's weight crushes my shins.

Zaire flies over the top of me like superman and hammers the door with his shoulder.

The door flies backward—the man with it.

I whimper.

Zaire jerks me all the way inside and yanks the door shut.

Falling back into his seat, Zaire's eyes chase around the car.

His gaze hits the visor, and he tips the flap down with a finger as keys drop with a musical note that means our escape.

A fist smashes against the window, and I give a shrill yelp.

The man presses his face against the glass.

"Zaire—oh my God!"

He jams the keys into the ignition and turns the engine over, commanding a repeat performance of the last place.

I slam my hands to the dash as Zaire squeals tires, backing out with such ferocity he doesn't bother to turn the car around, instead making his reverse a weapon of flight until we're in the right lane of the highway.

Slamming the gearshift into drive, he plunges his foot onto the gas pedal, and the car lurches forward.

Then dies.

Three figures are running toward us.

Gripping my hurt legs, I hop in my seat. "Zaire, we've got to go."

"Working on that, darlin'."

The figures grow large as they draw nearer.

He waits. Doing nothing.

"What the hell are you *doing*?" I screech, eyes bulging.

"Engine's flooded, got to give it a second."

Oh, baby Jesus.

Just as the first person grabs the handle of the car, Zaire turns the engine over again.

The engine flutters then ignites.

He softly pulses the pedal, and the engine roars to life like a lion.

"High performance," Zaire comments with a nonchalance that has me about peeing my pants.

We pull away, and the hangers-on must release their hold or be dragged behind us.

When I cry this time, it's in abject relief.

After a few minutes, the sun rises, and my relief turns to gratefulness that we lived to see another day.

Nineteen
Zaire

"Ten hours," I say, attempting to throw a conversational bone at Alexandra in an effort to gauge where she's at emotionally.

Her head rests against the seat. At my words, she tilts it to the side, facing me. Tired, abraded, dirty, and hopeless—she's still the most beautiful woman I've ever seen.

"Okay." Her head rolls back to face forward.

"Hey."

She doesn't look my way, but Alexandra's hand raises, and I take it. Our fingers coming together as though perfectly timed.

I elaborate, "Ten hours to Merit and supplies—answers."

"I know why they've come after me," she announces in a flat voice.

I knew there was more. But fleeing the fuckers that are trying to murder Alexandra wasn't the time to get every sordid detail. "Does this have to do with the Epstine kid porn empire falling?"

She sighs, fingers tightening subtly around mine. "That's

what I think. And I knew all the higher-ups. I can identify them."

"I can't figure out why your father would allow the abuse of one of his daughters."

"It's been my personal horror to ponder that myself."

Dawn plants slanted rays of sun, piercing the filthy glass we're entombed within. One slice of illumination strikes Alexandra across the bridge of her nose, freckles bold within the whitewash.

"I'm so glad to see the sun," she confesses as that swath of light broadens, encompassing her entire face, causing her copper hair to glitter like stoked coals.

"I never wanted to return home from boarding school." Her eyes stay on me as she confesses, "coming home meant the possibility of witnessing more abuse against Bridget." Visibly swallowing, Alexandra gives a reluctant shake of her head. "I wanted so badly to help Bridget, but the terrible truth was I felt like I was waiting until it was my turn."

"A turn that never came?"

She quickly nods. "But the damage was done. Men were monsters and even though—clearly—I have needs as a woman who is a sexual being like any other female—I couldn't embrace intimacy."

"You run."

Her face swivels to mine, and we share a beat of understanding before my eyes retrain on the ribbon of highway before us.

"Yes. If I can just keep going, I won't think—can't."

"Alexandra," I implore quietly.

"That's why Merit would watch my alcohol. Because I begged him not to let me get blackout drunk."

I suck in a breath at this admission. "A bit out of his purview," I say quietly.

"Yeah," she laughs sadly, her fingers worrying over the

material of her pants. "I thought he needed something to do since danger was just a vague ideal." Her laugh is more disbelieving snort than anything else. "Being as how acquiring a bodyguard was kind of a fluke."

"Not so bad a whim from where I stand." I glance her way.

"As it turns out, it was the best thing I ever did," she says in a husky voice. "I'm so tired of crying."

"You're not crying now," I point out, the corners of my lips lifting.

"Because I feel safe," she says with quiet conviction.

"You do?" I'm genuinely surprised. About lost everything—twice. Actually, three times if I count the hotel clusterfuck.

I barely got us out of all the near-misses.

Alexandra's soft laughter is a balm to my soul. "Hell yes. I thought I was a goner three times, and somehow—you saved the day. I bet you never thought in all your bodyguard jobs that this one would be the one where you'd go through all this."

Goose egg bodyguard jobs. *Tell her, Zaire.*

My lips part to confess all. Club Alpha, how I manufactured scenarios so like this one for pay, and ultimately—for love. The facts tremble on the tip of my tongue, even knowing that she'll be even more scared than she already is if Alexandra discovers I'm not a bodyguard.

"It's okay—you don't have to give me the gory details. I know this probably wasn't the worse detail you've ever been on."

It's the only detail I've *ever* been on if a person doesn't count all the nefarious scenarios I devised to vet potential billionaire love interests together.

I've been conniving as fuck. Many times. Putting in place horrible circumstances—a few backfiring badly through no fault of my own, though I've always felt like some of those things that happened *were*. The buts, ifs, and should-haves have piled up inside my head.

I don't want Alexandra to be in this group of faults. As a point of fact, I'm ready to employ some of my scheming now.

Forgetting the impulse to confess all for the moment, I say, "We must outfox them. Unfortunately, there's more of them than us. The outcome isn't certain, but we have a chance to survive if we play our cards right."

"How?"

"It's my experience," I begin, speaking a partial truth, "that doing what the opponent expects elicits a predictable reaction."

"This sounds obvious, but—" For a pounding second, she rolls her bottom lip inside her mouth then releases it, whetting my appetite for things we don't have time for. "You're saying we need to be unpredictable?"

"Sounds easy. It's not," I admit, having out-thought people in my time. And it's a bit like chess mixed with robbery. *You better know how to play and play well.*

"I want to live," Alexandra confesses softly.

God. I release her hand and cup the back of her skull, running my hand down her recently combed hair and gripping her nape.

Her head hangs.

"I"m not going anywhere, Alexandra."

"You're just one man, Zaire."

I look at her as long as I can without crashing the car. "I am the man who will fight to the death—for your life."

Unbuckling her seatbelt, Alexandra scoots over beside me and lays her head in my lap.

"That's really unsafe," I speak with a sternness I don't feel, loving the closeness of this woman I didn't know a week ago.

"You'll keep me safe."

I stroke her hair as we hurtle toward Croatia, thinking

about the guile I employ and how using it cannot be a good start to our relationship.

Alex

Some animal died in my mouth, I decide.

I open my eyes. I'm still on Zaire's lap and reach over, cupping my hand over his cock.

Zaire jumps, emitting a low groan. "Alexandra," he breathes. "My God, you almost wrecked us."

My smile is sly as I roll onto my back, propping my feet on the passenger door as I gaze up at his square jaw peppered with ginger stubble.

"You've been driving for over twenty hours without food." My eyes rest on the water bottles we swiped from the store. Funny how small things like robbery don't even scratch a person's moral surface when you're running for your life and you're so thirsty you'd drink your own pee.

Gross. I wrinkle my nose and Zaire looks down as I do. "What?"

"Thought of something icky."

"'Icky'?" Zaire's cheeks lift as he smiles.

"I was thirsty, and we stole the water bottles… *uh*, never mind."

I inchworm from beneath his arm and sit up, checking out the scenery. "Oh—wow," I say, awed, "the Adriatic Sea."

It's the same gorgeous turquoise I loved from Greece. Weird how the view doesn't really change, just my circumstances. The beauty is perceived so differently when one can relax and take it all in.

On the run, it's just a sea I can't enjoy because my mind is crowded with terror.

Zaire nods, fingers flexing on the steering column. "Mer's going to meet us in," he turns a Patek wristwatch over, continuing, "in one hour at the border crossing from Bosnia to Croatia."

"You phoned him?"

Zaire nods. "Of course the goddamned burner is dead now. I don't have my charger because of the debacle at the hotel. I'm lucky I had the emergency backpack handy."

"You stowed it inside my hotel room," I say, hiking an eyebrow.

He nods. "Merit did, but told me where it was located. I never believed the contingency would be necessary."

"Yet, here we are," she comments in a mournful tone.

"Yes—here we are."

"Love the touristy vibe on the thing. 'Visit Greece,'" I say ruefully, turning to locate the pack, and add, "Gross—bleh." I purse my lips. "It's got blood and stuff on it."

"We can't get mired down in bodily fluid allocation."

"Sick," I say, but I smile. "I guess we have to see the humor, or we'll never make it out of this alive."

"That's how I roll," Zaire quips.

I settle back into my seat and buckle up. A low growl sounds from my stomach, and I realize I can't legitimately remember when we last ate.

"I'm hungry too," Zaire says. "Been too cautious to stop. Figure Mer will have supplies when we get there. More water and food for sure even if it's just a pack of beef jerky."

"Beef jerky sounds divine."

Lifting a hand, Zaire presses his fingers against his closed eyelid. "Feels like I've got sand in my eye."

A pang of guilt flares, knowing he's done everything. The fighting, the driving. "Just tired."

Dropping his hand back on the steering wheel, he nods. "Yes. Beat, actually."

"I said I'd drive." My eyes dance around at the safe and mainly deserted highway in broad daylight. Doesn't seem too threatening.

A disinterested grunt sounds. "Nope, darlin'. If I fall asleep, it'll be the kiss of death. I'm a sound sleeper and have been deprived. My body would love to go to sleep, and another inconvenient slice of shit gets served up and—wham!"

"Groggy."

His hazel eyes, noticing not for the first time they're actually quite green, find me. "You have no idea."

A sign announces the border crossing in forty-eight kilometers. *Half-hour.*

Leaning over, I run a palm along his jaw. "Your beard is ginger."

A dull flush finds his nape, and his hand rubs the area. "I know I look like hell."

Shit. "That's not what I meant, I just—I don't know, like that we both have red hair, somewhere."

He glances at me, eyes darkening. "I happen to know you're a natural redhead."

"Pfft," I huff, slamming myself against the seat.

"I stepped in something?"

"Yes," I begin, furious. "So many stupid guys are always messaging me, or my assistant, who handles the hundreds of comments every day, to see if my pubic hair matches the hair on my head."

Zaire chuckles, brushing off my irritation with, "Masculine curiosity, Alexandra."

"Screw them," I blurt.

"Well, clearly, you chose not to, and that's why the facts remain in question."

I sit up like an arrow, face whipping to him.

He has a grin affixed.

I smack his arm. "Jerk!"

Zaire laughs from his belly.

After a few seconds, I join in. "Okay, so you do know the facts," I concede.

"And I plan to review them in the future," he says with a completely straight face.

I want him to.

I want a life where Zaire and I can be together like a real couple, not a pair of semi-filthy, weary, and scared humans who don't know if they'll see tomorrow.

I cling to my wish even as reality whispers to the contrary.

TWENTY
MERIT

Merit's exhale is weary, and he has an ass-ton of empathy for Zaire that he didn't before. Taking on Zaire's role by himself, without the team Zaire had used to employ in his Club Alpha days, has been challenging.

The careful crafting of events and circumstances that appear to organically occur to promote response was what Zaire used to do for a living, and it sucks.

He's decided fashioning circumstances that teeter on actual danger, to vet a person's character, takes a level of finesse Merit doesn't usually need to apply in his bodyguard role.

Merit tends to see every problem like a nail—and he's the hammer.

In this case, he orchestrated the Davenport connection to surface Zaire's protective instincts. Most men are protective over women, that's why violence against women still makes news—the women-abusers tend to be in the minority.

Merit wanted to showcase what Zaire was willing to do for Alex.

And in turn, they could gauge her response.

Little did he know Davenport wasn't the FBI operative he'd been told. Bad intel led to Zaire bashing the man's brains in, believing him intent on harming Alex.

Which clearly, he definitely would have given the opportunity.

"Did you—is this your doing?" Gia asks.

Merit rasps a palm over his face. "Some of it. Davenport had a role to play."

"Judging by the news, he played it a little too well."

"I didn't know he was playing two roles."

"This has turned into a PR mess, and now Alexandra is being torn through the mud, along with Zaire."

"And now that we know who Alexandra Frost really is—and she *doesn't* know, there's a greater possibility of every swinging dick being put into action."

"DNA results confirm?" Gia asks in her calculating way.

"The girl can't help any of it."

"I understand that, Merit—but perhaps Zaire doesn't want to be in a relationship with Alex, given who she's related to."

Damn. "That's fair, but keep in mind—we handpicked Alex. I tossed myself in front of her to be selected with the express purpose of infiltrating her life sufficiently to assimilate her routines and personality."

"Good call to get that DNA."

Not soon enough, clearly. "Actually, it was straight from the Club Alpha script."

"Shit—did Zaire take my DNA?"

Yes. "Sure did, you're the lawyer, didn't you sign the get-out-of-jail-free card?"

"Ex-lawyer," she qualifies. "I did. I guess because of our friendship and everything he did for Paco and Greta, I glossed over the fine print."

"Nice lawyering."

"Fuck off, Merit." Her words are cold, but humor warms them.

"I'll keep you updated—they'll be crossing the border shortly."

"How is that going to go?" She gives a short laugh. "Obviously, they're wanted—I don't know—*everywhere*, and that border is a passport-only."

"It's the part of the circus act that's the most fun."

"Zaire's really been put to the test, Merit," Gia states in a low voice.

"Yeah." He pauses for a second then says, "It was necessary. Zaire was wallowing, feeling like shit because his entire fortune was exhausted to repair Club Alpha's rep—to exonerate himself."

"Hey."

"I know, he wasn't alone. You, Paco, and Greta—hell, Denver—you guys were all great, especially when Zaire had too much pride to ask anyone to help."

"When he'd done so much for us." Merit can visualize Gia giving a sad shake of her head. "People before money," she intones cryptically, voice full of the things Gia lived through to be here in this moment, finally able to live her best life.

"Yes," Merit emphatically agrees, his thoughts touching on Chloe and how much he loves her, how furious he'd been—still was, about the vicious attack of two years ago.

How even after he and Denver meted a brutal brand of vengeance, the act still doesn't seem sufficient. The feeling of some undefined residual vengeance they're still deserving of, remains. A person can't kill the same human twice—however illogical it is for the impulse to exist. Because death is final, though that's not always the case with feelings. Emotions can live on—prosper.

"Merit?"

He comes back to the moment. "Sorry."

"What do you have in play for the border?"

Judging by the way Zaire handled one of the rest stop incursions, he'll have to put plan B into action. "He fucked up the four actors in the theater I set up at the rest stop. My intel says there were more encounters. A completely random man tried an attack on Alex." Merit drops his chin, weighing the dangers, both acceptable and unacceptable. "I don't want what happened with you and Denver—hell, Paco and Greta for that matter, to become a repeat performance."

"Merit," Gia begins like she's speaking to a slow child, "it already has. Beginning with sketchy Davenport."

"Minus a brain." Merit snorts. He'd have killed the man himself for the betrayal alone. To think that Zaire's instincts were the only thing that saved Alex.

And that's the only fact that makes him feel like this entire setup can go a bit further. Zaire's proven he has the instincts of a lion.

"Zaire's going to kill us when he discovers our duplicity."

"If he lives through it," he says, in his typical macabre way.

"Merit, don't talk like that."

"Can't help it. There are components in play that I could've never imagined."

"Would you have gone through with this had you known who Alex Frost really was?"

No. "I wouldn't have wanted to put Zaire at risk," he says with typical logic. "And I have done it anyway. Because that bit of red hair I extracted from her hairbrush—I almost didn't take it. Her parents were *so* well-documented. Why do that extra step, I'd thought."

"I always believed that family was a bit *too* neat for my taste, though I could have never imagined—" Gia admits.

Probably. "—too late, but I might not have been the right fit for this." His chuckle is dark, knowing.

"Too late to self-analyze. Just make sure those two survive

through this, Merit. Once they're out of Croatia, we can come clean."

"No." He shakes his head though Merit knows she can't see the gesture. "Not until we surface Alex."

"God, you see what happened. Our sources have watched them. Zaire communicated with you, told you what's happened with the traceable burner."

"Yes."

"What more do they need to go through?"

Merit thinks of his promises to Denver, to Paco and Greta, and answers with the bald truth, "Everything."

Zaire

We're fucked. Period.

My eyes sweep a border I've never anticipated trying to cross. With insufficient time to do any research.

In all fairness, I thought I'd be babysitting a rich social media princess, and the notice Merit gave me was short.

Alexandra turned out to be a wonderful girl worth guarding, and now I'm taking her to a border where passports will be required.

We don't have Euros to bribe with even if that *were* an option.

"They're not going to let us through," Alexandra says, voicing my precise thoughts.

"I say we ditch the car and hike in."

My eyes move to her shoeless feet, a consequence of racing from a metaphoric burning building, cheap hostel-purchase socks now filthy.

Damn.

"I can do it," Alexandra says, resolute.

Her feet will get shredded.

My eyes travel the gentle slope of sharp grass that blankets the low hills with the Adriatic Sea just beyond our purview.

"Your feet—they'll be mincemeat."

Her face whips to mine, and a smear of dirt hides her freckles from my gaze.

"I don't care, Zaire. I want to get away from these fucktards that are chasing us."

A laugh busts out.

"What?" she asks, vaguely insulted by my obvious shock.

"'Fucktards'?"

Alexandra gives a prim nod, which makes me laugh harder.

"Shut up." She crosses her arms. "Give me some credit."

Cars whiz by, a line forming so far away it's a many-eyed spider of blinking taillights of red.

Sobering, I straighten. "Okay, we have water, and I have the coordinates from Merit before I had to dump the burner."

"And where are those?"

I grunt. "Croatia."

Alexandra rolls her eyes. "Duh."

The corners of my lips twitch. "Not too far past the border," I elaborate.

Her stomach gives a loud howl.

"Food," I say, giving her a critical look. "You're melting away before my eyes."

"Nah," she says too quickly, plucking an invisible string off her linen pants, now completely worse for wear.

The green shirt I bought her from the hostel is tired as well.

"This too shall pass." An old expression I remember Pop saying when I was young.

"Not fast enough." Alexandra opens the door, pushing it

wide, and steps out, wearing the bright green scarf hiding the copper hair that's so identifiable.

Exiting the vehicle, I turn, grabbing the dilapidated pack from the backseat floorboards and slinging the lightweight load over my back. I settle the weight between my shoulder blades.

Instasweat begins to form on my upper lip and the edge of my hairline. I'd commit murder for my ten gallon, feeling naked without it.

I have, come to think about it.

"Oh my God, it's so hot," Alexandra groans.

I take her hand and we begin to walk up the slope of the hill, diverting west, the seaside a distant turquoise jewel bisecting a cloudless horizon.

"Don't they have troops or soldiers or something to stop us loose ends?"

I give a light chuckle. "We're loose ends?"

"Yes," Alexandra says, blowing a bright ginger tendril off her face then tucking the stubborn piece behind her ear to hide the escapee beneath her scarf. "Clearly, they're tagging my ass."

Yes.

We walk on, gradually becoming surrounded by fronds, the razored straw-type grass that begins to morph into harsh underbrush, boxing us in at all sides.

"Okay, not gonna lie, this sucks."

"Stop."

Alexandra halts, giving a tired sigh.

"Let me look at your feet."

"I'm fine, Zaire."

Our gazes lock. "Let me be the judge of that." Bending over, I say, "Hang onto my shoulders."

Alexandra grips my shoulders, and I carefully peel one sock from her foot.

She hisses as the material comes away from her abused foot, some of the fabric sticking against fresh oozing blisters. Maybe she'd have been okay if she'd worn the high heels.

On second thought—*Nope.*

Her arch is bruised from traversing rocks, heel lanced by the grass that looks exactly like it feels: like tapered green knives.

"Alexandra," I say softly. "You can't go on."

"We *have* to go on." Tears run down her face, her wounded feet flinching from the open air.

God *dammit*. "I have an idea."

Her silence fills the space as the arid rugged bushes touch us from all sides.

Seeing no resistance, I continue, "You ride piggyback."

Angrily swiping at her face, she says, "That's not funny, Zaire." Her eyes run over my face for a few seconds before she finally speaks. "You're not kidding."

"No."

I turn with my back facing her and crouch, placing my hands behind me.

"Hop on, darlin'."

A moment before she climbs on, I crouch a little lower. Gripping her ass cheeks, I hike her into position, adjusting her weight until it's stabilized at my high hip.

"How long can you do this?'

"Long enough."

"I weigh a lot."

Plowing through the bushes, I automatically navigate in a direction where the shrubbery is less dense, glancing at the sun in the sky, the shadows cast by the bushes to gauge time—direction.

After a few minutes, when I finally slow long enough to catch my breath, I ask, "How much?"

"How much what?" Her breath tickles my neck.

"How much do you weigh?"

"You ask the worst questions, Zaire."

"No, darlin', that's only one."

She tells me.

I laugh.

"Don't laugh, you jerk."

I squeeze her legs with my hands. "I'm laughing because *I* weigh almost a hundred pounds more than you."

"You're taller."

"I'm a guy."

She's silent for a moment. "Yes, I'm aware."

"Let me get us somewhere safe. Just let me do what needs doing, Alexandra. Stop overthinking garbage that doesn't matter. I know my limitations. I wouldn't do something I think will jeopardize us."

"Okay."

"Do you trust me?"

Her arms tighten around my neck. "Against my will, against everything I thought possible—yes."

I guess that's a yes.

I trudge onward, hoping like hell Merit will be at the end of the line because I'm flat-out of contingencies.

Twenty-One
Alex

We've traversed the worst of the underbrush as Zaire relentlessly hikes a broad swath around the border crossing.

I'm so afraid we won't be able to manage to arrive at the relative safety of Croatia and, supposedly, the sanctuary Merit provides.

From his back, I can just make out the arch of the border crossing and the steel girders that follow it to my right and east of our position.

My head's turned, and that's why I don't see them come at first, but Zaire says in a soft shout, "Off!" Then I'm falling, my palms slapping the ground a moment before landing with a bruising finality.

A man in fatigues that match the color of our surrounding vegetation shouts something in a foreign language and comes for Zaire with a knife.

Zaire crouches as the man attempts to stab him in the torso. Zaire slaps his forearm up, successfully deflecting the strike.

I hold my breath, beginning to stand, and something shifts

past me, lifting my loose strands of hair. I turn too late, and pain radiates in my stomach as a fist lands dead center in a perfect sucker-punch.

I fold, coughing and airless as I stumble backward, losing my fight with balance.

A second man had clearly circled around and ambushed me before I could even react.

Rage sets its teeth in my brain like a ferocious pit bull.

I land on my knees, and he moves in close, setting his right leg back to do a better job of kicking my head in.

I reach for his vulnerable nutsack with both hands, grabbing on, and fall forward, using gravity and weight to yank his testies to the ground.

He howls, sinking and punching my head in an attempt to release him.

Pain explodes, and I begin to cant to the right, hanging on to the prick's nuts like a lifeline.

We fall together in a tangle of limbs as we tumble over the slightly sloped piece of land.

Rolling downhill—rolling away from Zaire, we land at the bottom of a ravine with a small creek that bisects the natural valley.

He lands in the water first.

Attempts to stand.

I wince as I rise.

Our eyes meet, and he bares his teeth as he keeps falling to his knees. His balls are probably a mass of burning agony, judging by his expression and abbreviated movements.

I whip my head around, searching.

There.

I stagger to a small boulder I assume there's no hope of lifting. I pick up the rock, adrenaline seeing me through the motion.

He's just straightening to a stand, and I toss the boulder

from a yard away. The ground he gained is lost when the weight of the rock pitches him backward, landing him in the creek right on his ass.

With a primal banshee wail, I step forward, leaping on him.

Mewling, I know my choice has been made before I jump.

I suck the rock back up with both hands just as his hands find my waist to tip me over, nearly making the advantage his.

I lift the solid weight high, almost overbalancing as my control falters, the boulder shaking for a tremulous moment at the apex before I regain control.

I let it drop.

The rock lands on his skull, the sound becoming a nightmarish memory with the sound of a crushed watermelon as his face collapses under the force.

An involuntary, pre-puke cough punches out of my chest as I crab-walk backward off his body.

I slip, falling into the creek where blood and brains clog the small waterway, backing up to seek me as I scurry to escape the watery gore.

Flipping over on my hands and feet, I begin to crawl from the water onto the filthy waterline filled with a mix of leaves, sand, dirt, and damp grass.

Sinking my fingers into the small embankment, I drag my body upward as my useless socked feet slip on the slick terrain.

A shadowy figure appears, and I'm so blinded by tears and fear at first I don't know if it's Zaire—or if it's the other guy coming to finish me off.

The figure begins to run down the slope, slipping and righting himself in a jagged descent.

I'd know those hazel eyes anywhere, his gait, as Zaire approaches me.

I try to stand.

Fall on my ass.

With a choking sob, I plunge my arms into the air and feel the solidness when his hands make contact, wrapping strong fingers around me, and lift.

"Zaire!" I say breathlessly. "What—" I look up into his face, noticing through the fog of my panic he has more bruises.

But his eyes aren't on me, they are on the murder scene behind me.

I nod too many times too quickly. "I did that. I killed him—the border patrol guy."

"No." His eyes are on me now. Tender—compassionate. "Notice the lack of guns. The actual border control is gone."

"Gone?" I ask with stupid slowness.

"Dead," Zaire announces flatly.

"Oh." The world feels like it's beginning to tilt.

"Whoa, darlin'—I got you."

I focus on his face, measuring my breaths and concentrating on the fact I'm not dead.

After a painful minute of centering myself, Zaire searches my face, determining I'm not going to pitch forward in a dead faint, and says, "Let's grab his shoes for you." He glances at my feet then turns his attention back to me. "Clearly, they'll be too damn big."

"I can't..." I'm so ashamed I killed someone; I'm too scared to face the proof.

"Stay put," Zaires says, and I hear what he does as water splashes and low cursing reaches me.

He returns, lifting shoes that look wet. "Waterproof, thank fuck—but really? The socks are gone, but the shoes will work. He was a short fireplug." Zaire smirks.

The shoes look like they're only a couple of sizes too big.

"Put them on."

Zaire lowers me to the ground, and with trembling fingers, I pull on the shoes of the man I just murdered.

Zaire

Alexandra is crawling up the slope of the ravine she traveled down as I was busy avoiding a knife to the gut.

I didn't avoid the knife entirely.

After stripping the assassin down to his skivvies, I grabbed his clean socks, shoes that shockingly fit perfectly, and threw his camo fatigues on. It's practical, and that seems to be the order of the day.

I used my grimy button-down shirt as a tourniquet to turn off the blood from the forearm wound I sustained from his slashing offensive knife strike.

The material is now a blood-soaked flag on my forearm, but I probably won't bleed to death.

I begin a careful lope to where Alexandra struggles upward, my eyes taking in the bigger picture of the other assassin's body floating in a creek fouled by his fluids.

I reach her. Alexandra sits on her butt, gently swaying like a willow in the wind. She must realize I'm here for her, lifting her arms high.

Reaching forward, I wrap my hands around her arms and yank her from the ground.

She comes easily, falling against my chest and wrapping her arms around my middle.

"Zaire!" she cries.

Alexandra begins to ask me what's happened.

In rapid-speak, I explain what the men were.

Are they border patrol?

No.

Are they part of the group who wants her dead, and me—by default?

Hell yes.

"Stay put," I say.

Leaning back as I make the treacherous, slippery slope, I barely manage to avoid bottoming out on my ass.

I reach the creek's edge, and luckily, the brained dickhead has his feet close to where I need to grab the corpse.

Latching onto his ankles, I jerk the body just enough to clear the waterline and peel off his shoes and socks.

Eyes roaming his form, I decide the rest of his apparel is out, too soaked and bloody to repurpose to our advantage.

Trudging up toward Alexandra, I note her dark eyes are vacant, dry.

Shock.

Stopping short of where she sits like a limp rag, I sink to my haunches and tell her to put on the boots.

They're too big, but after assessing the body as a shorter man, I figure they'd fit a helluva a lot better than the size thirteens I borrowed off my guy.

"Do you want the good news or bad news first?"

"Bad," Alexandra says with flat automation.

"We still have some distance to travel, based on the coordinates that Merit gave us."

"How much?"

I pause.

Alexandra grimaces. "That bad?"

In the shape she's in—yes. "Five miles."

She takes a wet sucking breath, hand rising to cover her mouth. "I want to do it."

I take her shoulders, small within my large hands. "I'll help."

Slowly, her chin rises until those black irises are shining at me, through me. "I know—but what if there are more of them?"

I smile. "That's the good news."

Pointing to the spot where the ravine begins to slope to

our position, I indicate the silhouette of a backpack lit from behind by late-day sunlight cresting the top.

"If I'm any judge, there might be some useful things inside the assassin's pack."

"Assassin?" she whispers through dry lips.

I nod. "No other moniker fits. When people keep at you and all they're trying for is your death; assassins."

"Davenport?" she asks.

I think through her one-word question for a heartbeat. "At the very least."

Alexandra doesn't continue. Instead, she bends to the task at hand, closing the shoelaces over her filthy, bloody socks.

I shut my eyes and breathe deeply.

What I didn't tell her are assassins commonly work alone but can work in groups—pairs, as these two clowns clearly did.

Alexandra stands, skin pale. "All right, I'm ready." Her voice contains a tremor.

I chuckle, stepping forward and cutting an arm beneath her knees as I lift her like a groom on his wedding night.

But instead of the threshold, it's a steady gait to reach the top of the ravine's hill.

When we do, I carefully set her down, and Alexandra sinks to her butt as I root around inside the pack from the man I turned the knife on, gutting him like a fish.

I dropped my saturated clothes and now wear his.

Alexandra seems to notice and opens her mouth. Closes it. "Where are your clothes?"

Discovering and extracting food, my shoulders ease slightly from the constant tension. We have jerky, canned fish, and protein bars, and I answer without looking up. "I left them with the dead guy, and he didn't object when I stripped him. It's all good."

The silence is so heavy I turn to look at her, elbow-deep in the pack.

Tears crawl down her face. "I killed my guy," Alexandra comments woodenly, taking ownership.

"Hey," I say, knowing we don't have the time to linger here like sitting ducks, but if I don't fix this now, there will be no fixing it later, "he was going to kill you... right?"

My eyes search hers as I take in Alexandra's expression, watching the wheels of her memory slowly grind, replaying the horror I wasn't there to witness.

She finally whispers the affirmative I knew was coming, "Yes."

"I killed my guy too," I admit easily. I simply don't have the fucking time to self-recriminate, question, or evaluate my survival maneuvers.

Alexandra seems to shake herself out of the fugue she was teetering on, finally looking to me. "I guess they weren't 'our guys'."

My eyes lock with hers. "They were our guys to kill."

Twenty-Two
Zaire

My back groans as I readjust Alexandra's weight and take off, walking fast, her form wrapping mine like a monkey.

We'd eaten the bare minimum, and Alexandra claimed she felt better. That was one box ticked among a bunch of bad ones tallied by circumstance rather than choice.

Murder.

Check.

Starvation.

Check.

Terrorized.

Check.

Safety; not-yet-realized.

Check—check.

The sun sizzles into my path, beating the shit out of my face as I squint, moving parallel with the border crossing.

When I'm two miles in, I can't take another step and admit partial defeat.

The bald facts are: Alexandra is not heavy, but she's heavy after two miles.

I tap out, fingers lightly playing a fast rhythm on the top of Alexandra's thigh. "Gotta let you down, darlin'."

I feel defeated as her weight is slowly released and she unwraps her limbs. Her jerky stiff movements are proof of the soreness from being carried as she slides down my back.

For a moment, her face nestles between my damp shoulder blades as she wraps her arms around my torso.

I cover her hands with my own, and we stand there together, the sun bathing us in crimson light like blood.

Alex

After guzzling an entire liter of water, I wipe my mouth with the back of my hand.

"Better?" Zaire asks, twilight backlighting him like an escaped hornless demon.

I shake the disquieting image away with difficulty. "Yeah, I thought I'd die of thirst." My mouth snaps shut, realizing what I'd said. "Look at me using that word like it's no big deal."

The memory of a fragmented skull inserts itself inside my brain. I can't unsee the visual. Maybe I'll never be able to.

"Alexandra."

My chest grows tight, extremities beginning to tingle.

"Alexandra." His voice is more urgent this time.

My eyes rise to his. "Don't. Hit. Me."

Zaire sits up on his knees and walks to me just like that, cradling my face, the ghost of a smile riding his lips. "Are you panicking?"

I nod because speaking's not possible.

After a few raw seconds, I somehow manage to draw an inhalation that's normal.

Then exhale. Take another awful, labored breath.

"That's it, darlin'. Look at me."

My eyes sink into his as the last tendrils of the Mediterranean sun seek me and the sunset superimposes over Zaire's face.

I nod, eyes dry, heart full—mind... destroyed. After another minute or two, I say, "It's okay—I'm okay."

Zaire nods. "We need to trudge on. Daylight's almost gone."

I gaze down at my borrowed shoes and give a shaky, reluctant nod.

He stands, pulling me up with him. "Can you walk?"

No. "Yes." My feet are a mess.

That basic fact aside, I've learned something about myself I wasn't pressed to entertain before: I now know how much I want to live.

As a matter of fact, I'm desperate to.

My feet being wrecked no longer factors against the weight of my life.

We walk on.

Zaire

"I know you don't want to talk about it, Alexandra," I say quietly as we make steady progress for what I estimate is the last two miles.

"Yeah."

Chest tight, I admit my deficit, "I didn't protect you."

"Please," Alexandra says with a tired snort.

I look at her as we walk side-by-side. "I mean it. You hired me, and all I could take on was the one guy." And I wasn't even honest about who I really was, allowing the complicit omission of Club Alpha proprietor to remain unknown while Alexandra believes the bodyguard fable.

"He had a knife."

I shrug, still pissed about my role. My *unknown* role. "Didn't see the other dick."

That gets a laugh. "Yeah, they were *sneaky* dicks."

We both laugh softly, mindful of who could still be lurking in the dark.

Merit

"Grady, hand me my eyes."

Merit's sidekick for this routine-type-of-recon-that-isn't passes the night-vision goggles.

He doesn't bother to secure the chin and head straps but lifts them to his eyes, pressing them tight against his eye sockets. The lens caps annoyingly swing from their slim tethers.

Merit watches the two figures come to within several yards of our position.

Zaire is smart, taking the left flank and slightly rear position of Alex and navigating through the cloistered underbrush that allows some cover.

Merit takes in the approaching figures.

It's clear from her awkward gait that Alex has feet problems. He recognizes the zombie lurch of injured feet when he sees it.

Zaire holds his left arm at an odd angle.

Defense injury. "First aid box."

Grady glances at him for a weighted moment before replying, "You got it."

Lowering the goggles, when Merit is certain he can make

them out within true night's impending gloom, he retires the night-vision.

A sigh of true regret leaks out at the final, necessary step, and he tells Grady, "Release the Kraken."

Grady turns his head and speaks with soft deliberation into a collar mic.

Our men seep from the woods like an unchecked wound.

Alex

"Are we there yet?" I ask, attempting to lighten the mood for him.

For myself.

I catch his smile in the near-dark. "Almost."

I gaze at the murky forest line that Zaire claims is the meeting point, given it matches the coordinates he remembers and judging by the faded stars' soft illumination. Then there's the simple fact we'd finally have somewhere we could hide instead of being out here in the open.

Not *exactly* in the open. There's the shitty insufferable underbrush that's abraded every bit of my unclothed skin. I'd stupidly asked at mile four if we could escape the bushes to the open flatland that was located a tantalizing few yards away.

No, Zaire had instantly replied.

I'd halted the march, popping hands to hips, and glowered at him. Spent, hangry, dirty, tired, and just plain pissed off.

"We need the cover, Alexandra." His eyes had gleamed at me.

Cover, *schmuther.*

Grumping along behind Zaire, he'd gradually allowed me to be forward of him, saying we just head for the woods. There we could rest—have more food and water; maybe Merit would even be waiting.

His words had made me salivate like Pavlov's dogs. And I began to view the treeline like the finish line at a race.

I am a runner who can't run; the thought is almost comical.

Until the first dark figure appears.

"Alexandra."

"I see him."

"Get behind me."

"No."

Zaire looks at me. "I can't protect you if you offer yourself up like a target."

"You're hurt," I acknowledge for the first time, eyeing up his wrapped and wounded forearm.

Another joins the all-black figure.

Then a third.

I feel a lunatic grin seat itself on my face.

I'm determined I don't want to die, but I won't run—can't. I want to live so much I'm willing to entertain things I would have never believed I could. That I never imagined were possible to happen in the world I inhabit.

Then I think of what transpired against Bridget.

Anything is possible.

Any evil.

Any eventuality.

"You still have the knife?"

"Yes," I whisper in a thready voice, watching their unwavering approach as they divide, widening themselves from one another, the better to come at us at all angles.

My heartbeats begin to run together.

"Stand with your back to mine."

I do, pivoting as my feet shout their agony, healing blisters sliding apart again to weep their gore as I shift my footing.

"Move as I do."

I clench my eyes, only opening when the tension of Zaire's body thrums through my own in early warning.

The intimacy of fighting together is like a horrible dance.

Especially when only one partner knows the waltz.

Zaire

The warm weight of Alexandra at my back is a comfort and a torture.

The three armed men come, knives laid bare in their hands.

Gunfire is too loud. The distinctive racket of bullet exchange would alert the border patrol, a complication this group would logically avoid.

The first one holds up a hand, gloved and inky in the soft black of early evening, halting the pair who have moved wide of the center figure.

"Give us the girl. Just walk away, and you can live."

His eyes are white above the face mask. Impossible to identify. Maybe he's being real, telling the truth.

They take Alexandra and I'm off the hook. Simple.

He must make my smile because I can see from the easing of his shoulders that he thinks I'm in the bag, certain I'll take the easy way out and let these men take Alexandra to brutalize and murder.

Because I have no fucking doubt they won't simply kill her fast.

No way.

I sweep my eyes at the trio, cocking my head as my gaze lands on the center asshole. "Why don't y'all just fuck off." I nod, my arms surging to the right in the classic "exit stage left" style. Pure anger ruthlessly flows through me, lighting my system up for another go. "And when you're done fucking off here"—I point to a space between us—"make your way to the next country, and keep fucking off. In fact," I continue, warming to my impromptu rant, "don't quit on me until you fuck right off into the sea. We'll see how long your sorry asses last"—my eyes pin them to the spot—"treading water as you fuck. Right. Off."

Tension returns to the three musketeers like a wave begging to come ashore.

"Fine," Center Asshole replies in a clipped, one-syllable slur of anger and finality.

However, it's not me who saves the day but Alexandra.

I try to stop her, but the move is so unexpected my fingers brush the sleeve of the cheap t-shirt I bought her as she sprints past me.

"Alexandra!" I bellow, leaping after her as she slides into the first one like a home run at fourth base.

Her knife flashes a mercury streak as the stars give it their starved illumination. She lurches to the right, dropping, rolling over, and slicing the Achilles tendon of the first man as though choreographed.

He drops, clutching his leg with a hoarse shout.

Another lands on Alexandra, snapping her wrists above her and chopping the forearm that holds the blade.

The knife falls.

I howl her name like a wounded lion.

Closing in behind him, I jerk his head back like the Indians of old, dragging him back by the hair on his scalp.

Baring his throat.

Someone grabs me from behind, and I attach myself like a barnacle to the man who would murder Alexandra.

"Stop!"

What? I hesitate, recognizing the voice.

Standing, I move with the weight of the men, front and back, turning to face that voice with my two-man burden.

Merit stands before me; a cell beneath his chin illuminates a grim expression.

"What the fuck is going on?"

The one at my back shoves away, and my hands loosen from the strands of hair I had an iron fist within. The hairs cling to my fingers as he stomps away.

"Club Alpha is what's going on," Merit says.

I back away, not knowing who to trust—what to think as I keep them within sight and move to where Alexandra lays.

But her eyes are closed as though asleep.

I drop to my knees at the sight of her blood, hauling her into my arms.

No!

Twenty-Three
Alex

"Club Alpha is what's going on," Merit says.

Merit?

I shake my head. No, that's not right. I can't move, but I can feel something solid and warm around me.

"What the fuck is going on?" Zaire asks.

"Is she hurt?"

"Like I'd fucking let *you* examine her."

I try to talk. Can't.

Zaire, I say in my mind.

"She's trying to talk." *Merit.*

"Pretty hard to do since her throat's been cut," Zaire snarls.

My throat? My—*what's happened to me?*

"I'll explain later. Let me look at her and determine what's needed."

"Fuck you," Zaire grates.

"Okay."

I hear them come back but can't do anything.

His comforting cocoon is torn from me, and I land softly on the ground. Softly because another person has me.

"Open your eyes, Alex. It's me."

I will them open. At first, nothing happens.

Then my eyelids must cooperate because a blurry Merit comes into focus.

"What?" I try to ask, but a horrible stripe of fire flares, and I cover my throat with a hand.

"No touchy," Merit says with his typical sarcasm, gently moving my hand away.

Turning his cell, the flashlight element hits my face and I squeeze my eyes shut.

"Sorry," he mutters, trying to adjust the light.

When I sense it's off my face, I open my eyes. The strange light cast from the cell artificially warps his face into a sort of demented clown.

I try to swallow, and the pain lances.

Gasping, I instantly make the sensation worse and groan.

"Let me go, or I swear to Christ I'll rip your gonads off your worthless bodies," Zaire says from a fair distance.

"Chill out, Zaire," Merit says without looking then pats my arm. "You're okay. My guy gave you exactly what I wanted you to have. Nothing a little plastic surgery won't fix. Though the placement is saucy. You'll obviously need to refrain from speaking for a day or so."

What the hell is going on? His "guy"? But Merit's right. I can't talk—and clearly, I can't trust Merit.

How did things get turned around so quickly?

The sounds of plastic wrap and the rustling of paper signal a package being opened.

"Okay, I'm going to clean your wound and put some superglue in there, and you'll be as good as new."

A tear of frustration squeezes out of one eye.

"Don't cry, Alex. Be brave."

I am brave.

Fierce joy seizes me when I realize I was able to cut the jerk who cut me.

Merit swabs cleaning solution inside the wound, and the liquid burns like acid, setting the tender area on fire.

The only sound I'm able to make is an inaudible moan.

He pinches the folds of my split skin together, and I grip his arm, eyes bulging.

"Almost done," Merit says, eyes sliding to mine before returning to the task. "Gonna have to put a bandage on this too. Might have to run; don't want this opening."

I can't run. My feet are in tatters; my throat's been sliced and diced.

"Hey, Merit, I know this is your little soiree, but we've got company," Zaire says sarcastically.

Merit's face whips around, jaw clenched over a scene I can't see.

Oh God, oh God, oh *God*.

Planting my elbow, I hoist myself into a sitting position, automatically moving my hand to cover my throat.

My eyes scrub our immediate environment.

The man I cut has risen, one foot held off the ground, the toes of his boot barely skimming the ground while the other leg bears all his weight.

Good.

But it's the others who come that have me standing.

Four men tromp through the open plains that separate the scrub brush from the sanctuary of the forest.

"More of your fucking men?" Zaire asks.

"No." Clipped. Certain.

Shit.

The men who hold Zaire's arms drop his limbs and step back, widening their distance from Zaire, from each other.

I look for signs that we're lucky, that these dudes are

border patrol and can be reasoned with. They don't wear a uniform, unless a person counts wearing all-black.

"Darlin'."

I run to Zaire, the approaching men too far to intercept me.

They stop yards from where the one who balances on his leg stands, Merit a few feet behind him, Zaire and I together and behind Merit.

I risk a glance at the other two who have positioned themselves like bookends from where we stand.

I turn my attention forward.

Zaire puts his body slightly in front of me.

I move to grip his arm, my fingers closing around the wound drenching his makeshift bandage that was a shirt in its former life, and he winces.

My eyes move to his, and since I can't talk, I apologize with my eyes.

"Forget it, darlin'," he forgives instantly.

Zaire places his index finger to his lips. *Watch—listen,* that gesture says.

Robbed of my voice, I can't even scream when the first one speaks in an eerie repeat of the "guys" who are somehow Merit's.

"We know who you are, Lang."

Merit's chin hikes. "Good, then you understand I'll hand you your fucking asses given five minutes," Merit announces in a level voice.

The man at the left speaks again as though Merit hadn't just threatened him. "Let it happen. Give us the girl. You know who she is—the last loose end. Gotta tie that shit up, Lang. I know you're her hired gun, but just walk, man. Our bosses don't have a beef with you."

Zaire takes my hand, ignoring the two men who held him

so he couldn't come to my side when Merit was patching me up.

He begins walking toward Merit's position, towing me behind him.

Merit and his men no longer seem like the threat their theatrics indicated.

Club Alpha, Merit had said two times. *What does that even mean?*

The ones who stand in front of Merit are different. They hold none of the tension that Merit's men possessed.

Belatedly, I realize that the tension might have been their efforts to hold back from true harm.

I touch the wound at my throat.

Why did Merit's "guys" do that to me—what the hell *is* this? I'm beginning to wonder if they've got me confused with someone else.

The men in front of Merit are contained violence. Complacent in their upcoming task, they appear to be almost superficially relaxed.

For my murder.

I tug at Zaire's hand, wanting to flee.

He shakes his head. *Wait,* the gesture seems to say.

"I know who the girl is," Merit states in a flat voice.

I'm Alexandra Frost, my mind easily supplies.

"Our handlers say Jeffrey Epstine's spawn must end, just like the bio-daddy. We can't have any more leaks in the playground the elites have established. You know how it goes." He spreads his arms, leveling an aw-shucks grin at Merit, the glimmer of his blade bright as the stars lend their cold beauty to the honed metal.

Jeffrey Epstine? The ultra-perv that had the island so the rich could defile kids? The dude that committed "suicide" in prison?

He-I—*what? Bio-what?*

I feel my jaw drop open.

Zaire's eyes slide to me for a stuttering split second's appraisal before returning to the small army.

No! I mentally scream at him. I *know* who my parents are. Obviously, my dad's horrible because—Bridget. My mom was complacent in the crime against Bridget by not advocating, by shoving my ass out the door barely past toddlerhood to a boarding school where I blended in with all the other rich, unwanted children.

I can't be related to that pedophile. *No,* I deny.

Yet, here these men stand, claiming the opposite of the truth as I know it. My attention returns to the man and his claims.

"Your answer?"

Merit folds his arms, rocking back on his heels, and I die inside as I wait out his contemplation.

"No—you-highest-bidder-for-fucking-hire."

There's no warning.

They come, mowing through the first man who I maimed, one of them dipping low and cutting him close to the groin. Blood arcs, fanning out twenty feet from where he falls on his back in a nauseating burst of liquid. The stream of blood shoots toward us when the fallen man gets in a lucky strike as he falls, sinking his blade into the calf of the man as he walks away.

I back away from the silent carnage.

Two fall at Merit; there's no better description. One takes his left arm, and Merit reactively chops his throat with tight knuckles.

The man chokes, staggering backward as the second jerks Merit's arm behind his back, hiking it high.

Merit spins out of the hold and grips the arm that had his, bringing him forward and ramming the man's skull with his own. Lifting his knee, he plows it into the man's torso, following through with a jab to the head.

Movement comes from the left.

I scream as Zaire and the other two of Merit's men charge the two who are now loose.

One throws a knife from its blade at the closest of Merit's men, the blade spins, hitting with a smacking punch to the chest. He falls forward, sinking the blade the rest of the way with his landing.

Searching the ground, I find the bloodied knife I used to slice the one guy's Achille's tendon.

Pick it up.

Zaire and the man who is left come together to form a sort of barrier in front of me.

A furtive sound has me spinning around, and I reflexively turn the blade as I bring my dominant hand up.

The tip sinks inside the torso of a man who holds the twin of my own.

Our eyes meet, and my brain turns off.

The world narrows to a pinpoint; all that remains is him and me.

I drive the hilt higher.

In slow motion, his blade comes for my temple, seeking like a magnet to steel.

I duck, still holding the hilt for dear life.

His blade screams past my head so closely my loose hairs rise.

Fisting my left hand as I dip, I drive my fist into the base of the knife's hilt.

A pained yelp escapes me as the move radiates a numb streak of agony that zings from my fist to my shoulder.

A wet smack sounds, and the man who almost killed me tips like a felled tree, falling away from me.

I release the hilt, falling on my butt. My neck's a throbbing mass of fire, so beyond hurt I can't name how I feel.

Merit's crawling toward me.

Zaire rushes him, and Merit stands, clearly injured.

Zaire steps into him with a punch meant to maim, and Merit grabs his arm, taking him down.

I stagger to a stand, walking toward them as my eyes take in the bodies littering the ground. Their blood's colored like ink from the meager starlight and slim crescent moon.

Zaire spins out of Merit's hold and picks him up, slamming him on the ground.

"Stop," I rasp, hand to throat.

He doesn't listen, kicking Merit.

I run, grabbing Zaire by the thin t-shirt he wears.

Zaire pivots. Fist high, he sees it's me.

The meteor of his fist of flesh trembles, begging to finish the revolution of violence he began.

Slowly, he lowers his fist.

Grabbing me, he draws me into his body. "It's okay now, Alexandra."

"Stop beating up Merit," I whisper, mindful of my injured throat.

"Yes, you fucking hothead, stop beating me up."

We part, staring at Merit.

His face is pretty bashed up. His pale hair stands up in a shock of matted blood on one side of his head, and even in the low illumination, the bruises over his bare arms stand out in stark relief.

"I don't have a lot of time because those dicks"—he takes a deep breath, collects snot and blood from his mouth, and spits it with a sort of gross elegance, continuing—"tuned me up pretty hard, killed my men, and there will be more where they came from."

"First, you're going to tell me what in the absolute fuck is going on."

Merit slides his fingers through his short hair and grimaces as his fingers come away wet with his own blood. "What's going on is I'm running a Club Alpha game."

Zaire shifts his weight, looking uncomfortable. "Club Alpha's finished."

Merit shakes his head. "Nope, there was actually one more game."

"All right. Let's say this bullshit was true. Who are the players?" Zaire asks.

Merit is silent for so long I don't think he'll answer. Then he does. "You haven't figured that part out?"

"Fuck," Zaire replies in a voice like a deflated balloon.

I look between the two men. "What the hell is Club Alpha?"

"A dangerous game," Zaire says.

"Are we the players?" I guess.

Merit's dark eyes find mine. "Yes."

Twenty-Four
Merit

I fucked up. Big. Fucking. Time. He sees that now. Sometimes a person can't possibly intuit every eventuality, and Merit's found himself squarely in that position.

How was he to know that Alexandra Frost was the only bio-child of the king of all perverts when he'd scouted her as a candidate for Zaire?

Now Merit has to lie in the bed he's made.

Men died to surface the "players" emotions, their integrity —fortitude, in a game they all were not adept enough to participate in.

Small consolation that it appears Alex is more than even Merit gave her credit for.

Facing Zaire feels like a firing squad is staring back at him through their eyes. "We don't have time to thrash this out right now."

Zaire puts his hands on his hips. "No shit. Now what—I'll compartmentalize whatever y'all did to fuck with us for later?"

"I have a man—"

"One that's not dead," Zaire qualifies with a sarcastic grunt.

The effort to not peruse all the bodies on the ground is ugly.

Talk about compartmentalization.

Speaking of which, Alex looks a little green in the gills.

Merit gives a terse nod. "Yes. Grady," he says, jerking his chin in the direction of the woods. "He'll get us the fuck outta dodge."

His eyes run a swift line down Alex's body, taking in the obvious men's shoes and her shocky face.

Zaire steps in front of her, narrowing his eyes at Merit. "Don't think it."

"I'm not thinking anything but getting out of here, like I said."

He and Zaire have a stare-down while Zaire clearly does a mental workaround as to his limited options. No doubt Zaire sees him as public enemy number one, but Merit let the Club Alpha cat out of the bag, and now Zaire's got choices.

Clearly, Merit wasn't trying to actually hurt him and Alex. The separate matter of Alex being sought for sanction because she's the child of the ultra-whistle blower of child trafficking —had impeccable timing, he thinks, giving a mental eye roll.

"I want to go," Alex says, looking around as she cups her elbows.

Zaire shifts his weight, glaring at him for all he's worth. "Let's go." He begins to take Alex's arm and, with only a single step, she hisses.

Feet, like Merit suspected. "What's happened to her feet?"

Zaire swiftly explains.

Merit gives Zaire critical perusal. He's a mess too. Full of bruises, blood, and grit that's put him in sub-standard shape to carry her. If Merit was a betting man, he'd say Zaire already had carried her.

He lifts his chin, eyes raking over the awkward and tense way she holds herself. "Come on, Alex."

Showing them his back might be the bravest move of the night, and he listens to the rustle of grass as footsteps approach.

"I can take her," Zaire growls.

Right. "Fuck that, you're too beat up. Besides, don't be a dick—I'm fresh."

Zaire stomps over. Then, with a pause for dramatic effect, he lifts Alex and deposits her on my back.

As Merit adjusts her weight, Alex wraps her legs around his waist and neck. "Tighten your arms."

She does, and with a tired sigh, the dead weight of Alex solidifies.

Moving out fast, Zaire easily keeps pace with him as they walk-jog to the treeline and the safety beyond.

Zaire

I could kill Merit myself.

Of course, now that I know his actions are some kind of fucked-up Club Alpha lookalike, in turn, I've now been made aware he was funded by *someone.*

My mind runs through the possibilities like a deck of cards.

Paco and Greta come to mind first; a close second is Gia and Denver, who were patently quiet when I'd said I was shutting Club Alpha down.

Silent—because I speculate they were fucking scheming—is what.

Alex attempts to sleep on Merit's back. She's so exhausted and shocked out. Not that I like to admit how bad off *I* am. I'm right with Alexandra, barely able to keep pace with the much-fresher Merit.

My hands shake from exhaustion and hunger. Even my anger at feeling like I've been played by someone I consider a friend can't supersede those two bald facts.

I'm simply too spent to keep my rage engaged.

All I care about is getting Alexandra to safety and getting hard answers after we've been fortified with food and water.

We slow our pace as we hit the first of the sparsely spaced trees that surround our entry. Their canopies soon become so dense only filtered moon and starlight reach us to barely illuminate our footfalls.

I startle like a sleepwalker when a man steps from amongst a dense copse to the right of our position and instinctively tense into a crouch, residual adrenaline doing a slow pump through my beleaguered system.

"This is Grady." Merit jerks a thumb toward the dark figure.

I barely catch myself from slumping in relief.

Grady walks without sound, not bothering with introductions and giving the scene of my tired ass and Alexandra on Merit's back cursory attention at best, and hikes his chin at Merit. "Half a click to the road."

Hanging my head, I ask in a quiet voice, "Have any food?"

Grady's face swings in my direction. And as if he anticipated that question, he extracts something from the deep cargo pocket of his pants, bringing a package into view I immediately recognize as a pemmican bar.

I snag the rectangular package, tearing off the top with my teeth and spitting the remnant away as I take a giant bite, chewing like my life depends on it.

I walk to where Merit still holds Alex.

Her sleepy eyes open to slits. "What?" she slurs.

"Eat," I command, shoving the bar of tallow, lean meat and berries at the general direction of her mouth.

Alexandra licks her chapped lips and takes a bite, beginning to mechanically chew. Her eyes open wider as tastebuds fire off, signaling reawakened hunger. "More," she croaks in a low voice.

I smile, the movement hurting my abused face.

"You're bleeding, pal," Grady announces shrewdly.

My arm has steady rivulets of blood running down to drip on the absorbent forest floor.

Marvelous.

Grady silently lifts a water bottle.

Snagging the offering, I down the entire liter.

Give a burp, remember Alexandra's present, and laugh. Don't have to worry about manners until we're in the clear, but I had enough presence of mind to note it.

Alexandra gives me a tired smile and a thumbs up. "Nice." Her voice is a thread, the wounded throat prohibiting real speaking.

"Don't talk, darlin'."

Grady walks a water to her, uncapping it. Merit slowly releases Alexandra's legs, and she slides down his broad back.

I draw her against my side as Alexandra gratefully takes the water from Grady.

"How many?" he asks Merit while she drinks in abbreviated fits and starts.

"Everyone." Merit's pale eyebrow lifts. "And you saw our company, I assume?"

"Yeah. Wish we could have gotten out of here before the chode crew showed."

Merit nods, attention shifting to Alexandra. "Grady's going to carry you the rest of the way."

Alexandra gives an exhausted shrug, but the look on her face clearly says she would rather do anything but be carried.

Grady tosses his gear sack to Merit, who catches the small pack midair, shrugging it onto his back.

"Come on," Grady says neutrally, sinking to his haunches.

I watch the woman I'm falling in love with crawl onto another man's back.

I seethe.

But my anger is a banked fire compared to my exhaustion. My pride must take a back seat to her safety and the end-goal of expediting our escape.

Merit and I step into a pace behind them, and I ask quietly, "Tell me what the fuck is going on?"

He clenches his jaw. "Like you're already aware, Club Alpha deeds can intersect shit we had no way of knowing about."

Do I ever know that.

"Why did you play me? Chloe's dad?" I emit a low snort.

I catch his smirk when a patch of light spears a hole through the canopy above. "He's fine. Contrived."

"Dick."

"Probably," Merit replies carefully. "That little scene back there was actually our grand finale."

"Clearly"—I point to Alexandra riding on Grady's back—"she's not some shallow bitch."

Merit covers his mouth to muffle a laugh, his expression having a secretive feel to it. "Yeah, I think that's been established."

"You used my methods against me," I accuse.

We allow a bit of distance between us and Alexandra, but not too much.

"And it worked?" Merit asks insightfully.

Hell yes. I know I could love her—maybe I already do.

"Is she really"—*God, I don't want to say it aloud*—"the daughter of Epstine?"

Merit gives a grim nod. "One hundred percent certain."

"Would that knowledge have made a difference if you'd known before you put this into play?"

"You're assuming I didn't know when I got this ball rolling."

I had.

A drumbeat of silence pounds between us before Merit answers, "No, I didn't know, and, yeah—I don't think I would have gone through with it."

"Alexandra's too complicated," I say as a matter of course. Just the facts, man.

Merit shrugs, spreading his arms away from his body as though to say, *of course.*

Alexandra's lineage isn't her problem. Life offers chances at happiness that hide in between circumstances like needles in haystacks. A person has to be open to seeing what's offered, no matter how gruesome the timing.

The road comes into view like a mirage squeezing itself between tree trunks.

We speed our pace, and I never know how much Alexandra actually heard of our conversation until much later.

I had not been quiet enough.

Alex

I squeeze my eyes shut when I hear Zaire's damning words.

Alexandra's too complicated.

Tears I can't spare threaten, but I fight them off as the motion of the Grady guy undulates beneath me. I'm not crying on some stranger. I can't walk on my own because my feet are in ruins.

Survive, Alex.

I can't believe Zaire's just dismissed me after all we went through together.

My eyes latch onto the promised road and vehicle of transport to get us the hell out of this nightmarish bit of fuckery.

Grady slows, and it's then that I see the car is actually a black SUV with downed branches covering every inch of it.

A faint brush from low slung tree branches signals Zaire and Merit approaching from behind.

"Alexandra?" Grady says quietly, and gripping my wrists, he lowers me to the ground.

I lean against a nearby tree trunk, bracing my body with a hip. I tip my head back and roll my profile until half my face touches the rough bark. I move my face to the other side that's not still swollen and bruised from all the preceding altercations that run together inside my mind; an entire series of attacks and escapes.

I concentrate on breathing. Not the fact that Zaire told Merit I'm *too complicated* or that I had amazing sex with him that I believed meant something.

Nope.

Or the lovely "fact" that my parents might not actually *be* my parents and that I'm the bio-daughter to some kingpin pedophile.

Abandoning that horrible potential, I frown. Who *would* be my mother then? If that creep was supposedly my father, who would my mother be?

Branches are loud as they're swept from the vehicle.

Zaire comes to me, and I allow him to pick me up and carry me to the car where Merit opens the door just ahead of our approach.

When Zaire asks me a question while buckling me in, I shake my head, lightly tapping the wound at my throat as though talking hurts.

The words I have to say hurt way less than the realization of his abuse of my heart—his dismissal of facts we can't even prove.

And even if it were true that I was biologically related to Epstine—how can I be held responsible for my lineage? Does being related to a vile, evil man mean that *I* am an evil human being as well?

The men slide into the vehicle, and with the turn of a key, Merit pulls away from the sight of the massacre where I almost died.

Technically, I lived.

Even though now I feel dead inside.

Funny how a bit of information can murder a person without a weapon in sight.

Twenty-Five
Zaire

Alexandra is too quiet. Yes, her throat has a cut just deep enough to require a glue stitch.

That fact doesn't change the slide of her eyes when I try to look at her.

The shake of her head at every question.

We speed to a safehouse that Merit promised has the provisions we desperately need.

Yet, I'm distracted by the artificially created distance I sense growing between Alexandra and me.

Merit drives—Grady shotgun, as we navigate backroads, and he gives Merit short directions until, finally, we land at a dirt road that winds from the rutted main asphalt to a distant house beyond.

We pull up in front of a stone house, clearly constructed of indigenous rock. Two windows look down at us like beseeching eyes with a centered front door embedded so deeply in shadows its shape appears like a yawning mouth.

Shutting the engine off, Merit turns. The ticking of the cooling motor is ominous raindrops of sounds within the echo chamber of my thoughts.

"Everything we need's in here."

"Okay, then what?"

"Grab a shower, eat—drink. Then I'll brief you."

I look to Alexandra.

Her face rests against the glass of the window, lackluster eyes seeing everything and nothing.

"I'll get ya, darlin'."

No reply, no response. My lips part to ask her what's wrong besides the obvious, and Merit shakes his head from the front. "Later."

With a rough exhale to still a harsh reply, I push the door open, exiting the vehicle. Shutting the door with a palm, I cruise around the back of the vehicle and reach her side.

Our eyes meet through the dark glass of the rig, and for a blistering microsecond, I swear I see betrayal in that gaze.

Then it's gone, and those beautiful dark eyes shift from my dredge of her soul.

Moving away from the door, I lift the handle and easily lift her into my arms.

We quietly move to the front door, and an ominous portent of the future slows my steps.

The door I thought was so dark isn't.

It's colored a deep, uncompromising blood-red.

———

Merit

"Do you think you can manage a shower?"

Alex's feet are far worse than he thought. The crippling bruise at her arch encompasses the entire interior arch of her right foot. Her left is abraded everywhere, even her pinky toe did not escape the lance of the grasses and rough terrain.

Alex bites her lip, trying for brave and not doing half-bad.

"I can dress these wounds on your feet but—" he gives her throat wound careful consideration. The glue's held, but she shouldn't try to speak like she has been "No more attempts at speech."

Her eyes touch on Zaire for a moment before returning to him and giving the barest nod.

Merit frowns. There's some new, underlying tension between them he can't put his finger on. Wracking his brain, Merit can't figure out what's happened between the killing spree and now to warrant the vibe.

Shrugging mentally, Merit determines the priorities need to happen.

Getting them clean, dressing wounds to ward off infection, then stuffing them with food.

Alex looks dead on her feet, having dropped a few kilos she couldn't afford to lose.

Merit pats her knee and stands.

She gives him a wan smile.

Barefooted, Alex limps to the bathroom where the shower's already been turned on.

Alex shuts the door softly. Merit makes out the quiet sound as she latches it.

He turns to Zaire. "Get in there and clean up the instant she's done."

"Hot water?" Zaire asks.

"Tankless water heater."

Zaire's chin lifts in tired understanding. "Thank God for small favors."

They look at each other, the awkward pause growing between them.

Grady clears his throat. "I'll be outside, maintaining the perimeter until more men arrive."

"Affirmative," Merit replies without looking at him.

Grady leaves, and Merit narrows his eyes at Zaire. "Sit," he sweeps a hand in the direction of one of the small kitchen table's four chairs.

Zaire flops his ass down where Alexandra just sat and closes his eyes.

Merit unwraps a shirt that's begun to stick to the wound on Zaire's forearm, slowly pulling the fabric away from the cut. Zaire's eyes slam open. "That feels fucking *great*."

Merit's eyes flick to Zaire's. "Yeah, started to adhere to the wound."

"Well, I'm awake now," Zaire glares at him.

Merit smirks then states, "Did okay back there."

Zaire barely lifts his chin. "I've never been so glad for what you taught me than I was during that fiasco."

Merit tears away the last of the sodden shirt, and Zaire hisses through his teeth. "Damn, that sucks," he breathes the words out as the wound begins to bleed anew.

The knife wound is deep enough that Merit wouldn't be surprised an artery's been nicked as he studies the gash while blood continues to slowly ooze.

"Defensive strike," Merit states.

Zaire nods.

"Looks like he punched you," he notes, carefully rotating the arm as he scrutinizes the slash that presents puncture-like at one end then running to a shallow finish at its end.

"Hang tight, but—gonna drench this fucker and sew it right now."

"Let the fun begin."

Merit pours hydrogen peroxide into the ragged gash, and the edges bubble, mixing with the blood to become a frothing crimson mass.

"Fuck." Zaire leans forward, shifting from one ass cheek to the other. "Hurts like a bitch."

"Not like the next part will."

Their eyes clash.

Merit retrieves the first aid kit, pulling out a needle and thread.

A deflated breath leaks from Zaire as he grits his teeth.

To his credit, he doesn't pass out.

Alex

My head rests against cool tile as the hot water runs down my body, singeing my feet like acid as the heated liquid seeks every tender, raw wound and abrasion vested on my feet from journeying everywhere with only socks, running and fighting with barely a breath between charged events.

I've lathered my hair twice with shampoo. Half a bottle of conditioner had been under the sink, and I use the entire thing after rinsing my hair to squeaky-clean, letting the creamy mass sit like a slick turban piled on top of my head. Cleaning every bit of myself is a luxury as I use the medicinal smelling soap everywhere, leaving my feet for last. I carefully wash them, panting through the pain as the water beats on my back and body, breaking apart the topknot of conditioner.

Sinking to my butt, I place my feet beneath the heated spray of water and comb through my now-untangled hair. When every bit of it is free of knots, I carefully stand and step back underneath the spray while I come up with a plan.

I *will* leave this place, and Merit will help me.

I'm not staying or pretending to stay with a man who believes I'm too much work because of the supposed blood running through my veins.

Yanking the tap off, I carefully remove myself from the shower and dab the towel on my feet first.

They're a wreck but clean. The bruise in my arch is a

mystery—no idea how I got it—but the center of the area is so tender I can barely put weight on it.

The other cuts are more manageable.

Merit told me there were clothes and shoes that would fit, and of course, he would have known what fit because he was creeping around in my closets, setting me up for whatever this Club Alpha crap was.

I pick up the carefully folded panties, bra, sweatpants, socks, and tennis shoes.

It takes nearly five minutes to get the socks on, and with that chore done, the shoes go on last. After the final lace is loosely tied, I breathe out a sigh of relief. When I go to stand it feels like a cloud of yum after surviving the last forty hours with nothing.

A billow of steam releases when I exit the bathroom into the tiny space, and I'm greeted by a vision of Merit at a stove, cooking. His all-black ninja outfit is so incongruous with the cooking posture I laugh aloud, immediately regretting the unconscious move as pain spears the slice at my throat.

He and Zaire turn. Zaire's face is open, his smile more so, and it feels as though my heart is being stabbed; the chill of the blade of his betrayal turns my marrow to ice.

Survive, Alex.

I gingerly walk toward them. When the smell of the food hits me, I'm suddenly ravenous, keying in on what's in the pan instead of the chaos of my emotions.

"Hungry?"

I nod, and Zaire scoops a huge portion of some kind of beef stew into a deep crockery bowl.

"I'll try not to choke as I eat."

Merit snorts. "I have bread too."

I tilt my head at that and slide into one of four seats at a small dinette made of what looks like reclaimed wood. Or maybe it's just that old.

"Are you a baker and a cook?" I ask just above a whisper, touching my throat as I speak.

"No. Actually." Merit ducks his head, giving a sheepish smile. "Grady made this from whatever was lying around, and there's bread shops in town. He dressed like a local and bought supplies."

I cram a bite inside my mouth, the flavor burst from the stew an indescribable heaven of savory notes, rich fat from the meat, and the fact my stomach hadn't had anything but two bites from some weird protein bar scrounged from one of the packs.

Zaire sets a huge hunk of bread in front of me, and ignoring the butter in favor of speed, I grab it, take a huge bite and tear it off from the main oblong piece.

I chew as fast as I dare without choking, take a swig of chilled milk from a glass, and dig back in.

Without talking, I work through the first bowl of stew, and when I get to the bottom, Zaire gets me a second.

I look at him, and his lips twitch at the corners in obvious amusement.

Which makes me want to bawl. Glad my hunger and trauma can amuse his stupid Texan ass.

He must see something in my expression, and I quickly look away so he remains clueless about my mindset. I attempt a few words before he can dig around, asking questions I don't plan to answer. "Did you eat?" I ask in a hoarse whisper.

"No talking, Alex." Merit frowns. "And, yes, Zaire ate after my torture session."

They exchange a look.

I let my face fill with the question, and Zaire raises his arm, showing off a neat bandage that covers the wound instead of the blood-sodden shirt he'd used as a temporary bandage.

"Oh." Despite my anger over his dismissal of me, I care.

I wish I didn't.

I wish I didn't have the image of us coming together to struggle through; to try and reconcile the purity of the encounter and how easy it was for Zaire to throw it away.

I mime sewing with a needle and thread.

Zaire nods, shooting a sour look at Merit. "Barrel of monkeys."

I shiver, imagining the pain of being sewn up with no numbing medicine.

"I'll grab a shower now that you're done." Zaire's eyes search mine, sensing something's amiss but not sure what.

I try on a smile, and he seems to accept that, walking away.

"Don't get the bandage wet!" Merit calls after him.

Zaire flips him off.

Merit chuckles. "Classy."

The door shuts.

My shoulders ease.

Merit parks another bowl of stew in front of me, and I pat my stomach. "I don't know if I can eat more."

"Eat," Merit says, pushing the bowl toward me with his index finger.

Our black eyes meet, the shades identical.

"Explain Club Alpha, please." There. I can be polite.

"Zaire isn't a bodyguard."

My stomach drops as Merit watches the rainbow of my expressions.

"It was a setup. Chloe's dad's heart attack was theatrics to lure Zaire into position."

Oh my God. "So you *lied*?" I whisper, and the pain from my throat silences me.

Merit puts his fingers to his lips then nods, holding up a palm. "For a reason. A damn good one.

"Zaire Sebastian was the owner of Club Alpha, an elaborate matchmaking entity. The premise is to find 'the one', and it was billionaire's only. They each put in fifty million dollars.

Zaire would come up with complex circumstances designed to surface the character of all the players. In that way, the billionaire could rest assured that their 'chosen mate' was not into them for just their money but for who they are."

My mind reels. Finally landing on the fact that Zaire is not who he purported himself to be.

He's not a bodyguard. He's some rich boy setting up rich friends.

But I remember his words about how he didn't have any money. Something's not making sense here.

Merit carefully watches my face. "It's not what you're thinking. He saved my friends. He has a gift, Alex. He's so intuitive it's scary. He matched people who, at first glance, you'd never think them possible together as a couple." He spreads his hands to his sides. "And then they were."

I point to myself, taking another bite of my cooling stew, and find my appetite has definitely departed for the time being. I push the remainder away.

"Yes, you were the one we all agreed would be worth shooting for."

"Does Zaire have billions?" I ask, using my voice despite his warning.

Merit shakes his head. "No. He was wealthy by any standard before Club Alpha was railroaded by the Feds," Merit explains in a low voice warmed by his anger, adding, "and others."

I nod, crushed. "So you were hoping Miss Moneybags would dig Zaire and he'd live happily ever after with *my* billions."

Nice.

Shoving the chair away from the table, I stand, backing away from a man I thought I could trust, who I thought literally had my back.

I can't trust *anyone* now—feeling hemmed in, trapped.

Merit grips my upper arm, ebony irises searing into mine. "No—Alex, that is *not* it."

The crack of flesh is loud in the acoustics of the stone house when I slap Merit. "That is *exactly* it," I say in a furious whisper.

"What the fuck is going on?" Zaire asks, his eyes taking in the scene of Merit gripping me as my slap surfaces on his face in the form of an angry red handprint.

We simultaneously turn, and there stands Zaire, deliciously dripping wet, looking hot.

The fucking liar.

I jerk my arm out of Merit's grip and stalk over to Zaire, so furious I literally see red.

"This is what's going on." I shove him, and he staggers back a step. I touch my throat as his confused stare meets mine.

"Stay away from me," I say in a fierce whisper as I brush by him.

Twenty-Six
Zaire

My eyes roll over the stark outline of a raised handprint against Merit's fair complexion. "What the fuck did you say to her?"

"The truth."

"What kind of truth?" I ask slowly, fearing the worst.

"Club Alpha. She knows you're not a bodyguard, what you used to do after lawyering—everything."

Damn. "Thanks for tossing me under the bus." I plug my thumb against the center of my bare chest. "*I* wanted to tell her after we'd rested, eaten—cleaned up. Why didn't you allow me that?" My hand falls as I stand there, dripping all over the floor.

"Because I'm the one who put you in place without you being aware, Zaire. I needed to come clean with Alex what my role had been—what it is now." He chuckles, rubbing a hand over the angry mark on his cheek. "She wasn't impressed."

I tighten the towel at my waist and stab a finger in his direction. "That was all theatrics. You just made shit a whole helluva lot harder for me, partner."

"Yes." Merit plants his feet wide, folding his arms across a muscular chest.

"Did you explain I didn't know my role—that I didn't even know there was one?"

"Alex didn't give me a chance." He rasps a hand over the slapped cheek again with a chastised smile.

"You've left me a goddamned mess."

Merit's dark eyes level on me. "So fix it."

I rip a hand through my hair, noticing the absence of my ten gallon, and sigh.

"You've got a few hours before we head out again. This place is only good for a day, tops."

Great. "Why?"

Merit's chin dips, his black stare hard on my face. "Because these fucking assassins are hot on our trail. I wasn't planning on this—them. I've alerted the financial backers, and money is in place to get us stateside."

As long as Alexandra is safe. "All right, wonderful. Now I have to come clean on everything in a reactionary way, instead of easing her into it like I'd planned." I shake my head. "And... Alexandra only has partial information."

"Not the best part. Because it's possible she has the impression—"

"—I'm after her money."

Merit's chin dips in acquiescence. "Remember, she's not supposed to talk."

"Thanks, asshole."

I wheel around, heading in the direction of the room we were supposed to share.

Alex

That miserable man. Coming out there in his towel, looking all perfect when all the while Zaire is like the rest.

Zaire had seemed like *such* a gentleman.

And I'd been a fool.

The locked door shudders under a pounding fist.

I jump out of my skin. "Go away," I try to say, but I can feel the wound flex that's located exactly over my Adam's apple. The cut's awkward placement is like having an abrasion on a knuckle. I never realized how constantly I swallow until this happened; and the added frustration of not being able to talk correctly.

My reply can't be heard over the pounding.

"Alexandra, let me in."

Zaire.

Figures. "No," I whisper, backing away from the locked door.

Silence.

Then a thud comes at the other side, and the door quakes inside its frame.

I run to the door and quickly unlock it, swinging it wide.

Zaire stands a few feet away, one leg planted behind him and the other bent. It's clear from his posture that his plan to charge the door can't go through because I'm standing there.

He straightens, chest heaving, hazel eyes flashing angry fire. "I want to explain things."

I shake my head viciously, pointing in the opposite direction, wanting to stomp my foot for emphasis but knowing it'll hurt like hell if I do.

"You're going to listen."

Slowly and with deliberate emphasis, I raise my fist then stick my middle finger up, mouthing *fuck off* as I do.

"By God, you will have the manners sufficient to hear me out, darlin'." His eyes lock with mine. "Or this will not end well. This, I *can* promise you."

I slam the door in his face and back up.

Prick.

He plows into it as he turns the knob, slapping it wide.

Merit appears behind him. "What the fuck is going on?" His eyes ask me if I'm okay.

I'm just fine, thank you very much. Hell hath no fury like a woman scorned.

And at the moment, I'm so scorned I could set the universe on fire.

"Merit, you've done enough damage. Piss off." Zaire steps through the threshold and slams the door, setting the lock, and turns to face me.

I cross my arms, giving him an incineration glare.

My feet are too hurt for me to run, my heart too shattered to pump blood, my brain too confused to think.

But my soul attempts to connect with Zaire even after all his treachery.

He's so gorgeous I feel the heat of arousal flood when I know he's a lying fucker—that I shouldn't want him.

"Darlin'..."

I stick my arm straight out and resprout my middle finger.

"Okay," he says and steps into my arm, grabbing it and bending it behind my shoulder blades.

I struggle, and his eyes dilate, first running from my eyes then downward to my lips.

"You dick," I manage, so low I can barely hear myself.

"Yes."

He doesn't even deny it.

Zaire's eyes are tender on my face, without a drop of guile. "I'm the dick who loves you, you silly woman."

I swear my breath stops, piling up inside my lungs as heat swamps my body.

Denying him, I shake my head, trying to buck his hold. But he's too strong.

"Listen to me."

I still, too tired to fight, horribly weak to the logic he might feed me after that intro.

"I was a lawyer years ago and hated it. I attended university and pursued that occupation for my dad—he wanted a son who was a lawyer. But I *knew* there was something different for me out there." He sweeps his free hand vaguely in a gesture meaning outside the walls of the stone cottage to the greater world beyond.

"I began Club Alpha on a lark. However, as I began to craft the basis of the chessboard I envisioned such a thing could be, I became intrigued at the international flavor of extreme, real-life game playing, pitting circumstances against unsuspecting potentials. Club Alpha was not for spoiled billionaires but for those with a lot of money who wanted what non-billionaires want." His golden eyebrows rise, and he releases my arm.

Pins and needles stab me as feeling returns to the limb, and I rub it, retreating a step from his dangerous nearness.

Happiness, I guess a nanosecond before he says the same word aloud.

That one word hangs in the air between us, bearing the weight of the next. "My last two Club Alpha scenarios went south. The players fell into far more danger than even I could have invented. In fact, the FBI was sure that there was more to Club Alpha than a dangerous and expensive game to vet players' integrity and motivations."

He cards irritated fingers through hair that is damp and beginning to curl around his ears as the tendrils dry. "I lost everything I had, fighting court battles to clear my name, the enterprise I had begun from the ground up. My lawyer friend spent eighteen months of her life fighting along my side. In the end, Club Alpha was exonerated of any wrongdoing, but my wealth was all but depleted."

"So you latched onto me," I whisper, touching my throat as traitorous tears carve paths of sadness down my face.

Zaire grips my shoulders, eyes brimming with smoldering honesty. "Never."

I hang my head, daring to hope—too cautious to entertain his words.

"Look at me."

I raise my face, and Zaire puts a finger beneath my chin. "Merit set this up with the help of former clients so that I could have what I'd given to them—a 'pay it forward,' so to speak. I was no more aware of being a player than you."

What?

His eyes run over my face. "I'm pissed too."

We laugh, and the discomfort at my throat aborts the laugh almost as soon as it began.

"Did you think I could betray and hurt a woman made vulnerable by our mutual circumstance?" Zaire searches my eyes. "What kind of worthless turd of a man would I be?"

Slowly, I move into the shadow of his body and press the uninjured side of my face against his bare, heavily muscled chest. "I was so hurt," I admit in a soft voice.

"Shhh," he says, cupping the back of my skull. "I'd rather die than see you hurt."

I pull away, tipping my head back so I can look up at him.

"What?" his eyes linger over my expression. "Whisper it."

"You said to Merit that I was 'too complicated'."

He nods. "I did say that, but it was in response to something you clearly didn't hear."

I wait, and when Zaire seems to sense I won't continue, he does, "Merit didn't know about your real biological history when he started on a 'Club Alpha' course of contrived events. Like me, Merit would have cut bait and run because the risk by association would have made the game potentially too dangerous for the players to actually live through."

Truth, I think.

Our gazes lock.

"And it *has*. The game has become very dangerous, Alexandra."

I give a painful swallow and a teeny nod.

I watch as Zaire sees a new question fill my face before I can ask.

"Ask."

I cover my throat, "You love me?"

"If there's such a thing as 'meant to be together,' it's us, darlin'. I feel like it always was."

"What," My hand stays on the wound as though that will keep the cut from reopening, "'always was'?"

Zaire maintains eyes contact, his hands moving to rest at my lower back as he draws me against his pelvis.

I can't help but notice he's happy to have me there.

"Us," he answers as he bends over me.

I tilt my head, heart back to beating, thoughts sliding back into place, and just like that, the softest kiss I've ever received makes me whole again.

Twenty-Seven
Zaire

I back Alexandra up toward the bed and carefully lower her down on the mattress.

Wide eyes wait, but desire mixed with uncertainty is not what I want to see.

Then Alexandra does the unexpected, springing my cock free of the towel with two fingers and her will.

She presses her lips to the end of me, and my prick jumps to attention.

I fist her dark copper hair, winding my fingers through the silky texture of still-damp locks.

"Let me adore you," I say quietly, feeling vaguely vulnerable for saying the words, but I mean them from the bottom of my racing heart.

Alexandra shakes her head, bringing an index finger to her lips in the universal gesture of *quiet*.

Then her supple lips are on me, driving down my length, a hand cupping my balls as she does.

"God," I say, beginning to push her head down as Alexandra's rhythm becomes expert, syncing with her hand, the subtle push of my hips as she pleasures me. "Stop," I say.

With a smack, she releases me.

I shudder from the sensation at my sensitive tip.

My fingers leave her silky hair.

Her legs dangle off the bed, and I bend, placing my hands high on her interior thighs and pushing her legs apart as I swim between them, my cock shivering as the tip brushes her t-shirt.

I strip the borrowed top from her body, unlatching the plain white bra next.

Her perfect breasts chill in the air of the room, nipples puckering for attention.

I lave first one, swirling my tongue around the stiff peak. Cupping her other breast, I give it equal attention.

"Pants. Off," I command.

"Bossy," she says so quietly it sounds like a word carried on the air between us. My eyes run over the bandage at her throat, and I'm instantly pissed at Merit.

"You have no idea," I say, vanquishing the thought from my mind. Foreign thoughts have no business between Alexandra and me.

She carefully pulls off the loosely-knotted tennis shoes. Once free of those, she kicks off the sweatpants and panties.

Taking her in, I do what I've wanted to since the moment I saw her at the door.

Sliding my hands beneath her thighs, I lift her, and Alexandra puts her arms around my neck, thighs tight at my waist.

My cock has already sought her wetness without any guidance.

I never release her from the prison of my gaze as I begin to take her standing up.

"Zaire," Alexandra breathes as I gently rock inside her slick heat; the arousal from having sucked me off makes everything just that much more intense.

Knowing Alexandra was turned on while she pleasured me heightens my own arousal.

I will my cock to new heights, seeking that sensitive spot that's high and deep. Going for the powerful orgasm, I pump as I hold her in the center of the room.

My cock rubs the place over and over, each rock going deep and sliding over that area like my life depends on it.

"More," Alexandra says, face flushed, head tipped back, lips parted.

Moving my hands to her ass cheeks, I drive deep, pinning her body against my dick, giving a subtle swirl of my hips before the next plunge.

I know when she'll come because Alexandra stills, leaning back and tensing in my arms before her release bolts, racing over the top of us.

Hard contractions hug my cock, thumping around me like a delicious heated glove, and I can't hold my own release back as the load from my body fires, punching the bulls-eye of her hot center as I plant myself deep inside.

We hang together, suspended in the middle of danger, lust, and love keeping us together like glue, and revel in the stolen moment.

After a second, I begin to soften within her and know I'll have to eventually withdraw.

Taking in the glow that surrounds her like an aura, I know I'll never want to withdraw. From her body—from her life.

From Alexandra.

Alex

Sex isn't always about fucking, I think with crude reflection.

Sometimes—and I feel like that happened to us tonight—it's actually a thing of beauty.

There's only one unlit light in the room, a crude bulb dangling from the plastered ceiling of the bedroom, and the singular wall socket holds an archaic nightlight plugged into it and burning softly.

That sole light casts the vestiges of poor illumination over us.

None of that matters.

The dilapidated surroundings, my assumptions, the danger that seeks us from every corner.

What I used to be, what I might be.

A man's love can't define me, but I find knowing the emotion binds us—upholds me.

Before my eyes, I sense myself becoming a new creature, someone who has a chance at happiness, not the shell of my prior existence.

"What are you thinking?" Zaire asks. His face is shadowed because the nightlight backlights him. I find I don't need to see him clearly; the fabric of his voice is layered with the texture of his feelings for me.

He flicks a lock of my long hair over my shoulder, then brings it back to his nose, eyes closing as he inhales deeply.

The small gesture has me closing my eyes. I'm washed and cleaned with cheap products I never would have used before, and none of that matters to Zaire.

It's a piece of me, and he clearly likes all the pieces of me.

"I never get tired of looking at you, Alexandra."

My eyes open and he drops my hair in favor of kissing my lips.

We lay on our sides, Zaire's feet hanging off the edge of the bed we never used.

As our tongues twine, he draws me against the line of his

body, and I feel his erection come back to life and laugh softly, my throat giving a pang from the movement.

"What?" he draws back, searching my face.

A pleased little smile lifts my cheeks. "You're hard again," I whisper in awe. It's been minutes since we were just together.

"Yes, darlin', you clever witch—you've got me under your spell."

"So, I could just command you." I flutter my eyelashes, carefully clearing my throat. "Sorry, *cast* a spell on you, and you'd have to..."

"Perform," he mocks then adds with a degree of happy resignation, "Probably."

"Wow," I say, fingers briefly touching my throat.

He frowns. "Your throat hurts?"

"Only when I talk," I say with a wee bit of sarcasm.

He chuckles. "No small thing."

I shake my head, and sudden melancholy creeps over me. "I was thinking about how good it feels to have someone love me."

"So why the sad face?" His fingers smooth the furrow I didn't know was between my eyes.

"I want this to be over," I whisper, thinking about G being gone—my social media account seems so shallow now, so unimportant. My luxury travel becomes ominous, considering I was a sitting duck all that time and didn't know it.

I would have been dead had it not been for a fluke of circumstance that brought Merit into my life because he made it clear that the men who are after me as a "loose end" had nothing to do with the Club Alpha thing.

I lift a hair running along the top of Zaire's ear and touch the errant curl that's almost a stubby ringlet.

Zaire squashes it with a hand. "Need a haircut. Hell—I needed one before I took the job."

"You're not a bodyguard," I state in a flat voice.

"No—but I'm skilled enough to do the job, I'd say." Irony colors his voice.

"Definitely." I don't bother to keep the tremor out of my voice as memories of him dismantling men as they came for me fill the crevices of my brain.

"Hey," he says, turning my face to his. "I think you made me be more, bring more. When a man has something to fight for, we can do incredible things. Things we would not think were possible before. So, yes, darlin', I was always a bodyguard for you. I would have guarded you for free—once I got a load of those big dark peepers and discovered you weren't just beautiful on the outside but here." He places his large hand over the swell of my upper breast, my heart beating below his touch.

I cry, and Zaire gathers me close, pressing my body against his larger one.

"It'll be okay, darlin'. Sleep on this, and tomorrow, everything will look better."

"And then we run again," I whisper.

Zaire doesn't answer, though I know he hears me.

His embrace tightens as I swiftly drift into a dreamless sleep, worries and resolutions racing after me kept at bay by the man who holds me tucked within the safety of his arms.

Tomorrow

"Think fast," I say, tossing the gory pack at Zaire.

With casual grace, he lifts his arm as the pack flies at him, fisting the straps and opening the top to presumably check on the contents.

"Pathetic," he announces after a few seconds of perusal.

"Merit will have more stuff," I say in an almost normal tone of voice. Six hours of sleep had done wonders.

"Stuff?" his eyebrow rises at that.

"Knock it off," I say, walking over to him and giving him a light punch on the arm. My eyes catch sight of the bandage around his forearm, and I drag a light touch over the white gauze. Glancing at his face, I ask, "How bad?"

He shrugs. "Fifteen stitches bad."

I whistle then instantly regret it.

Zaire sees all. "Hey, quit making noises with your throat."

"You like my noises."

We exchange a private look.

Grady walks into the main room, and Zaire's body tenses.

"Chill," Grady says, biting into a bright green apple so aggressively the sound cracks into the sudden silence of the room.

I startle. *Color me jumpy.*

"Rig's gassed, time to book."

His mossy green eyes run over the pack. "That's fucking hammered." He smiles. Then the expression turns upside down. He uses the half-eaten apple to point at the pack. "Is that what I think it is?"

I look where he's pointing and see some junk that's solidified over part of the word "Greece" on the pack.

"Yessiree," Zaire says.

He grunts. "We're not that low on resources. Hang tight."

Zaire and I stare at the pack as I think of how the "junk" got there, and the memory is enough to kill my appetite.

Slowly, Zaire removes each item and spreads them on the table and, without a moment's hesitation, walks the deflated pack to the door and moves to go outside.

A flutter of panic seats itself in my guts at the thought of him being removed from my presence.

"Zaire," I call out as loudly as I dare.

Don't leave me.

He turns, dawn's pale light seeping all around him like treacherous fog. Fingers of ethereal light peel away the cornered shadows as low illumination scatters through the open door.

Zaire assesses my face instantly. "Garbage." He lifts the pack.

I nod, not trusting myself to speak and feeling like a fearful, clingy girl. Instead of a woman who just survived an ordeal. Several, if you count them separately.

I turn away from the disquieting image as the front door closes behind him.

Taking a deep breath, I squelch my unease and take stock of the meager contents.

More pemmican, which I found savory but bland. A pair of panties for me and boxer briefs for Zaire. A single toothbrush and about a quarter of a tube of toothpaste plus some rainbow-hued Euro currency, crumpled and discarded like trash along with a few coins.

Merit breezes in, a fragrance cloud of the same cheap but functional soap following him from his recent shower.

His damp blond hair lays flat across his skull, untouched by a towel.

"Hey," he says by way of greeting.

"Hi," I whisper back.

"Throat's better," he states.

I nod.

His lips twist. "Did you two kiss and make up?"

I frown.

He chuckles. "I'm glad. It's the reason we're up to our armpits in alligators."

His eyes scan the interior. "Where's Zaire?"

I touch my throat, speaking carefully, "Took the garbage out."

He grunts.

"Seen Grady?"

I nod. "He's getting another pack."

"That one's got DNA on it, so, yeah, slick thinking."

Gross.

The door slams open.

I spin, breath held.

Merit lifts an arm with a gun attached to it.

Zaire's eyes are wild.

"What?" Merit asks, nodding the end of the gun to a point above Zaire's shoulder.

"Grady's dead."

My stomach leaps. A bubble of terror bursts so bright and large my body feels like it's exploding as oxygen finds me again, slamming into my deprived lungs like a punch.

Zaire launches at me, and I duck as his arms drag me to the ground.

Gunfire explodes, and I scream, forgetting to be careful, and the fragile healing of the wound at my throat gives.

I begin to bleed as Zaire covers me with the protection of his body.

Twenty-Eight
Merit

Fuck me running. Uninvited company—again. And Grady dead. This is why he doesn't get close to people. In his line of work, people age out before friendships have a chance.

He gives a moment's pause before engagement, lamenting the loss of yet another man.

A good one.

Merit flicks his eyes at Alex, Zaire dragging her across the floor and out of harm's way.

Let me live for Chloe, Merit has time to wish, and like a scene from a Clint Eastwood movie, he strides for the door, shooting as he walks, plunking melons like a fruit melee as the enemy storms the door in a neat juggernaut.

Merit moves out of the way just as a bullet embeds above his left shoulder, the crack of splintering wood echoing above the firing squad.

Movement at his left alerts him, and his eyes shift to the peripheral motion.

Zaire is opposite Merit, holding a Glock with the business end trained at the door.

Ominous silence fills the space like the portentous eye of the storm.

There are two entries to the stone cottage. The bullets can only penetrate the few openings that present themselves. Because of the age of the structure, there are two doors and four windows.

Merit doesn't look around for Alex but knows, if Zaire's on his feet with a gun, she's secure.

Then the impossible happens.

Alex wails into the stillness, a hollow siren's song of grief. As though a ghost that had been haunting her had finally come to life.

With grim resignation, Merit turns and gets the shock of his life.

Alex

Zaire holds his hand over my throat.

I shake my head, physically removing his hand and replacing it with my own.

I point to Merit. *Help him*, my eyes plead.

Watching Zaire mentally work through committing to leave my side is painful, but in the end, practicality wins out.

He protects me better by joining Merit now.

Zaire shuts his eyes for a moment then nods, getting to his feet.

I press my fingers against the wound at my throat to staunch the flow of blood.

Zaire grabs a gun from the kitchen table that hadn't been stowed yet, and I say a swift grateful prayer that it hadn't been.

As I crouch beneath the table, the quiet is only broken by the steady, loud ticking of an ancient wall clock.

Tick, tick, tick.

A furtive noise sounds behind me and I twist around, eyes diving into the gloom of the hall where I know the only other door of the cottage is stationed.

A woman walks slowly toward me, partially hidden by the dimness within the long hall.

At first, I'm so surprised by the appearance of a female among the onslaught of male assassins and players in the intricate web of Club Alpha machinations I sit there in a stupor.

Then as the gloom of the hall releases her form, the face of the woman is revealed.

I crawl from beneath the table and stumble to standing.

Forgetting my throat, my safety—basically everything, I make a sad plaintive wail upon recognizing who she is.

What force in the universe would give me Bridget back now? When danger is everywhere and I don't know if anyone will live another moment.

I stagger forward, taking in the more mature features, the flaxen hair—the black irises so like my own.

Randomly, I notice she looks like Merit before I crash into her and confess all the things I wish I could have that last time I saw her, some almost fifteen years prior.

"How—oh my God, Bridget," I say. I declare my love, my remorse; I lay bare my shame. Through all this she stands benignly before me, taking in my words, my emotions as though she's a human sponge.

When more people come to stand behind her, the tears that run down my face begin to dry as I take in who has her back.

Shakily, I withdraw from her body, becoming aware that blood has joined my tears.

Reality begins to penetrate the shell of my shock.

Her smile turns to a point behind me. "Merit," she greets.

What's-what's going on?

"What the fuck is going on here, Bridget?" Merit demands.

I whip around, staring at Merit, cataloging somewhere in the back of my mind that Zaire stands with as much surprise filling his face as I must have.

Retreating a step, I gain the two of them in my sights. My eyes go first from Merit, then to Bridget. Finally, my attention lands on the men who stand behind her.

"Oh my God." Puzzle pieces click together I'd never dreamed possible.

"God doesn't play a part in this, unfortunately for you, dear sister."

Bridget's dark eyes are banked with low fire. The fire of rage fueled by insanity.

I back up another step.

She moves forward, eating the space I'd created between us.

"Who do you think runs Daddy's little playground now, eh?"

I shake my head, taking in her honed body, the scars—both superficial and deep, that litter her body like measles.

The coal-black eyes stay on me, so cold on my face.

"Bridget—" Merit begins.

She holds up a palm. "Don't interfere, cousin."

Cousin. My eyes move to his. "Is this Club Alpha stuff?" My fingers move to my throat, slick with blood.

Bridget tosses her head back and gives a laugh from her belly.

Gooseflesh rises in response to the slightly hysterical pitch as the noise owns every patch of my bare flesh.

I shiver, wanting Zaire so badly I can hardly live in my own skin.

"My second cousin doesn't have anything to do with us, Alexandra. This is all about you and how *I* was the one who sacrificed her childhood so you could be the promised one." Her eyes glitter at me like marbles. "Just keep fucking the men, Bridget—and one day this empire will be yours. Not once..." Bridget steps forward. "Not *one* time did dear old dad allow you to be touched."

"I'm sorry, Bridget," I whisper from my abused throat. "I didn't know any of this."

Her smile is tight, stretched like plastic wrap across her face as she steps into my space as tight as she can, only inches separating us. "But you were *so* glad it wasn't you—weren't you Alex?"

Her eyes, so like my own—hold my gaze prisoner.

I can't lie. "Yes," I whisper.

"Yes, she says." Bridget twirls away from me.

I see the knife then. It's the type that is flat on one side and serrated on the other.

I am so sorry that Bridget was used like that. But the one thing Zaire has done for me is to absolve the guilt of a preteen who couldn't do anything about a horrible circumstance. A violation perpetrated against someone I cared about. My sister.

In my periphery, I sense Zaire inch closer.

"Bridget," I try in a low voice.

She whirls, bringing the knife up with her.

I gasp, pinwheeling backward, and almost lose my balance as I try to keep from bleeding to death and avoiding my crazy, knife-wielding sister.

Zaire grabs me from behind and hauls me against him.

I can breathe again in his arms.

"Jeffrey Epstine had many children from his child surrogates."

My body stills against Zaires.

"I've dispatched all of them. You are the only one who remains." Her head turns in Merit's direction. "You were adopted and didn't know any better. I don't kill the males because they can't breed."

Her attention returns to me. "But you—you can't be spared. Besides," she says, raising the tip of the knife, and taps the dull edge against her chin in a contemplative gesture, "you are culpable, comforting me when the men had their way. Poor Bridget." Her laugh is a witch's cackle. "When all the while, I plotted *your* death. Let Alexandra *Frost*"—she pauses, letting the fake last name sink in—"have a little bit of life and then"—she mimes grabbing something from thin air and fisting the invisible thing as though caught—"steal it like *my* life was stolen. Who do you think bumped daddy-O off in prison?"

A nightmare.

"I saved you for last, Alexandra. It took years and more money than I cared to spend to find every sperm stain left from our wonderful father, but I did."

I'm inside a living nightmare.

Zaire's arms tighten around me.

"Boys," she kicks her head in the direction behind her.

Men come forward.

"Don't make me kill my own blood," Merit says in a low voice full of resolution.

"She must die, Merit Lang."

"I don't know what Alex supposedly did to you, but there's other ways to fix this."

Mercenaries march toward me.

"She'll suffer the way I did," Bridget says, backing away.

Gang rape, I think as a dozen men fall into position.

"Subdue the men—careful with my cousin," Bridget adds.

Her eyes move over my shoulder to where Zaire stands. "She cares for him, so *fuck him up.*"

"Not on my watch, you fucking psycho," Zaire says in low warning.

Guns are absent but knives flash.

I tear myself from Zaire's arms, running for the door with thundering footsteps tearing after me.

My mind doesn't think, body driving forward.

Flight.

Zaire roars behind me, engaging those at the end.

Someone grabs the back of my hair, dragging me backward. Bridget wraps her arm in all that length, yanking my head back and raising the knife.

I could eat the feast of her hate as the emotion bears down on me, knife frozen above my vulnerable neck, ready to eagerly kill me.

"Alex, down!"

I sight down my contorted body, and like a dark angel, Grady lies over the steps, leveling a semi-automatic machine gun into the space.

I allow my weight to succumb to gravity and fall.

Bridget's surprised face rises.

The bullets take her backward, bucking her body as it shakes from the rounds.

A body I held after atrocities.

A body that falls on top of mine like a slaughtered doll.

I try to get away, but her weight pins my legs.

Grady steps over us both, cutting down all who remain standing, the kick of the weapon smoothly jumping with the execution.

I lay my head down on the floor, my eyes meeting those of my dead sister.

Zaire

What in the absolute fuck? My eyes run over the posse up the ass of the lunatic in front of us.

It's clear this *is* Bridget by the way Alexandra behaves. The gambit of emotions race across her face: shock, elation, fear—panic.

I'm also aware Alexandra believed Bridget was dead. Now she's come back from the grave and not in a good way.

When Bridget verbalizes her plans, it's clear Merit and I aren't meant to live, regardless of him being some supposed far-flung relation.

There's no way out, no back-up, no escape—outnumbered.

Doubling down on my emotion is easy; I can't have those men taking Alexandra from me—hurting her with the intent I see etched in their eyes like a prophecy.

When Alexandra runs, I move into the men at the same moment Merit does, our guns out of bullets—our wills full of ammunition.

We're outnumbered, and I can't keep eyeballs on both the female maniac *and* the dozen men.

Merit and I work through them, killing half inside of minutes.

When the shout comes from the front door, I swing my attention to Alexandra.

Psycho Bridget has used her hair as a handle, fisting the length and wrapping it around her arm like a snake.

"Alexandra!" I bellow as a knife sinks into my thigh.

I turn too late as another slash lands.

Falling to my knees, another blade moves toward my face.

Then the attack halts in its tracks. The knife begins to spin and falls as my aggressor is cut in half by a fiery spray of light and tapping noise.

His body separates at the waist as though torn by the hand

of a giant; the upper torso topples backward, the legs flopping beside me.

Bodies drop on the floor like the clear-cutting forest of humans.

In the sea of corpses, one figure remains standing.

Merit.

His dark eyes are light compared to the blood that covers every inch of his head, neck, and face.

He says something but I can't hear, my body growing rapidly cool.

Still, my eyes hunt for Alexandra.

Oh... there she is. *Settle down, darlin'*—she keeps screaming my name over and over again.

Funny, I can't hear very well either.

The noise dims along with the vision before me, turning the edges of my consciousness into smoke I can't grab, wake from.

So I don't.

Twenty-Nine
Alex

"They're doing everything they can, Alex," Merit says soothingly.

"Is he—"

"I know as much as you do."

Zaire's been in surgery for hours as the surgeon attempts to stymie internal bleeding.

The surgeon is a private one that the backers of Club Alpha provided as a contingency. Zaire's receiving top-notch care. Not that I can relax enough to appreciate that.

I lean back against the hard hospital chair and silently stew about every detail of the last few days that's now been revealed.

Bridget was Interpol. She used all her connections toward the end-game of locating every single human Jeffrey Epstine had fathered. Leaving the only one she had a personal connection with for last.

Me.

"I should have guessed we were related." Merit shakes his head, giving my face some scrutiny.

"Not very much. Like she said, cousins." I can't bear to

utter her name. Not yet. Maybe never. I touch my throat, feeling the fine texture of stitches beneath my touch.

Contrary to what Merit had said, I will have a scar. That's okay. I survived, and it's okay there's a reminder. I'm grateful to be alive.

Thinking of Zaire in there fighting for his life, I keep my grief in check by the slimmest of margins.

"I'd only met her a couple times," Merit says, rubbing a hand over his freshly washed hair. "Same circles. I'd protect high-profile people, and sometimes our paths would cross when I was beating feet around the globe. In fact," Merit confesses quietly, "she's the one who told me her number one hobby was genealogical research."

No kidding. "You never knew about what happened?"

Merit shakes his head. "I wanted this Club Alpha thing to work for Zaire; his friends did. I scoured your past, except for some boozing tendencies—nada." He winks.

"Yeah, well—what happened to her scarred me too. I will never go through what she did, never imagine how awful it was. But somehow..."

"Bridget blamed every single female child who didn't have to live through what she did. Her cheese had completely slid off her cracker."

"Definitely," I agree, sad.

Sad for a Bridget who never got to grow up normally, who later used all her talents to craft a plan of vengeance. In a way, she hadn't ever lived. Existing solely to kill others isn't living.

A person like that would already be dead inside.

"Bridget got the fortune," Merit says. "Epstine left everything to her, but she had to be emotionally eviscerated before she inherited, and the instant Bridget got the money, she killed him."

"Why would any father ever do that to his own daughter?"

I whisper. Though the plastic surgeon who patched me up said I could speak normally, I'm gun shy.

Poor choice of words, Alex.

Some wonderful human got us clothes, and I'm wearing jeans, shoes, and a t-shirt without a spot of blood on them.

Merit's similarly outfitted as we wait.

"Is Grady okay?" I ask suddenly, believing I'll never forget the image of him at the stairs as a crazed Bridget and I hung in the balance of my murder.

"Yes. We'll have to ask Zaire why he thought Grady was dead."

"Didn't he have a head wound?"

He inclines his head. "Yup, and those bleed like a bitch."

We laugh as a stress reliever.

"He's 'under observation,'" Merit says with a hint of humor.

"I always hated that expression—like a bunch of people with big popcorn buckets are sitting around waiting for a muscle to twitch."

Merit snorts. "You're funny—cousin."

I lift my fist, and we bump knuckles. "I could be related to someone worse," I concede.

Silence grabs the moment, both of us thinking of our mutual crazy relative, now dead.

"Thank baby Jesus for Grady," Merit comments after a few moments.

"He saved the day." My voice is full of the simple joy of being alive.

"You have no idea."

"I think of the plans I saw in every one of those mens' eyes and have a pretty good clue as to what would've gone down, given that she was so crazed to kill me she jumped the gun before her cohorts could make good on the threat."

Then Grady killed them all. "Is Grady okay with, you know, what he had to do?"

Merit leans back against the chair back, crossing his legs at the ankles. "Mentally?" Shrugs. "Grady's as mercenary as they come. He made his deal with the devil ages ago."

Huh. Okay.

I ask quietly, "What about you?"

"We've met the same demon, Alex."

"Don't say that." I touch his arm. "If it hadn't been for you and Zaire, those guys would have taken me apart, piece by piece, because I'm that creep's bio-daughter."

Merit's silence is so weighted I sit up, shifting in my seat to face him.

"What?"

"I don't want to be the one to tell you, but you'll find out, and I'd rather have you know from me."

He waits.

I nod.

"Your parents were killed on the autobahn yesterday."

My mouth drops open, and every memory—all of them fake, of course—comes rushing into the river of flashbacks flooding my brain. It doesn't matter that my parents actually weren't, that they were playing a part.

I had believed.

Opening my mouth, I instantly close it. Carefully covering my throat with my fingers, I ask quietly. "Accident?"

Merit shakes his head. "There are *no* coincidences. That's the story."

"So it's all over the news?"

"Yes. But now that Bridget has been surfaced for her crimes, you and Zaire have been exonerated of all wrongdoing."

"Not before everyone thought I'd done a bunch of horrible things."

"Yes."

The thought of Zaire and me being tossed into prison for something that wasn't our fault is ludicrous. However, I can see now with Bridget's connections, she could've framed Zaire and me for all the carnage, leveraging her vast wealth like a sword and striking the killing blow.

"Wait a second." I sit up straight, feeling somewhat guilty that, though shocking, the main emotion I feel from the news of my "parents" death is relief.

"What?" Merit's lips quirk in amusement.

"That means I'm technically broke, too." I look to Merit excitedly, "I'm not actually a 'Frost'."

I raise a palm and Merit high-fives me. "Ah... Alex."

"Yes," I say, leaning back with an almost euphoric giddiness.

"Most folks wouldn't be too keen on learning they are penniless."

I shut my eyes, reveling in my newfound independence from wealth.

"I'm not 'most folks'."

Merit chuckles. "No shit."

Zaire

"No racing, no hockey, and no aerodynamic sky diving."

I blink. "What about sex?"

The doctor's eyes twinkle. "I think that might be okay."

Alexandra blushes to the roots of her hair.

Looking between the two of us, the doctor taps his clipboard with all the fun facts from slicing and dicing me and says, "I'll leave you two alone."

The doctor leaves, and Alexandra shifts on the edge of my hospital bed. "I'd punch you if you weren't an invalid."

I glower. "I'm not an invalid. You heard Doctor Serious—I'm cleared to get after you properly, darlin'."

My girl's eyes fill with water. "Don't you dare cry, Alexandra." I lift my arm, and all the snakes of plastic drips follow the motion as I cradle her jaw.

She leans into the gesture. "I can't help it." She sniffles. "I thought she'd kill me, and when she, when she..."

"Died."

Alexandra gives a jerky nod. "When she died and the danger was over, I saw you lying there in a pool of your own blood."

She takes the hand that was just on her face with both of hers.

Eyes steady on mine, Alexandra says, "I knew then that I couldn't lose you. There was no way that life could be so cruel to take you from me, Zaire Sebastian."

"Darlin', I wasn't planning on it."

We smile.

"Guess what?" she asks.

"I have no idea."

"I'm broke."

My eyebrows hike. "Come again?"

Alexandra nods happily. "I'm after you for *your* money now."

Mind spinning, I realize that she's not a Frost anymore, remembering all that Merit had told me after Alexandra and I had our initial meeting after my surgery.

Her false parents are dead. Bio-daddy was killed by psycho bio-daughter in a staged prison "suicide."

Good riddance, I think without a hint of mercy. "I've got enough for both of us." Not really, but what the hell.

Her smile widens into a grin. "Oh?" Alexandra's eyebrows shoot up.

I slowly shake my head. "I've got a mil—that's it."

Without replying, she leans over me, kissing me softly on the lips.

Her dark eyes are solemn. "After everything I've been through, money doesn't mean anything."

I couldn't agree more.

Merit

Sometimes shit works out.

When Alex finally leaves Zaire's hospital room (because the nurse kicked her out so the poor lovesick ape could sleep) and starts down the hall, she appears to float.

Happiness keeps her afloat.

Wait until Alex gets a load of the special visitors he brought here.

They stand at the end of the hall, and finally, after she's mid-way to where we stand, Alex trains her eyes their way.

Halting, her eyes widen, taking in the sight, and with a small gasp of delighted surprise, she begins walking again.

Then she runs, crashing into Genevieve with an enthusiasm that has Merit catching the girls before they fall.

Crying and smiling, Alex hugs every one of her staff she presumed was dead.

After ten minutes of happy reunion, Alex turns a narrow-eyed stare with barely-veiled suspicion, which Merit confirms with a shrug and says, "Club Alpha."

She slaps him again.

The blow is much softer than the first one.

4 weeks later
Zaire

"Where's your cell?" I ask, lifting Alexandra's hands to my lips and pressing a soft kiss at the top of her hand.

Today she wears her coppery hair in a loose braid with faded jeans and a deep violet t-shirt that clings to her body, simple ultra-thin gold hoops glint as she turns her head to regard me.

"I did it."

She sounds so serious I wink at her. "What did you do?"

"I officially canceled my Tiktok."

"Ah," I lift my chin as I thread our fingers together. Opening the door to the movie theater, I sweep my palm forward to let her pass through.

"Thank you," Alexandra murmurs as she bestows a gorgeous smile on me.

"Your followers are going to gnash their teeth and weep," I state.

Alexandra lifts one shoulder, saying nothing, though I know it bothers her a bit—to let her followers down, her people as she thinks of them.

Lots has happened in a month. The primary change is Alexandra doesn't feel the same about her job—her life—she claims I turned all of it upside down. In the very "best way" were her words.

I touch the rim of my ten gallon and frown at how stiff it is, missing my old one something fierce.

Have to break it in, I reckon.

Walking to the counter, I order her favorite: a large tub of popcorn with extra butter.

I order red vines for myself.

Alexandra turns to smile at me, and the scar at her throat puckers with the movement, and I'm glad it's the only one she has, besides the mental ones. Those take longer to heal.

But I'm not going anywhere.

I don't know how I'm going to do what I want to, but then divine intervention inserts itself.

"I need to use the restroom."

I nod. "I'll pay, darlin'."

"You'll have to. I'm broke, remember?"

"I do," I say, tipping the stiff brim of my hat.

Alexandra laughs softly as she strolls away.

Turning to the cashier, I lean in, requesting the most bizarre thing he's probably ever heard.

After a few seconds of confusion, he does as I ask.

We're just finished with our scheming when Alexandra returns and we walk into our movie.

Alex

You don't have to die to go to heaven. I've arrived.

Zaire and I are never parted. Jobless, we meander through our new lives together, figuring out the new path as we go.

It's the only way I want it.

Simple things, like our weekly matinee movie, are a new favorite routine I adore.

Grabbing another handful of popcorn, I hit something solid.

What the hell?

I poke Zaire.

"What?" he asks inside the empty theater. Because no one comes and sees movies on a Wednesday at noon, apparently.

Except us.

"There's something weird in the popcorn box," I whisper, forgetting that my throat's healed now, except for the scar my plastic surgeon says will eventually heal.

Zaire doesn't care, and neither do I.

"Let's see what the mystery thing is." Zaire takes his cell from his front pocket as the movie blares on without us.

Tapping the flashlight feature, he aims the strobe of light into the bucket.

It's a small box.

I wrap my fingers around it, lifting it off the half-eaten popcorn it sits on top of.

Zaire follows with the light.

With trembling fingers, I open it.

A huge diamond sits in high prongs.

I whip my face to Zaire. "Is this—"

"Yes."

"Do you, am I going to...?"

"I hope so."

I snap the box closed and throw my arms around his solid neck. "I love you," I whisper in his ear.

"Not more than me."

We pull apart, leaving the movie theater and the bucket of popcorn behind.

———

Zaire takes my salty, buttery hand in his, and I transfer the box with my engagement ring to the other hand.

"Wait."

We stop. I pull my hand free, dusting the salt off the box where a swath of butter bathes the top, and I laugh.

Snapping the box open, I look at the diamond again.

It's a black gem, darkly sparkling as the early afternoon sun strikes the facets.

"A black diamond," I say, loving how unique that is.

Zaire watches me admiring my ring in its box then slowly plucks the ring from its nestle within the velvet slit.

His clean fingers avoid the butter and salt and manage to slip it onto my left ring finger.

"Black is so unusual." I turn my hand in every direction, thrilled with the glittering ebony facets winking back at me.

My smile is so big it hurts my face.

"I chose it to match your eyes," Zaire admits quietly.

I begin to cry because that's just how thoughtful this beautiful man is.

The man I will marry.

Thirty

Zaire - One month later

I pad quietly to the door, wondering who—for the love of all that is holy, has come to my penthouse door at nine o'clock on a Sunday.

Alexandra's still asleep, having been plagued all night with nightmares. Those horror movies don't play inside her mind every night anymore, but half the nights of the week she sees blood, gunfire, and murder.

Tearing the door open before a second chime can sound, I grip the thick wood, glaring at whoever dares disturb our five minutes of peace.

My normal pleasant disposition has taken a leave of absence.

A courier stands there, gazing up at me with the nonplussed expression everyone who doesn't make enough money to put up with attitude has.

"Zaire Sebastian?"

"Yes."

He thrusts a clipboard at me with a manilla envelope clipped neatly to it, addressed to Alexandra in care of me, and on top of that rests a return receipt registered mail—signature required by an actual human.

"I'll need to see your ID too," he says after a few seconds.

I spin on my heel, traipsing to the acres of quartz kitchen countertop where I dumped my wallet the previous night. Snatching the wallet from the surface, I inchworm my Texas State driver's license from the clear plastic sleeve. Finally freeing it from the tight compartment, I walk the plastic rectangle back to the door.

The courier studies the ID briefly then, "May I have that for a moment?" His dark eyebrow quirks.

"Sure, be my guest." I lean against the doorjamb, wearing only jogger pants and soccer-style slip-ons.

Laboriously, the courier prints the ID number on the receipt then turns the clipboard to face me.

"Sign here."

I sign.

Quite a process to see whatever is contained within the manilla folder, I puzzle.

He unclips the document and hands it to me.

"Have a good day," he says with such a lack of enthusiasm I smile as he leaves.

Shutting the door, I slowly walk to the kitchen, and setting the folder down on the countertop, I ready the Keurig for our morning coffee.

Alexandra likes it when I bring her coffee.

Naked.

I grin, remembering all the places inside my rented penthouse we've christened.

My smile fades as I ruminate about the past month of fighting the press, lies, and the push-back Alexandra's received from a disgruntled following who still want her to be *that woman*.

People don't understand that you can't be who you were when you go through the things Alexandra did.

That *I* did.

When a person discovers the parents that raised you aren't the actual bio-parents. Then on top of that revelation; said parents are "accidentally" killed before Alexandra was able to find closure? Lots of stress.

Heaps.

Alexandra lives with me now. The move was an easy decision. We decided to make a fresh start. She and G have been busy planning the wedding on a budget.

My lips quirk, a bit of a learning curve on that one. A lot of "I wants" became "I don't needs."

The lease expires on this penthouse at the end of the month and we're toying with "where next?"

Sliding the manilla folder away from the brewing coffee, I open the fridge and snag heavy whipping cream, setting it on the counter.

I close the fridge, and a sleepy Alexandra is revealed.

Her long ginger hair cascades to her waist, and the cropped tank top with tiny spaghetti straps is worn *sans* bra, paired with loose "boy shorts" as she calls them.

I get a half-boner from the sight. "Hey," I say in greeting, and wrapping fingers around her nape, I pull her in, giving Alexandra a kiss on her forehead.

Yawning, she stretches that lithe body toward the ceiling.

I trail a finger over a nipple through the thin material of the cami. She lowers to her flat feet. Taking the hand that touched her, Alexandra presses a kiss over my scarred knuckles.

"Who was the asshat that rang our doorbell in the middle of the night?"

Gazing out the windows, I laugh.

Sun streams in from the nine-foot, floor-to-ceiling,

tempered glass, non-opening windows, bathing Alexandra in early morning light that turns her hair to spun copper.

"Not *quite* the middle of the night," I comment, turning as the sound of the first cup spurts its last drop of brew. I stir in the cream and add a dollop of whipped cream I dragged out from a separate container.

As I hand it to Alexandra, she mentions how spoiled she is.

"My queen," I reply.

We share an intimate look.

Then I remember the manilla folder. "Courier came with this for you."

The envelope is addressed: *Alexandra Renee Frost - Epstine.*

I cringe a little when her eyes stutter after the hyphen. Alexandra said she'll take my name without regret.

Alexandra Sebastian has a nice ring to it, I decided.

I ready my cup and the Keurig begins its racket.

She turns the envelop over, notices there's an unbroken raised seal on the back, and frowns. "This is weird."

"At least, it's not another request for a tell-all book," I throw over my shoulder.

Her eyes find mine. "Or more requests to return to Tiktok."

"Exactly."

Opening the silverware drawer, she withdraws a steak knife and slices the folder open, breaking the seal and sliding out the thick packet of documents.

My coffee finishes, and I turn, pouring in just enough cream to lighten my java from black to a deep brown color.

I stir.

"Zaire." Alexandra's tone has me spinning to face her.

"Unless I'm an idiot..."

"Not possible," I say instantly.

She pushes her hair behind one ear. "I am the heir to the Epstine fortune."

I take a sip of coffee, unsurprised by the news.

Mainly because I made sure it happened, though I could not be sure my, and a few other key people's, efforts would prove successful.

"Doesn't it stand to reason you would be? Bridget killed everyone else..." I shrug, not copping to a thing yet.

"But there were all sorts of male children." Alexandra gnaws lightly on her bottom lip, distracting me again.

"True, all younger than you. The will said very specifically there would be one living heir, the eldest of which would need to be found and substantiated through viable DNA sampling."

"Wait a second," she says, giving me a suspicious look. "You don't seem very shocked." Alexandra puts her hands on her hips. "And you're a fountain of information. Wait." She points a finger at me. "A geyser!"

"I'm not."

"Were you behind this?"

I nod.

Alexandra sets the papers down, coming to me as I set my steaming coffee on the countertop, and winds her arms around my waist, tipping her head back to study my face.

"Why?"

"That part's easy—I want you to have something good from all the bad.

"It's more than we could ever spend," I state, waiting for her reaction.

Without a minute's hesitation, she announces, "I know exactly what I can do with the money."

I smile, my love for this compassionate, generous woman I will marry overwhelming me.

"I will give most away to all the other children who are

harmed by people like," her exhale is wounded, yet she bravely continues, "my father." Those last two words end on a whisper, but she says them.

"Good choice," I say, scooping her against me.

We stand like that for a long time, coffee cooling, bodies warmed by our love.

Epilogue
Merit

"A toast to the bride and groom," Merit announces to the packed house, raising his champagne flute and wrapping his free arm around Chloe.

The tight group moved heaven and earth to make a wedding happen like the one this last Club Alpha couple deserved.

But by God, it *did* happen.

After the inheritance was summarily doled out, Alexandra Frost was free of ninety-nine percent of the Epstine fortune via charitable donation to free kids from child trafficking, retaining just enough money so her luxury travel of the future would include only one key person beside herself: Zaire.

Buying a working ranch on a hundred acres, complete with livestock, small lake, and an old mansion to fix up is their next stop, and Merit couldn't be more pleased.

"To Zaire and Alex, may this be only the beginning of all great things to come."

The crystal stems lift, winking like a million tiny suns as the outdoor venue has a rare day of full sun with cool temps.

His eyes meet those of Paco's and Greta's—their two kids smiling and laughing noisily.

Gia and Denver wear grins that outshine everyone except Zaire and Alex themselves.

He feels privileged to be the first to hear the happy news that there will be a small Sebastian on the way.

Zaire's ten-gallon hat sits on the table as he and Alex stand, raising their champagne flutes and twisting arms, taking a traditional first sip from each others' glasses .

The exchange is tender, the passion touchable.

Merit sips from the champagne, lowering his glass as Chloe slides her arm around his waist, sinking against his side.

He kisses the top of her head, gazing out at the crowd of family and friends with a lightness he hasn't felt in years.

If there's one takeaway from this life, it's how damn lucky he is to have found an ending as happy as theirs.

THE END

Got a *Billionaires' Game* Hangover? [Continue your dark thriller journey] HERE if you loved *Club Omega*, you won't be able to put HER down!

HER: A LOVE STORY

⭐⭐⭐⭐⭐ "Emotively moving - gripping and *sensual*..."

👉 Never miss a new release! Join TRB News for exclusive updates, early access, and special offers.

📚 **Your words are powerful!** If you enjoyed *Club Omega*, please share your star rating and thoughts to help other readers discover their next favorite author. *Thank you!*

Continue your journey with more of TRB/Marata Eros' thrilling novels:

THE PEARL SAVAGE

☆☆☆☆☆ "A real page-turner!"

NOOSE

☆☆☆☆☆ "**Raw, edgy... graphically** painted."

BLOOD SINGERS

⭐⭐⭐⭐⭐ "One hell of a ride!"

CLUB ALPHA

⭐⭐⭐⭐⭐ "It's action-packed and so suspenseful....

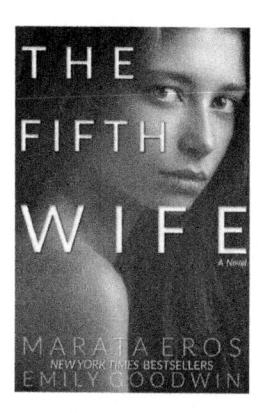

THE FIFTH WIFE

★★★★★ "Absolutely fantastic dark taboo toxic romance. Loved it…"

THROUGH DARK GLASS

★★★★★ "One of the best and I have read many!"

BROLACH

⭐⭐⭐⭐⭐ "...oh hot hot **hot**..."

The Token 1 - Provocation

⭐⭐⭐⭐⭐ "**Crazy good**. It draws you in..."

EMBER

⭐⭐⭐⭐⭐ "This story is... **explosive!**"

HER: A LOVE STORY

⭐⭐⭐⭐⭐ "Emotively moving - gripping and *sensual*..."

THE REFLECTIVE

★★★★★ "'...futuristic writing, hard characters, **powerful...**"

REAPERS

★★★★★ "One of the **best!**"

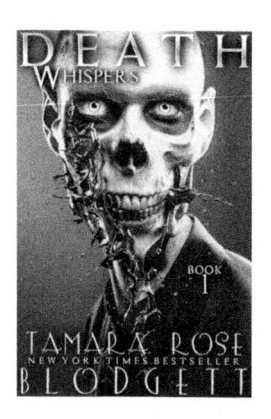

DEATH WHISPERS

★★★★★ "HUNGER GAMES, 50 SHADES and DIVERGENT, anyone?"

A HARD LESSON

★★★★★ " ... **HOT! HOT! HOTTT...!**

PUNISHED

★★★★★ **"Unputdownable from Start to Finish!"**

Enjoy a special treat! Read on for an **exclusive bonus chapter** from one of Tamara Rose Blodgett's unforgettable stories...

BONUS MATERIAL
Becca - Then

HER
A Love Story

***New York Times* BESTSELLER**
MARATA EROS

Copyright © 2021-22 by Marata Eros
All rights reserved.
No part of this book may be reproduced in any form or by any electronic or mechanical means, including information storage and retrieval systems, without written permission from the author, except for the use of brief quotations in a book review.

Glass roars like a tornado inside our car as the windows simultaneously break.

Disoriented—I violently float—landing with a harsh impact that, much later, I'll never remember, no matter how hard I try.

I don't think anyone wakes up on the day of their death and believes they're going to die. Especially on their wedding anniversary—with the most important news of their life left unsaid.

Ultimately, the car murdered my husband. His 1971 second-gen Camaro.

That, and the black ice.

Even in death, James saved me because he went through the windshield first.

I followed. Not because I wanted to but because I was flung in the same trajectory.

But I can't think about that right now.

Slapping a hand on the wet pavement, I push off and scream, clutching my hand to my side.

Can't breathe.

I lie back down, and that's when I see him.

James lies supine as though sleeping. If it weren't for the pool of blood spreading around him, I'd think he was waiting for me.

Waiting for news he won't ever hear.

Reactively, my gut coils at the vision—the knowledge of what that still body of my husband means.

Dry heaves begin to wrack my body, and I shriek as the pain in my ribs robs me of oxygen, every breath feels like crushed glass.

My eyes move back to James, latching onto the profile of his face. I've always told James his face is like a Greek god. Square jaw, Roman nose—aquiline features.

But there he lies like a shattered, life-sized doll.

So much blood, I think as his life's liquid spreads like black ink across the road.

Doing a frantic visual hunt of the bridge I lie on, I search for people—help.

A noise penetrates the fog of my consciousness. Turning my head, I whimper at what the movement costs me.

The Camaro has flipped on its back like a disgorged turtle, and one of the stock wheels James loved so much is performing a lazy backward rotation.

Something wet trickles into my left eye, and I close it.

My right eye sees just fine, and James' sportcoat is stuck between the jagged pieces glass of the broken windshield like food in teeth.

I look away for a moment before my eyes unerringly shift back to James.

He's so still.

I bite off a yell with the first laborious movement toward my husband.

I need to help him.

The crawling is the worse thing I've ever done.

Time is lost.

My eyes shut. Then open.

I'm closer.

A wail of something jerks me awake. I'm only a few yards away now.

One more press and I'll be next to him.

Time is lost.

When I open my eyes, there are people everywhere, at least their voices are.

Mist rolls in between the suspension supports of the bridge as twilight's strangeness steals reality, and a lone figure strides toward me within the dying ethereal light.

I rapidly blink.

James.

Relief sweeps me and tears threaten. *He's okay after all;* all that stillness was illusion.

The figure appears to move with that self-contained assurance James possesses—has always possessed.

But as James draws nearer, I note the height—intellect warring with want.

My heart pauses its elated rhythm.

The curves that only a woman's body maintains are backlit in stark relief by artificial lighting of streetlamps blinking on for the night.

The confident stride, the singular purpose, and that sense of imprisoned energy while in motion are all reminiscent of James.

My dead husband, my mind whispers with sinking finality.

When the law enforcement officer halts then sinks to her haunches beside where I lie, one glance at her face, and I know.

The light from a streetlamp above us shines on her face, illuminating every plane, every angle, every curve—the smoky color of her eyes.

Dark with concern.

"No," I deny.

My fingers bite at the asphalt as I attempt to heave myself to standing.

The pain levels me, and I fall, scraping my knee because my stockings have gone to hell.

Jerking my head up to look for James, I shallowly pant through the horror of my ribcage.

That's when I see it.

A lone bright red high heel, tipped on its side, lies beside a body bag where James had lain just moments before.

I look at my feet and notice it's a match to the one I still wear, my other foot bare of the screaming scarlet heel.

I don't throw up then because I haven't eaten in hours; my stomach's empty. I wanted to be hungry for our special night.

This wasn't a night I'd order a salad and be on a diet.

James. My breath is a scorching bubble of anguish in my chest.

The female officer comes in behind me.

She'll lie. The falsehood will be that everything is going to be okay.

Officer MacKenzie Flint doesn't articulate platitudes. She holds my hair away from my face while I take turns throwing up nothing and screaming from the pain.

My ribcage is shattered.

But not nearly as much as my heart.

―――

Mac

I kick my head back on the headrest of the driver's seat and mutter, "More fucking cutbacks," as I listen to the latest lies on the news.

I viciously punch my finger to the on/off power button.

The guillotine comes down on the soundbite, and my exhale from the blessed silence shoots out in a slow stream of relief.

Rory's angular face turns to me, fingers curled around the top part of his bulletproof vest as the vapor lights outside the McDonalds sweep the interior of our cruiser with bluish-white illumination. "Why do you *listen* to that garbage?"

I smirk. "Because I'm a closet sadist."

He barks out a laugh. "Or maybe not that much in the closet."

I narrow my eyes at my partner and hike a brow. "Fuck you—what are you? A priest?"

Rory does a mock-shiver. "Hell no. That—wow—just wow. Now *that's* perverted."

I grin.

My cell chimes simultaneously with Rory's, and that smooth kick of low-level adrenaline thrums through my body at the sound.

Probably a useless 911. Somebody shoved something into an orifice to see what would happen. Or my fave—someone's mad at a neighbor for blowing leaves onto their driveway (though it's late for that).

Like the wind has nothing to do with the leaves blowing themselves silly.

Clowns.

I depress my thumbprint and the screen opens. Face recognition is too slow in the dimness of the cruiser.

Rory sees the stats first.

"MVA."

Motor Vehicle Accident. Huh.

We put the patrol car into gear—lights and sirens on.

The witness places bodies on the ground.

Sometimes the police are babysitters; sometimes we enforce—sometimes we're the stand-in for the morgue.

Wish everyone knew our first and most important role is to protect.

"He's gone," Rory says the moment we pull up.

Our mutual gazes sight the body right away. There's a stillness in death. A person sees death enough, and the very omission of animation is the biggest tell.

We exit the patrol car and take in the scene with our eyes; then our secondary senses come online.

At first, there's no sound.

With my back against the driver's door, Rory and I visually sweep the scene again, catching sight of a couple of people at the edge of the bridge and immediately dismiss them.

Like a shutter from an old-fashioned camera, I catalog.

Old race car upside down.

Click.

One dead body.

Click.

My eyes do a brief stutter over the next detail.

A red shoe steals the horror show, lying very close to the body on its side.

That belongs to a woman.

Click.

My head whips back to the dimness of the little-traveled bridge.

A female lies on her side, chest heaving, presumably the owner of the lone high heel.

I begin moving while thoughts seize me.

My eyes shift to the corpse a few yards from the woman's position, and the gears of my mind write the three-second narrative.

Married. One dead, nice clothes.

Date night.

Click.

The female is crawling toward the dead guy.

Nope.

I begin long-striding my ass over there. There is no way that woman is going to see her husband's brains all over the road.

I get to her, blocking the line of sight to the male.

Her chin rises, and I get the first true look at her face, a handy streetlight revealing details.

Containing my shit is second nature. And, God help me, it's the middle of a scene, but at the end of the day, I'm just a human being, and I never become more aware of that fact than I do at this moment: the fragility of emotion that reminds us of our humanity—and vulnerability to it.

Blood mats the hair to her temple. Dark eyes are wide with the beginning of shock. Skin paled to alabaster in the odd light of day's concession to night.

She is breathtakingly beautiful.

Click.

Slowly I squat, my ass almost resting on my heels, not wanting to make things worse by making sudden moves.

Do your job, Mac.

She needs to be assessed and stop crawling around until that happens.

Paramedics will arrive.

She'll be okay.

Our eyes lock, and a frozen moment of perfect understanding flows between us.

"No," she says in a wounded whisper, and the tone clenches something inside my body.

I just saw the world in those dark eyes. Not how I see it but how she does.

Turning away from me, she begins to haul herself upright.

Nope.

I move in to grab her.

She screams.

I startle like a rookie before I realize something is clearly busted.

Then she sinks to her knees and begins dry-heaving.

Fuck.

I squat down on a knee, my other leg bent, and pull back all that long dark hair.

She gives hoarse coughs between heaves.

Broken ribs. I lean down beside her temple. "Hey now," I say in a low, soothing voice.

Her head hangs, and I realize I still have a hold of her hair and let go.

The curtain of hair falls around her.

"He's gone, isn't he?" she says to the ground.

Her grief pierces me.

Fuck.

"Yes," I answer softly, hearing Rory's words in my head: "You've got the finesse of a gorilla on crack with delivering news, Mac. Leave that to me, Ms. Sensitivity."

He can always get a laugh out of me.

I'm not feeling that humorous at the moment.

The woman slowly lowers herself to the ground, trying to curl up into a fetal position.

I've never seen tears like hers.

They're mammoth, rolling down her face like gems of wet despondency.

The next thing I know, I've picked her up as carefully as I can.

She tightens a fist on my vest, and my utility belt shifts uncomfortably against my back, my hips.

I hold her anyway as she silently cries, automatically tucking her head beneath my chin.

When the medics come, I find I don't want to let her go.

Ever.

Mac

Not gonna lie, I'm shaken. To my core.

When the paramedics came, I backed off, handed the woman over to the pros.

"Think her ribs are busted," I'd commented like an out-of-body experience. When you work scenes, a lot of times, it's the same paramedics most of the time.

You get to know them.

George had looked down at me as I held the woman on my lap.

"Okay, Mac—thanks." He'd lifted a brow like *the fuck?*

"Right," I'd said.

They laid the stretcher down, and George and a female partner I didn't know took her from me, laying her on the stretcher, and she gave a small whimper.

More tears.

I had begun to back away.

Her eyes had met mine briefly without reprisal, accusation, or expectation.

Why had I felt guilty about leaving? God *damn*.

I'd turned on my heel and began to walk away. I hadn't *run*, but it'd been a hard thought.

In the periphery, I catch sight of Rory jogging to catch up with me midway to the patrol car.

"Hey."

"Hey," I answer without looking at him.

Out of the corner of my eye, I see his eyes run over my face. "What's goin' on? Ya seem rattled."

Lie or be honest? Lies never come easy to me. "I am."

His chin jerks back, brows popped high. "Why? Totally typical MVA—and no boozing to get lit over. Black ice, heavy engine, light back end—dude lost control."

I nod. Got all that, seen it—duly noted.

Swallowing hard, I let my partner know what I couldn't admit until right now. After all, partners in law enforcement are like a married couple without the sex and domestic division of labor.

"Felt something."

Rory snorts. "That clears shit up, Mac. Love it." He rubs a circle over his vest and gives me the *barf it out* look.

"For the woman. Felt a connection."

Rory's silence has us locking gazes over the roof of the car, our hands gripping opposing doors of the vehicle.

"You mean like"—he swipes fingers through his shorn hair, and the pitch of his voice takes a dive—"you *dig* her?"

Shame fills me. I'm crushing on a victim at a scene, for fuck's sake. A heterosexual female trashed by shock and injuries, and I'm thinking about ... fuck.

I'm thinking about how gorgeous she is.

And other shit.

"Fuck," Rory breathes. "Not gonna lie, Flint—this vibe check is *not* you. You're"—he waffles his hand—"a love 'em and leave 'em type."

Truth.

When I don't fill the silence with words, Rory's dark brows slowly lift. "She's not *gay*, Mac."

My exhale is disgusted. "No shit?" Not disgusted with Rory's insights but with my own lack of checking my shit at the door before I entered the scene.

But in my own defense, I've never had a bleep on the screen before this moment. This night. Every scene, every time—it's just my job. It's always about The Job.

"Okay, this is weird as fuck, just saying."

I open the driver's side door. "Don't."

"Fuck that."

He opens his side, and we slide in at the same time.

In classic guy mode, Rory doesn't address my comment again.

Until the next time.

Because, of course, there is a next time.

Becca

"I'm sorry for your loss," the doctor says in a pat, conciliatory voice.

Right. *Wonderful.* "Thank you," I reply in a flat tone.

After the appropriate pause, he continues, "Now, there's nothing we can do for the fractured ribs, but you're very lucky—there were no internal punctures or bleeding. You'll be sore, but nothing else was broken—you don't even have a concussion."

He smiles like this is the best news of the century.

I want to strangle him.

"Now," he hesitantly begins again, probably noticing how I practically growl at him, "for pain management, we have a few options, depending on how you're tolerating your rib situation."

Rib situation. "No meds," I say automatically and a grief so pure, so powerful and unexpected has me covering my mouth with my hand as tears fill my eyes, overflowing the dam of my hand, dripping over my fingers.

Dr. Steinman shifts his weight, fingers imperceptibly tightening on the clipboard that no doubt holds the reins to all my injuries and stats.

Except one.

"I understand some people don't like to take medication..."

One fortifying inhale later I say, "I'm pregnant."

In the good doctor's defense, he tries to school his expression, but the information I just blasted at him makes that impossible.

I'm a busted up, pregnant woman of a certain age who unexpectedly lost her husband of almost two decades a few hours ago.

"Well..." His face screws up, and then he appears to shore himself up. "Congratulations."

I nod, letting my hands fall to my lap. "Thank you," I manage in a whisper.

He clears his throat, loosening his tie that peeks from the top of his white doctor's coat. "Is there... someone?" An awkward silence fills the gap between this and his next question. "Is there anyone I can contact?" he finally manages.

My mind has zero thoughts. Then, suddenly, there are too many. "Has my cell phone been recovered?"

He begins to back away toward the door. "I'll get a nurse to locate your belongings. But typically, the police collect personal effects from the—the accident," he finishes quietly, the last word barely above a whisper.

"Well, there's no one to contact unless I have a phone or something." I look around the sparsely furnished room as fresh tears bloom and note there's nothing to anchor me here.

Just a white room that has the medicinal hospital smell and not one personal thing to remind me I'm me.

The feeling of being set adrift overwhelms.

My hand goes to my belly. I realize that part of my dry heaves has to do with how sick I've been feeling. And whatever man thought up the term "morning sickness" needs to go right to hell because it's more like "all-day sickness."

Just as a nurse enters my hospital room, Dr. Steinman says, "I'll be back to check on you in a few hours." With a relief he can't hide, he escapes.

"Let's get you cleaned up," she says briskly.

I scan her name tag. *Mary*.

Her kind eyes run over my face and body in quick assessment. "We'll get you a hot shower then some food."

I pull a face.

Hers shows only compassion.

"Do you know?" I ask quietly, hoping I don't have to repeat things I'd rather not dwell on at the moment.

She nods. "That you lost your husband and you're expecting? Yes. Do I know you'll survive all this? Yes."

My breathing is shallow as I try to ride the next wave of grief.

"Why did he leave me?" I ask in such a low voice I know Mary can't hear it.

"He didn't."

My eyes slowly rise to meet hers.

Mary shakes her head. "It feels like that now, but in time, your perspective will change, and you'll come to understand there's nothing we can do to change the course of some events. Your life is *not* over, Rebecca."

My nods are swift, my tears swifter.

First, I move my legs to the side of the bed and moan from the pain.

Mary holds her arm out. "It's easier for me to be a human post and you hang on."

Okay.

I slide my rear off the bed and shudder a starved exhale out. Take an experimental inhale and about die when I choke and gag on the pain.

Mary waits out the coughing fit.

When I'm done and shaking with fatigue, we shuffle to the shower, and she turns on the hot tap, holding her hand out to gauge the temperature, adding a small amount from the cold tap.

With a nod, Mary carefully turns me and unties my hospital gown.

"Can you wash yourself while I stand here?"

No. "Yes."

It's a horrible process that is laborious, slow, taxing, and a bit embarrassing.

Mary waits through all of it.

I silently suffer on the trek back to the hospital bed with the only piece of happiness—my own blood and the microscopic pebbles from the road no longer mat my hair, though Mary had to wash the tangled locks because I couldn't lift my arms.

When I finally lie back, I sigh then groan because it wasn't a smart move.

I shut my eyes then remember my manners at the last moment. "Thank you, Mary," I say quietly.

She pats my knee, and her sharp eyes notice the protective hand I have covering my belly.

"It'll be okay," Mary says, eyes compassionate.

I think she says those words because, in the next moment, exhaustion takes me, and I fall into a fitful sleep filled with dreams of the dead.

HER: A LOVE STORY

"Emotively moving - gripping and *sensual*..."

THE TOKEN 1

Provocation

New York Times BESTSELLER
MARATA EROS

Copyright © 2013-14 by Marata Eros
All rights reserved.
No part of this book may be reproduced in any form or by any electronic or mechanical means, including information storage and retrieval systems, without written permission from the author, except for the use of brief quotations in a book review.

———

"You're dying," Dr. Matthews says. Two words. Final. Complete. Desolate.

I feel my fingers clench the armrests of the chair underneath me, but the rest of my body remains numb.

If his words aren't enough to convince me, I see my silence is a prevailing annoyance in his day.

Dr. Matthews walks stiffly, making his way to the softly glowing X-ray reader.

I flinch when he slaps the photo of the soft tissue of my brain against the magnetic tabs of the lit surface.

The light glows around the tumor, immortalizing the end of my life like an emblazoned tool of disregard.

Just the facts, ma'am.

I sway as I stand, gripping the solid oak of his desk. It's very large, an anchor in the middle of his prestigious office full of the affectations of his career.

I walk toward Matthews. His hard face is edged by what

might be sympathy. After all, it's not every day he tells a twenty-two-year-old woman she's got moments to live.

Actually, I do have time——months.

It's just not enough.

I look at the mess that's my brain, at the damning half a golf ball buried in a spot that will make me a vegetable if they operate. My eyes slide to the name at the bottom. For a split second, I hope to see another name there. But my own greets me.

Mitchell, Faren.

I back up and Matthews reaches to steady me.

But it's too late.

I spin and run out of his office as his voice calls after me. The corners of my coat sail behind me as I slap the metal hospital door open and take the cement steps two at a time.

I see my car parked across the street and race to it. My escape, my despair, is a thundering initiative I can't deny.

I miss the hit as if it happens to someone else. Only the noise permeates my senses as light flashes in my peripheral vision, mirrors against sunlight. I tumble in a slow spin of limbs. My body heaves and rolls, hitting the asphalt with a breath-stealing slap. I lie against the rough black road. My lungs beg for air, burning for oxygen, and finally I take a sucking inhale that tears through my lungs. The wet road feels cool against my face as I watch someone come into my line of sight. My body burns and my head aches. My arm is a slim exclamation point from my body, my fingers twitching. I can't make them stop. I can't make anything stop.

Powerless.

The doctor is too late with his condemning words. I've already died. I know this because the man who approaches is an angel. A helmet comes off hair so deep auburn it's a low-burning lick of flame. He swims toward me like a mirage, walking in a surreal slow motion. I blink, and my vision blurs.

I try to raise my arm to wipe my eyes and whimper when it disobeys my command.

My angel crouches down, his eyes a deep brown, belying the dark bronze of his hair. "Shhh... I got you." His voice is a deep melody.

I sigh. Safe.

I try to focus on him but the helmet he parks next to his boots becomes three as my vision triples.

There's a scuffle and I try to move to see what all the commotion's about. The angel wraps his warm large hand around my smaller one and smiles. "It's going to be okay."

That's when I know I'm not in heaven.

That's what people say when nothing is okay.

I flex my hand, grab my isometric handgrip, and do my hundred reps. So fun—a little like flossing my teeth. I put on the kettle with my good hand and turn the burner on high.

Flex, squeeze, release, flex again.

I get to a hundred and switch hands. As I go through my daily ritual, I flip open my Mac and browse my emails.

Faren, can you cover my shift? Faren, can you come in a half hour early? Faren, can you bring the main dish for the office pot luck?

Delete, delete, delete.

I'll say yes because it's hard for me to say no. Tough lessons in life have taught me that.

I put my handgrip on the corner of the end table, glancing at my left pinky and frowning. It's almost straight. Almost. No one can tell unless they're looking for it. No one ever looks that hard. Humanity glosses over shit.

I leave my laptop open and walk back to the stove. Depression-era jadeite salt and pepper shakers stand dead in the middle of a 1950s pink stove. The combo reminds me of an Easter egg. The kettle insists it's ready, bleating like a sheep. I lift it carefully, deliberately, using all the muscles of my hands as I've been taught.

As I teach others to do.

I pour the hot water over the tea bag and sigh, forcing my bad hand to thread through the loop of the tea cup handle. My dexterity is returning. I've pushed myself so hard that my hand rebels, willfully abandoning its hold on the cup.

The porcelain shatters, and shards fly on the wood floor of my tiny apartment above the main street where I live in deep anonymity. The pieces splinter in all directions, and I sigh. I want to chop off my hand.

I want to cradle it against my chest because it still works. Just not perfectly.

Like my life.

"Another headache?" Sue asks.

I nod, my hands falling away from my temples as I reach for my patient folder. I grip it with both hands and scan who's up first.

Bryce Collins. Pain. In. My. Ass.

I grin. I love the tough nuts to crack. They make it all worth it. I stride to my torture chamber, pushing the door open with my hip and search through the sea of work out equipment and hand held physical therapy implements to meet the sullen gaze of a seventeen-year old athletic prodigy.

A prodigy with a chip on his shoulder so wide I could drive a truck through it. Well I have my own dings and dents. We can compare later.

Right now, it's all about the work.

"Hi, Bryce."

He mumbles a reply as I hand him the first merciless task. The huge rubber band fits around the pole in the center of the room. Mirrors line the wall and toss back our struggles.

And our triumphs.

I watch as he half-heartedly goes through the motions of his straight leg kicks. When he reaches twenty I scoop my hand down and latch onto his hamstring and he groans at my touch. "Bend your knee a little," he does while giving me a look that could kill. I stare neutrally back until his gaze drops and he finally digs in.

An hour later, shaking and sweating, Bryce's huge and muscled body lumbers outside my door. He pauses as he opens it, looking at me with pissed off brown eyes.

"I hate you, Miss Mitchell," he says and means it.

I smile back. I totally get it. Bryce needs to hate me to get better. It beats hating himself. I nod. "I know."

He walks out, and I run my finger down the patient appointments for the day. Kiki makes her loud entrance, and my lips twist. She balances chai tea in both hands, staggering in too-tall heels that sink into the nearly bald carpet.

"Gawd!" she huffs as she winds her way through the ellipticals, weight machines, and treadmills. She leans against the walking bars that run like railroad tracks for those with dual injuries. Like both legs not working.

I swallow and force my smile back in place.

"Take your tea, you ungrateful bitch," she squeals, handing me my tea.

I blow on it. A touch of honey and ginger rise through the vapor, and I grin over the rim of the cup as I sip through the little slot.

"So?" I ask in a purr.

Kiki is pure drama. It's only Monday, so we have the entire week to build up to a crescendo. Mondays are usually sedate, so I brace myself. I have thirty minutes until my next client arrives to be tortured into wellness. Kiki smirks, sets down her tea, and moves to the pole. I give a furtive glance around the gym, hoping no one comes in.

"Got a..." She wraps around the pole and slides down it seductively, letting her butt cheeks split as she wiggles and bounces at the bottom. She springs up, the front of her hoohah a hairsbreadth from the cool metal. "Ginormous tip this weekend from a richie!"

She thrusts forward, wrapping one slender leg around the pole, and I groan. She does a little mock-hump against it and grins at me.

Kiki is so inappropriate I could die. But she's my drug and I'm hers. We fit together because we're so different. She's an exotic dancer who's also a senior at Northwestern State.

She makes great money, and she also does serious gym time, packing in an hour six days a week. It's important to not look too striated, Kiki claims. No "guy-look." Just tits, ass, and curves with definition. I designed the workout for her because I'm intimately familiar with the human body. I didn't set out to be, but life had other plans.

The sins of the past become the direction of our future.

Kiki pouts, leaves the pole, and saunters toward me. "You're no fun."

I roll my eyes. "Okay... I know I've got to ask the burning question or we'll get nowhere."

She perks up. "You got it, sister."

"Who was it?"

Kiki always takes stock of clients. Men think they know so much, but women could rule the world if we came together. I sigh. Kiki notices regulars, high tippers, newcomers and flags the creeps. She's scary uncanny. I came to watch a set at the prestigious strip club, Black Rose, and went away shocked.

Shocked by the clientele, shocked that Kiki could dance that well for such a short time, and shocked by the moolah.

"The owner," Kiki whispers as if we have a secret.

I shrug. "So?"

"It's Jared-effing-McKenna, baby!" Kiki is offended by my deliberate ignorance. Her brows rise to her hairline, and her dark eyes are wide with clear disdain.

Mine are steady with indifference.

The wheels of my memory spin. *Oh yes.* Jared McKenna. *The* Jared McKenna. Greek god. Adonis incarnate. Hercules. Playboy, womanizer, money mogul.

I slowly nod. Let's add "strip club owner" to the repertoire. I remember the detail of *why* he has so much money and want to forget as soon as I do.

Kiki pouts and tears off the lid of her tea. "Anywho... he was with someone, and his pal tipped me big time." She sips her cooling tea, gazing at me with "cat that ate the canary" eyes.

"Okay, the foreplay is killing me. How much?" I take a small slurp of tea, and she tells me. The tea sprays out of my mouth, and Kiki grins at my klutzy-ass move.

"Five hundred dollars!?" I choke some more, and tea dribbles down my chin.

"It's okay, baby... it *is* a mind-blower. I mean," her hands go to her ample chest in patent disbelief, "my nipples got hard and he didn't even touch me," she says sincerely and I burst out laughing. My headache is gone for the moment, my Monday morning lethargy lifting.

Five hundred bucks is an assload of cash, especially for one night of dancing half naked. It's more than I take home every week. *Just one tip.* My schooling is done, my career path set partly because of circumstance. Kiki is high on drama, but doesn't always say things without a purpose and I narrow my eyes at her.

"Spill it," I demand.

Kiki's lips twitch and she chucks her empty cup in the

trash. "This type of gig could be the thing to get you out of that dump in downtown."

I scowl. I like my downtown dump.

"Faren!" she wails.

I shush her before Sue comes in thinking someone died. Of course, with all the sounds of torment she's heard since I began working here last year, nothing should faze her.

Kiki relents and switches to a softer tone. "You could own something. Something nice."

I know this. I've been to her condo overlooking Pike Place and Puget Sound. Her view of downtown is magnificent. And expensive. It had to set her back five hundred K. I rent my death trap for nine hundred per month, and it's a studio in one of the tortuously small cobblestone-lined alleys of Seattle. At least it's on the fifth floor. The stairs are murder, but if I want two windows that actually face outside, that's what I can afford. Sometimes the freight elevator works; otherwise, it's exercise. The location allows me to walk to my upper-scale rehabilitation clinic. No need to use my beater car. That much.

"You don't have to give this up," Kiki says quietly. She knows I won't budge on that, and she of all people knows why.

Rehab's not a well-paying profession. But there's more than money, sometimes the soul needs edification.

I look at what Kiki has and what I don't. I shove those thoughts away. She's my best friend. She's seen me through everything. Dark shadows press in, and my headache returns with a throbbing vengeance.

Kiki frowns. "Another headache?"

"Yeah."

"I don't want to argue, Faren. You've got to know that." Her root beer eyes peg me to the spot. The sweep of her dark hair lays like chocolate silk past her full breasts. "But with your looks"——she throws her manicured hands in the air——"you could shake your booty a little and work a side job. Get a place in your same area... you could own something."

It's an old argument. Her penthouse is nearly paid for while mine's a rental with a landlord that cares more about the rent than maintenance.

Her eyes swim with knowledge, and I set down my tea. It's too cold to drink anyway. Her words put the last nail in the coffin of my resistance. "Something secure," she adds in a whisper and I let her hug me. I cling to her and try to believe my financial troubles and dark secret can be erased by taking off my clothes for strangers

Kiki loves me more than I love myself.

She loves me enough for us both.

———

Sue glances up when I click off the light off. The sky is darkening as I slide my last patient folder through the glass partition. She has that look in her eyes and pushes a business card through the slot.

It bears a doctor's name: Dr. Clive Matthews.

I give Sue a sharp look, and she shrugs, giving my hand a maternal pat. My eyes burn with tears from the spontaneous gesture.

Sue notices my emotional struggle and ignores it. "He got rid of my migraines. Miracle worker, I say." She nods and glances at the card significantly.

I notice the appointment time and sigh.

Sue doesn't drop her gaze. "How much longer are you going to struggle through those bone crushers?"

I don't answer, and she nods in her knowing way. "That's

what I thought, Miss Mitchell. You'd have just come in suffering worse than your own patients."

Sue's right. She knows it, and I do too.

I take the card and stuff it in the pocket of my smock, Dr. Seuss cats cover it in a smear of red and blue.

"Thanks," I say grudgingly while I grab my coat.

"Welcome," she shoots back in triumph as I hear the door whisper closed behind me.

I look at the card again as the cars, people, and city noise encapsulate me in the comforting rhythm of downtown. The smell of fish, food, and sea mingle, and I begin the short trek to the dank alley with the entrance to my apartment.

I have two weeks to prepare myself to go back into a hospital. I hate hospitals. They're all about death.

The thought of returning is almost enough to get a proper panic attack going.

Almost.

The Token 1 - Provocation

"***Crazy* good**. It draws you in..."

Acknowledgments

I published both ***The Druid*** and ***Death Series***, in 2011 with the encouragement of my husband, and continued because of you, my Reader. Your faithfulness, through comments, suggestions, spreading the word and ultimately purchasing my work with your hard-earned money gave me the incentive, means and inspiration to continue.

There are no words that are sufficiently adequate to express my thankfulness for your support.

I truly feel connected to my readers. It is obvious to me, but I'll say the words anyway for clarity: a written work is just words on pages if they are not read by my readers. As I write this I get a lump in my throat; your enjoyment of my work affects me that deeply.

You guys are the greatest, each and every one of ya~

Tamara
xoxo

Special thanks:
You, my reader.
My husband, who is my biggest fan.
"Bird," without who, there would be no books.

Special mention:
Jackie
Dawn
Susan
Erica
Liz
Cherri-Anne
Theresa
Bev
Phyllis
Eric

About the Author

www.tamararoseblodgett.com

<u>**Tamara Rose Blodgett**</u>: happily married mother of four sons. Dark thriller writer. Reader. Dreamer. Beachcombing slave. Tie dye zealot. Coffee addict. Digs music.

She is also the ***New York Times*** bestselling author of ***A Terrible Love***, written under the pen name, Marata Eros, and 80+ other novels. Other bestseller accolades include her #1 bestselling **TOKEN** (dark romance), **DRUID** (dark PNR erotica), **ROAD KILL MC** (thriller/top 100) **DEATH** (sci-fi dark fantasy) series. Tamara writes a variety of dark fiction in the genres: erotica, fantasy, horror, romance, sci-fi, suspense and thriller. She splits her time between the Pacific NW and

Mazatlán Mexico, spending time with family, friends and a pair of disrespectful dogs.

To be the first to hear about new releases and bargains—from Tamara Rose Blodgett/Marata Eros—sign up below to be on my VIP List. (I swear I won't spam or share your email with anyone!)

SIGN UP TO BE ON THE **TAMARA ROSE BLODGETT** VIP LIST https://tinyurl.com/SubscribeTRB-News

Connect with Tamara:

Website: www.tamararoseblodgett.com

TRB for Hire @ Fiverr (helping other authors become writers!)

Follow Marata Eros on Bookbub

Also by Marata Eros

💚 **Read more titles from this author** 💚

A Terrible Love (NYT & USA Today bestseller)

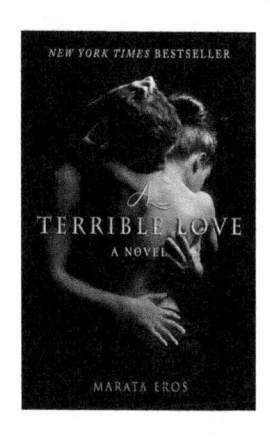

The Reflective – REFLECTION

Punished – ALPHA CLAIM

Death Whispers – DEATH

The Pearl Savage - SAVAGE

Blood Singers – BLOOD

Noose – ROAD KILL MC

Provocation – TOKEN

Ember – SIREN

Brolach – DEMON

Reapers - DRUID

Club Alpha – BILLIONAIRE'S GAME TRILOGY

Dara Nichols Volume 1 – DARA NICHOLS (18+)

Her

Through Dark Glass

The Fifth Wife (written with NYT bestseller Emily Goodwin)

A Brutal Tenderness

The Darkest Joy

My Nana is a Vampire

CLUB OMEGA
Billionaires' Game Trilogy
Book Three

***New York Times* BESTSELLER**
MARATA EROS

ISBN: 9798418488459
Copyright © 2021-22 Marata Eros
All rights reserved.
No part of this book may be reproduced in any form or by any electronic or mechanical means, including information storage and retrieval systems, without written permission from the author, except for the use of brief quotations in a book review.

Cover art by: *Tamara Rose Blodgett LLC*
Edits by: *Dawn Y*
Proofed by: *Susan P.*

Printed in Dunstable, United Kingdom